The Wicked Waif

Blackhaven Brides
Book 11

MARY LANCASTER

Additional Dragonblade books by Author, Mary Lancaster

Imperial Season Series
Vienna Waltz
Vienna Woods
Vienna Dawn

Blackhaven Brides Series
The Wicked Baron
The Wicked Lady
The Wicked Rebel
The Wicked Husband
The Wicked Marquis
The Wicked Governess
The Wicked Spy
The Wicked Gypsy
The Wicked Wife
Wicked Christmas (A Novella)
The Wicked Waif

Unmarriageable Series
The Deserted Heart
The Sinister Heart
The Vulgar Heart

*** Please visit Dragonblade's website for a full list of books and authors. Sign up for Dragonblade's blog for sneak peeks, interviews, and more: ***
www.dragonbladepublishing.com

Chapter One

I N THE HOWLING gale, battered by driving, freezing rain, Dove's small boat fought its way through massive waves. Rowing against the wind and the tide, he'd struggled to get close to what was left of *The Phoenix*, but he could see no one clinging to the wreckage.

He stopped rowing to listen for any cries through the storm and imagined he heard something, a sort of inhuman wail.

"Did you hear that?" he yelled to his companion, Cully.

"Can't hear a thing over this!" Cully shouted back. "Don't see no one else, though. Do you want to go back?" Releasing the side of the wildly tossing boat, he lunged across to Dove to take the oars. Dove gave them up with relief, for the strain had made his old wound ache. But at least he'd given Cully's arms a rest.

"Pull for the shore!"

Clinging to the side of the boat, Dove slid along its length and threw himself onto the other bench. He imagined he heard the wailing sound again—a trick of the raging wind, no doubt, for Cully was right. Even holding the lantern higher, he could make out no human shapes in the savage water. Anybody discovered now were more than likely to be dead, for no one could survive for long in these temperatures.

Still, as Cully pulled on the oars to take them back to shore, aided this time by the tide and the wind, Dove continued peering about him. Among the wreckage of the ship and its cargo of wooden boxes, some of which had spilled their contents, the waves tossed up odd human possessions—a boot, sailor's trunk, even what looked like a comb.

Dove wondered grimly how many lives had been lost this night.

He and Cully had pulled several men from the sea since *The Phoenix* had broken up so dramatically on the rocks beyond the harbor, but he knew the sea must have taken more. The other rescue boats were mostly back ashore now. Everyone had given up finding more survivors.

Hurled by a crashing wave, a large wooden crate almost landed on top of the boat before it swirled beside them in the sea instead. Dove leaned over to fend it off, and again he heard the wail, a wild shriek of panic, of pure fear. At the same time, he was sure the sides of the box moved, vibrating, lifting.

"Hold!" he yelled at Cully, thrusting the lantern at him.

Obeying through habit, Cully stopped rowing and took the lantern from him. Only when Dove seized the rope, captured the box, and began to haul it into the boat did Cully protest.

"Sir, we got no room for cargo!" he shouted. "Let it go, ain't our problem."

But Dove was working from sheer instinct. The unlikelihood didn't occur to him until much later. A wave battered him as he dragged the box over the side and he fell back. With an oath, Cully helped settle the box. Dove grabbed the knife from his belt and began prying open the top while Cully glared at him as if he'd gone mad.

"There's going to be water!" Cully warned, lifting the lantern higher to show him. But when Dove finally tore off the lid, a human being reached out of the murky water within and let out a wild, terrible cry.

Cully staggered back in horror, but Dove, letting the poor creature cling around his neck, hauled the figure out with one arm and then kicked and shoved the leaking box back over the side.

"Row!" he barked, pulling the last semi-dry blanket from the box under the bench and wrapping it around the freezing, shivering mess in his arms. It appeared to be female.

Cully didn't need to be told twice. He was already rowing as hard as he could.

Pulling the woman down onto the bench beside him, Doverton

hugged her to him. But in truth, he had precious little warmth left to impart, for he, too, was freezing cold and wet through. She felt tiny and thin, so delicate her bones seemed liable to break under the least pressure, as though she clung to life by a mere, frayed thread.

And in fact, by the time the other soldiers helped them pull the boat up onto the beach, he thought the thread had broken, for her body no longer shook and her eyes were closed as she slumped against him.

Doverton carried her ashore himself. Dr. Lampton, the town's best physician, strode past him and paused.

"I think she's dead," Dove shouted above the storm.

Lampton thrust his hand under the blanket, unerringly finding where her pulse should be. In the light from the lanterns on the beach, Dove made out blood on her head and on his own hands and coat.

"Not quite," Lampton said curtly. "Put her on the wagon with the others. I'll tend them all at the vicarage."

The wagon waiting in the street was full of shivering, injured sailors. Since there was no room for her to lie flat, Dove sat on the wagon with her to prop her up against his chest. "Tell the men to return to barracks!" he called to Cully. "We've done all we can here."

As the wagon moved forward, the woman suddenly took a deep, shuddering breath and began to shake again. She flung out her hand as though trying to ward off something, so he took it in his, murmuring, "There, you're safe now. You're safe."

After the first tug to be free, she clung to his hand. Her open eyes, wild with fear, stared up into his and in the brighter street light, he saw that she was young, perhaps barely out of her teens. Her face was wracked with pain.

"Safe," she repeated. Her eyes fluttered closed again, but the shivering didn't stop.

Mr. Grant, the vicar, had opened his house as a makeshift hospital. His wife and her maids had made up mattresses and bedrolls in the reception room and supplied dry clothes and blankets. The fire was lit and the whole house felt cozy as Dove paused with his burden in the reception room doorway. Dr. Lampton had arrived faster than the wagon and was kneeling by one of the sailors. The others huddled on mattresses, draped in blankets, drinking hot tea, or groaning with injury.

"Major Doverton!" Mrs. Grant, the vicar's wife, hurried along the hall to him with her arms full of blankets. "Who do you have there? Does he need the doctor at once?"

"She," Dove corrected automatically. "And I suspect she does."

"Ah, bring her in here," Mrs. Grant said, indicating the room across the hall. "I didn't know there were any women on board. Do you suppose she's the captain's wife? He hasn't asked for her."

Dove didn't imagine he would, if he kept her in a box. However, this was not the time for speculation. He followed Kate Grant into her drawing room and gently laid his burden on the sofa as she indicated. Mrs. Grant rang the bell before helping him wrestle the poor creature out of her outer clothes and boots.

"Perhaps you'd fetch Dr. Lampton from the other room," she said to Dove when the maid answered her summons.

Taking this as it was intended, as a discreet *Go away*, Dove left them to get the rest of the woman's wet clothes off and strode to the other room.

Dr. Lampton was just rising from one patient and turning to the next.

"Doctor, I've brought your new patient who seems in need of urgent help," Dove said. "The half-drowned female with the head wound."

Lampton grunted, giving the next man a brief examination. "You'll do for now," he told him. "Drink your tea."

He straightened and faced Dove, frowning as though the message had only now penetrated his mind. "The female, yes." He swung around and addressed the huddled man closest to the fire. "You did not tell me there were females aboard."

"There weren't," the man snapped, straightening. Presumably he was the captain. "My wife does not accompany me to sea, and my officers are not married."

Lampton was already striding away as though he didn't much care for the captain's explanation or lack of it.

"She needs to be warmer," Lampton said at once as his new patient shook violently enough to vibrate the sofa. "Much warmer. A warming pan and more blankets. Kate, is she injured anywhere other than her head?"

"I saw no sign of it," Mrs. Grant replied, hurrying off to do the doctor's bidding.

Lampton scowled at the wound as he cleaned it with gentle hands. He was a man of many contradictions, but Dove rather liked him. "It'll need stitched," he observed. "Any idea how it happened?"

"I can guess," Dove said quietly. "We found her in a box."

Lampton's eyes flew to his. "In a—"

"Exactly. Nailed shut, floating in the sea with the rest of the cargo."

"Stowaway?" Lampton hazarded, threading his needle.

"Possibly. Only, who nailed her inside?"

Lampton held the needle in the candle flame. "Sounds like you need to interview our captain."

"Oh, I intend to," Dove said grimly.

"In the meantime, I suggest you get yourself back to barracks and change before you end up with pneumonia. You've done a noble night's work."

Dove blinked at this accolade. Lampton spared him a glance. "I know it was you who organized the rescue and saved many lives directly, too. They all owe you a debt."

Dove colored uncomfortably. "Fiddlesticks," he said carelessly. "I'll take myself off." Before he did, he glanced down at the unconscious girl and made a discovery.

Lampton had pushed her mass of dark hair to one side, away from her face, which, pale and still, basked in the center of the candles' glow. Her skin was flawless over delicate bone structure, her features fine and pleasing, from her perfectly arched eyebrows to her slightly pointed chin.

"God, she's beautiful, isn't she?" Dove said without meaning to.

Lampton didn't look at her face. "If you say so."

Without warning, the girl let out a cry and her whole body jerked. Her hands flew out, thrusting at the doctor, pushing at air. "No, no, no!" she panted.

"Hold still," Lampton ordered, not unkindly, holding his needle and thread well out of reach. "It will hurt less."

But it was doubtful the girl even heard him. Dove strode up to the sofa and bent over her, catching her hands. "You're safe, remember? The doctor is helping you."

Perhaps she recalled his voice, or perhaps she simply ran out of energy, but she stilled, her wild, terrified eyes coming into focus on his face. "Safe," she repeated blankly.

"Quite safe."

Her hands twisted, but not to be free, merely to cling to his. Her breath came in huge gasps. "Don't let the dark come back. Don't leave me there."

"I won't," Dove soothed. "But you have to hold still so the doctor can close the cut on your head. If it hurts, squeeze my hands. It will be over in a minute and then you can sleep."

"I don't want to sleep," she whispered, but she lay perfectly still, grasping his hands, staring at him, while Dr. Lampton worked. She didn't cry out or complain. Only her frowning brow twitched occasionally in response to greater pain.

"What's your name?" Dove asked, to distract her.

Her frown deepened, but she didn't answer. There was still confusion in her eyes, and it was far from clear what she understood or even saw. She seemed to have latched on to him as the one safe and stable thing in her surroundings.

"This is Mrs. Grant," he told her as their hostess returned to the room with a warming pan. "She's the vicar's wife, and you're safe in her house."

Her eyelids fluttered. "Cold," she whispered. "Why am I so cold?"

"You'll be warm again very soon," Dove assured her, afraid suddenly she would not live long enough to know that warmth.

Dr. Lampton cut his thread and stood up. "Make her as warm as you can, Kate. Without burning her. I've a couple of fellows to see in the other room before I go."

As Lampton left, Mrs. Grant covered the warming pan in a blanket and slipped it under those already covering the girl, who seemed to be asleep once more. Since her grip on him had relaxed, he helped spread more blankets over her.

For a moment, he stood looking down at her. For some reason, he didn't want to leave her.

"I would hate for her to die alone," he blurted.

"Someone will stay with her all night," Mrs. Grant promised.

"You can't," he said. "You have a newly born baby."

"Oh, she is four weeks old, now, not so newly born. But I am also blessed with a house full of servants and helpers. Don't worry, Major. I think you need to look after yourself now."

DOVE FOLLOWED MRS. Grant's and the doctor's advice, for he had no wish to add an infection of the lungs to his health failings, and he had already put a strain on his barely healed wound tonight. Retrieving his horse, he galloped up the hill to the barracks with the wind behind him, glad of the brief respite of warmth at the vicarage.

Once in his own rooms, where Cully had revived the fire, he peeled off his wet uniform, rubbed himself roughly with a towel, and donned dry clothes. He was fastening his coat when Cully appeared with a nip of brandy, which Dove greeted with a delighted smile.

"Excellent idea," he said, taking the glass and toasting him silently. "Have you changed your clothes?"

"Yes, sir, bone dry now! And the rain's gone off, more or less."

"Good. Did the others all get back safely?"

"Yes, sir."

"I think they—and you—deserve a tot, too. I'll just nip over and see them."

Before he could, however, a peremptory knock sounded at the door. Cully opened it, and Dr. Morton, the regimental physician and surgeon strode in.

Dove scowled at Cully who gazed back fearlessly.

"I asked him to come," Cully said. "No harm in that, is there?"

"None at all," Morton replied. "You did right."

Cully cast Dove a grin of triumph and went on his way.

"Thank you for coming," Dove managed. "But I'm fine. What's more, I'm only just warm and dressed, and I have no desire to take everything off again."

"You won't have to. Just unbutton the pantaloons a little and push the rest upward. Sit here, Dove, and let's get it over."

Electing not to prolong the fight, Dove sighed and obeyed.

Morton brought the lamp nearer and peered closely at the giant, jagged scar across his abdomen.

"It hasn't opened," Dove said patiently.

"No, I can see that. But no thanks to you. Rowing in a storm indeed! Organizing is your forte. There were other men to do the rowing."

"Well, Cully did most of ours," Dove muttered. "To be frank, I'm sick to my back teeth of sitting still, shuffling papers, and issuing orders. I'd rather die *doing* something."

"Well, there's no need to hurry it," the doctor retorted, feeling his abdomen. "Does that hurt?"

"A little," Dove admitted, refusing to wince. "But that will go after a night's rest."

"Well, be sure you get one. You don't seem to have re-torn any of the muscles, and I can't feel anything inflamed."

"Then I'm fine." Dove's lips twisted. "For now."

Morton rose and gripped his shoulder. "I wish it was different, Dove. You don't deserve this."

Dove shrugged. "I've already had longer than many."

"And many more are alive because of what you did."

"I don't regret it." He forced a smile. "I don't even regret not dying on the field. Every day is one more than I expect. Only I refuse to die of boredom, Morton. You know that."

"Well, you've got away with it again," Morton said gruffly as Dove readjusted his clothing. "Just remember we want you around for as long as possible."

Dove watched him go. "Thank you!" he called after him when the door was almost shut. "I am obliged to you, as always."

Morton's hat flapped through the crack in the door before it closed. Dove's smile was twisted as he rose. One more duty and then he would go to bed.

The men who'd helped in the rescue were mostly from Captain Blackshaw's company. Blackshaw was notably absent from the barracks, although meant to be on duty. But Dove tracked his men down without difficulty, satisfied himself as to their health and was mightily cheered for his order of extra rations.

Then, looking forward to his bed and a good, long sleep, he left their hut and strode back in the direction of the officers' quarters in the main house. However, he hadn't taken more than a step before he saw Blackshaw, clearly returned with friends from a long evening carousing.

"Evening, Dove!" someone called to him from the group, and he raised his hand in brief acknowledgement.

He did not stop to talk, for he meant to deal with the discipline in the morning when he was not dog-tired and Blackshaw was more likely to be sober. But presumably, Blackshaw had noticed where Dove had come from, for he detached himself from his cronies and weaved toward him.

"Major," Blackshaw drawled with a hint of insolence Dove had been ignoring for several weeks. "Checking up on my men?"

Dove regarded him. The man was indeed drunk. Not for the first time, either. With a certain sympathy for anyone recently returned from battle, Dove had already closed his eyes to several minor breaches of duty, but now his patience had ended. It was time to call a halt, and it would not wait for morning.

"Yes, as it happens," Dove said coldly. "Since I could not rely on you to do so." He smiled glacially. "You'll be glad to know the colonel will receive an excellent report of their conduct tonight."

Blackshaw's frown of confusion was enough to reveal he had no idea what Dove was talking about.

"While you were in the tavern, your men distinguished themselves rescuing the sailors off a ship wrecked in the storm." Dove took a step closer. "*You* will be somewhat conspicuously absent from that report. Be grateful. And careful. Or I'll devote a whole report just to you. Do you understand me? Or do you want it in writing?"

Even in the flaring lamplight around the grounds, Blackshaw's flush was obvious. He made an aggressive attempt to stare Dove down, but was too unsteady on his feet. It looked more like an owlish stare. And perhaps he saw the hint of contempt in Dove's eyes, for his own fell in submission and he weaved his way back to his friends.

Dove walked on. But on the gusting wind, he could hear Blackshaw demanding of the others, "Who does he think he is?"

"He thinks he's your superior officer," Kit Grantham said wryly. "And he's correct."

Chapter Two

DOVE'S HEADQUARTER DUTIES were hardly arduous, especially since Colonel Gordon had returned. Being off-duty the morning after the storm, he rode down to Blackhaven to satisfy his curiosity about the wreck. And to find out if the girl from the box had survived the night, for her beautiful, haunted face disturbed him at least as much as the reasons for her being shut inside a box while the ship sank.

To his surprise, the vicarage seemed quiet. The servant took him at once to Mrs. Grant's drawing room, though he couldn't help glancing across the hall to the other reception room. The door was open and the mattresses had all been removed. There was no sign of the sailors.

When he walked into the drawing room, Mrs. Grant was laying her tiny daughter in a cradle under the window. There was no sign of the girl he had left there last night.

His heart sank. "Is she…?"

"No, she's alive," Mrs. Grant said at once. "But she was very agitated, seemed to have terrible dreams, and when she woke, she seemed not to know where she was or even who she was. Dr. Lampton took her to his new hospital where she can be better cared for."

"Among the fallen women and the diseased?" he said with an unreasonable surge of annoyance.

"Among her fellow unfortunates," Mrs. Grant corrected, waving him to a chair. "I mean to visit her later today. Come with me, if you wish."

"Thank you," Dove said. "I'll probably go there myself when I leave you." He hesitated. "She gave you no clue what had happened to her?"

"She gave us no clues about anything. Dr. Lampton believes there is some sickness in her mind, whether caused by her head injury or the trauma she suffered." Mrs. Grant shook her head. "Poor little waif. Who would possibly have shut her in a box while the ship sank?"

"I have a few questions for the captain," Dove promised. "I take it he and his sailors have gone, too?"

"Two are in the hospital. The rest are on the beach with the captain, collecting what they can from whatever of the wreckage got washed ashore."

Dove gave a twisted smile. "Grabbing it before the locals can?"

"Well, around here, the locals probably have enough brandy!"

Dove regarded her. "Did he seem like a smuggler to you?"

"Not particularly. Do you think he was?"

"I don't know. With brandy in his hold, he could be. Where did he sail from, do you know?"

"Liverpool, he said. Bound for Sweden." She smiled. "You are pursuing the mystery, Major? Under orders?"

"If we pursued every smuggler, half the town would be on trial," Dove said wryly. "But the girl in the box is another matter."

"I asked the sailors who were here. None of them seemed to know anything about a woman on board."

Dove rose to his feet. "Well, perhaps I'll just step round to the hospital and see if our waif can tell us anything."

THE HOSPITAL WAS a new charity, begun with donations from the Earl of Braithwaite, Lord Wickenden, and Captain Alban, among other wealthy residents of Blackhaven and its environs. Dove was sure Mrs. Grant, who was wealthy in her own right, had also contributed, as had the foreign princess who was apparently engaged to marry Dr. Lampton. Lampton was the chief physician, although Dove understood a couple of other doctors also gave their time to the project.

Dr. Lampton strode across the foyer as Dove was admitted. "Ah, Major. Have to dash, I'm afraid. Broken leg at Black Farm. If you've come to see the girl you rescued, Mrs. Fenton will show you the way."

The woman who had admitted him led him upstairs, where he could already hear the sounds of voices speaking loudly as though to a naughty child.

"It's rude to turn your head away when someone is speaking to you. You must answer Mrs. Brown!"

"Just leave her, she'll come around," someone else advised. "Come on, love, eat a little of this and we'll go away."

"Leave it for her," a third voice advised.

The first voice didn't agree. "Take it away and she'll talk as soon as she's hungry!"

"Mrs. Cross!" exclaimed the second voice.

Mrs. Fenton knocked on the door and stuck her head in. "Major Doverton is here, wanting a word with the new patient."

The third voice laughed. "We'd all like a word from her! Come in, Major. I'm Mrs. Brown."

She was a severe looking woman, though spotlessly clean. As she stood aside, he saw her underlings all clustered around the narrow bed nearest the door. In the other bed, equally narrow, a skinny young woman wrapped in shawls with a baby in her arms looked anxiously toward him.

His gaze dropped to the first bed. Although it was dry now, he recognized her hair and the position of the dressing at the side of her head. She lay very still, on her side, with her back to him.

"She won't say a word, sir," he was informed, "no matter how kind we are to her. Closes her eyes so she don't have to look at us neither."

Dove walked past them and around the other side of the bed. She did indeed have her eyes tightly shut, though he was sure she was awake.

"Good morning," he said, looking down at her. "I am glad to see you alive, at least."

Her eyes flew open and met his gaze. For an instant, his heart seemed to stop, for her eyes were more beautiful than he remembered, large and sparkling blue-grey. As she searched his face, her breath caught, and she sat up so suddenly he reached out to stop her.

"Slow down, you'll make yourself dizzy after such a bump on the head."

But that did not appear to concern her. "You're real!" she exclaimed in delight. "I thought I had imagined you."

"I wish you better dreams." He glanced at the women who stood gawping with their mouths open. "I'll sit with her for a little. I'm sure you have other duties."

A snigger came from the girl with the baby in the other bed, but Dove pretended not to hear.

The girl from the box was frowning. "Then if you're real, are the others? I remember another man with a grumpy face and kind eyes."

Dove, who had no difficulty in recognizing Dr. Lampton from this description, said only, "Yes, he stitched your head and saved your life."

She frowned. "No, *you* did *that*, didn't you? You pulled me out of the darkness."

It was an odd way of describing it, but he let it pass. She seemed to be concentrating on separating her dreams from reality.

"A beautiful lady with a friendly smile?" she asked doubtfully.

"Mrs. Grant. You spent last night in her house."

"Then the women in white caps like maids were real, too?"

"Probably," Dove said with caution.

"And the crying baby?"

"The Grants do have a young baby."

She let out a breath. "Oh good. Because although it sounded like a baby, I was so afraid it was actually me." She rubbed her brow. "And a handsome man who tried to talk to me? I wouldn't speak. Was I rude?"

"I suppose you were if it was Mr. Grant the vicar. Your host."

"Oh dear." She bit her lip. "I've been very confused, had such nightmares. I don't know who anyone is or what they'll do."

"No one in Blackhaven will harm you. What were you doing on the ship?"

Her eyes came back into focus. "What ship?"

"*The Phoenix*. It sank last night in the storm after being blown against the rocks at the headland. Did someone take you aboard? Did you stowaway?"

The frightened look came back into her eyes. She swallowed. "I don't know. I don't remember being there at all."

He perched on the edge of her bed and took her hand, which clung to his as it had last night. "Don't worry," he soothed. "Just tell me what you do remember."

"Darkness," she whispered. "Again. I couldn't breathe. There was no air, no light." Her fingers dug into his skin. "And then there was water, freezing cold water, and the whole world was spinning. I kept falling. The water was in my mouth, my lungs...I was drowning. And then my head was above the water again, and I kicked and shouted. Then I was upside down and fell some more. And then you pulled me from the darkness..."

Dove covered her hand on his. "We found you in a wooden box. How did you get there?"

She shivered, a strange fear clouding her eyes before she dropped them to their joined hands. "I don't know,"

He patted her hand. "Never mind. Tell me something else. What is your name?"

Her eyes squeezed shut, forming tight lines in her skin. "I don't remember," she whispered.

Dove had come across this before, in one of his men who suffered a brutal head injury in battle. "Never mind," he soothed. "Instead, think of someone calling a little girl to come inside for dinner. They call her a lot because she's a mischievous little thing. What name are they calling? What name comes first into your head?"

She frowned. "Tillie?" she said doubtfully.

"It's as good a name as any other. Do you remember your parents' names? What they look like?"

Her eyes widened. She shook her head.

"Then you don't remember where you came from?"

Miserably, she shook her head again.

"*The Phoenix* sailed from Liverpool, I'm told. Does that help?"

She stared at him. "It's all darkness before you pulled me out." Her fingers gripped convulsively once more, then released him in quick embarrassment. "I'm sorry. It's a little…frightening. To know nothing, to remember nothing."

"I can imagine. It should come back to you in time. For now, it's important to remember you're safe. The people in the hospital want only to help make you well. As do all the people you remember from last night."

"You are all very kind." She blinked away sudden tears. "And I have only been frightened and rude."

"I think that's understandable."

A smile flickered across her face as she regarded him once more. "You're an army officer," she observed, taking in his uniform. "The women called you *Major*."

"Major Dominic Doverton of the 44th," he introduced himself. "Our barracks are here in Blackhaven."

"I am very pleased to meet you," she said cordially, and yet there was a hint of fun in her eyes, an appreciation of the humor in observing the conventions in this most unconventional situation.

Doverton would have liked to look at her a little longer, but he caught sight of the redoubtable Mrs. Brown in the doorway. Rising unhurriedly, he said, "Miss Tillie, I hope I may call on you again."

"Oh, yes! That is, if you would be so kind. And Major?" she added as he began to walk around the bed.

He glanced back at her.

"Thank you for saving my life."

"Glad to be of service," he said lightly.

Mrs. Brown followed him from the room. "She told you her name?" she said eagerly. "Who is she? Where is she from?"

"She gave me *a* name," Dove corrected. "Plucked from the air. Whether or not it's hers, neither of us know. She remembers nothing before being in the water last night, and understandably that frightens her. So be patient with her."

"Of course," Mrs. Brown said, bridling.

Dove smiled and thanked her, which clearly mollified her, and went thoughtfully downstairs.

As he rode back through the town, meaning to go down to the shore to speak to the sailors, he turned right off the high street instead and went back to the vicarage. There, he encountered Grant, walking across from the church.

"Greetings, Major," the vicar said cheerfully. "Come and have luncheon with us. Or with me, at least. The baby changes Kate's plans whenever she can!"

"Oh, no, I won't intrude," Dove said at once. "I was just hoping for a word with you and Mrs. Grant."

"About the girl from the box?"

"Yes."

"Come in," Grant said, leading him straight to the drawing room, where Kate bounced up to meet him before she had even seen Doverton.

"Tris! You're home early, for once," she exclaimed. "Oh, and you've brought the major. Have you seen our patient, sir?"

"Yes, I have," Dove said, taking the seat she offered. "She has no memory of anything before being in the sea, so far as I can gather. She doesn't even know her name, though she's picked 'Tillie' for now. I'm not sure it suits her."

"In what way does it not suit her?" Grant asked, amused.

Dove shrugged. "I suppose because my mother had a maid called Tillie. And I don't think she's anyone's maid."

"Why not?" Grant asked.

"She speaks too well to be anything other than from a well-educated family."

"You think she is a duchess in disguise?" Grant asked, grinning openly.

"No, but—"

"She might be," Mrs. Grant interrupted.

They both blinked at her.

"I never heard her speak," she admitted. "But her clothes… I didn't notice last night because everything looks like a rag when it's soaked in sea water. But now that they're cleaned and drying, I can see quite clearly that the dress she wore, her underclothes, her pelisse, her boots—all are of the highest quality."

"It makes her wealthy," Grant said. "It doesn't make her a duchess."

"What do you have against duchesses?" Dove demanded. "But you're right. It doesn't mean she's noble. She could be the daughter of some cit or mill owner, or even a governess left a fortune by her dotty employer. Either way, it puts a different cast on what happened to her. She's no stowaway, no unfortunate fish wife who got on the wrong side of smugglers. She's a lady of means. And most people would think twice before putting such a lady in a box."

THE GIRL WHO had called herself Tillie—for no reason other than the name had popped into her head—watched the major leave with a mixture of disappointment and hope. For the first time since she'd wakened in the cold, wet darkness, she felt some sense of certainty, rooted in the person of Major Doverton, the man who had pulled her from the darkness. His very existence soothed her, his presence cheered her, and she hadn't wanted him to go. On the other hand, she felt so much better for talking to him. And she had hope of seeing him again.

For now, since she could not remember before, her life had started last night in the storm. And she hadn't made good work of it so far.

She let a rueful smile curve her lips and became aware her gaze was locked with that of the girl with the baby in the other bed.

"Have I been rude to you, too?" she asked.

"Lord, no, miss. You don't need to talk to anyone you don't want to."

"To be honest, I didn't know if any of you were real," Tillie confided. "I thought I might still be dreaming." She shivered. "I was in a nightmare where I knew nothing..." And feared plunging back into the darkness. "Your baby doesn't cry."

"No, he's good as gold, isn't he?" the girl said proudly. "He opens his little eyes, I feed him and change him, and he goes back to sleep."

Tillie leaned out of bed to see him better, and the girl, obligingly, drew the shawl away from his face. Tillie smiled. "He's beautiful," she said warmly. She raised her gaze to the proud mother. "But this is a hospital. Is he ill?"

"He were lying wrong. My ma wouldn't have the midwife or the doctor for shame."

"Shame of what?" Tillie asked blankly.

"I'm not married," the girl said defiantly.

Tillie frowned. "I've a feeling you're better off with a baby than a husband."

A surprised laugh escaped the other girl. "Well that's a novel way of looking at it! Anyway, Mrs. Grant—who's the vicar's wife and has a gorgeous little baby of her own—called in when my pains were starting, and then Dr. Lampton came anyway. He brought me here and turned the baby so he could be born. But he says neither of us is strong enough to leave."

"Are you content to be here?"

"Yes, for I don't think I could cope on my own. Got no energy. And they're kind here, hardly lecture me at all. I'm Annie, by the way. Annie Doone. And this is little George."

"After the king?" Tillie said, and then frowned. How did she know the king was called George when she didn't know her own name?

In any case, Annie shook her head. "After his father."

Tillie looked at her. "What happened to his father?"

"I don't know." Annie said. "It's like he vanished off the end of the world."

"Except there is no end," Tillie said, hoping to comfort. "It just goes all the way round until you're back where you started. Perhaps your George—big George—will end up back here with you."

Annie smiled, though tears glistened in her eyes.

Distracting her, Tillie said, "Annie, is there a looking glass here?"

"I've got one," Annie said proudly. "In the drawer. Borrow it whenever you wish."

Tillie reached down and opened the drawer in the bedside table between them. She found an old hand-held glass with several cracks, but she took it anyway and sat up, peering at the face that stared back at her.

She touched her eyes and cheeks and lips, as though the contact might turn them from a stranger's features into her own. From her appearance, she was no older than Annie, but that didn't really help. She tried lifting up her hair, as it might look pinned, but nothing looked familiar to her.

"You're very pretty, miss," Annie assured her.

"So are you, Annie," Tillie said. "But I'm not sure it helps either of us."

Chapter Three

LUNCHEON IN THE hospital was a decent meal that Tillie didn't really want, then suddenly wolfed anyhow because as soon as she started, she realized how hungry was. She had no idea when she'd last eaten.

Annie ate with gusto, too, and then invited Tillie to admire little George's beautiful eyes, for the baby had wakened and she was about to feed him. Tillie slid out of bed in her borrowed night rail to get a closer look and agreed that she had never seen more beautiful eyes than George's.

"Mind you," Annie pointed out. "To all intents and purposes, you haven't seen many eyes, have you?"

"I suppose not."

"Major Doverton's eyes are very fine," Annie mused.

Tillie smiled. "Do you think so? I am sure they are nowhere near George's beauty." Though it was true they were very fine. Dark and deep, with lurking laughter and hidden pain. She glanced from the baby to Annie. "Do you know the major?"

"Lord, no, we don't exactly move in the same circles! He commanded the 44th, or at least those left behind when the rest went to Spain. Until they all came home again with Colonel Gordon. The men like him. And the quality folks in town. But he's a bit of a mystery."

"How so?" Tillie asked, intrigued.

Annie shrugged. "He just doesn't mix much. He never goes to the tavern or misbehaves. Goes to the assembly room balls sometimes. I hear some have cast their lures out to him but he never bites."

"Then he isn't married?" Tillie asked in surprise.

"No, not that I ever heard."

There was no reason for that to please Tillie and yet it did.

"What are you doing out of bed, Tillie?" Mrs. Brown demanded from the doorway. "Doctor said bed until tomorrow at the earliest!"

"Well, it's almost bed," Tillie wheedled. "I only stepped across to see little George."

"Then oblige me by stepping back and making yourself decent to greet Mrs. Grant."

Tillie bolted back into bed. She had already apologized to Mrs. Brown and the other staff, but she owed Mrs. Grant rather more. However, the vicar's wife sailed into the room without waiting.

"Oh goodness, there's no need of formality," she said. "We are all women, after all. Why, you are looking so much better than this morning!"

"I feel much better," Tillie acknowledged. "And I owe you so much gratitude and so many apologies, I don't know where to begin."

"Then don't. We'll take it as understood. For in truth, I did nothing but lend you a sofa and ask my servants to look after you."

"But I was unappreciative and rude," Tillie said. "Will you pass my apologies also to Mr. Grant?"

"Of course, though there is as little need." She turned to the other girl. "And how are you, Annie? Both doing better, I hear."

"Definitely, ma'am," Annie said fervently.

For a few minutes, the two exchanged baby news and experiences, to which Tillie had nothing to contribute, although she drank it all in until Mrs. Grant turned back to her.

"Major Doverton tells me your name is Tillie."

"Maybe," Tillie said cautiously. "I have a feeling I heard it a lot. Or perhaps said it a lot. And I remembered the king's name is George!"

"And the queen's?" Mrs. Grant asked mildly.

"Charlotte."

"And their eldest son?"

"George, the Prince Regent. I do seem to know these things. I know we have been at war with France for years and are now at peace. I could recite you the countries of the globe—although I will spare you—but still I could not tell you a thing about myself."

Mrs. Grant, who carried a book under one arm, set it on the bed beside her. "And can you read the title of this?"

"*The Mysteries of Udolpho*," Tillie read, picking it up and looking at the spine. "By Mrs. Radcliffe."

"Have you read it?"

Tillie frowned. "I don't know. But I do know Mrs. Radcliffe writes delightfully gothic romances."

"Keep it," Mrs. Grant said. She seemed to be looking at Tillie's hands on the book. "Perhaps if you read it, it will help jog your memory. Who knows? At least it will entertain you."

"Thank you," Tillie said, touched. "I think I will enjoy it."

"Now," Mrs. Grant said, a little more briskly. "Providing Dr. Lampton sees no harm in it, Major Doverton would like you to meet the crew of *The Phoenix* tomorrow morning. Would you object to that?"

"No...will he be there?"

"The major? Oh, yes."

Tillie gave a quick smile. It might have been relief, or pleasure. She couldn't tell. She lifted her gaze to Mrs. Grant's face. "Do you know him well?"

"No, I can't say I do." Mrs. Grant regarded her thoughtfully, then added, "He is a much more private person than many of the officers in Blackhaven. But I do know he is a good man. He has helped many people here, including friends of mine. And he organized the rescue last night, as well as bringing you and several others ashore in the storm."

"I think he has a tragedy in his life."

Mrs. Grant blinked. "If he does, I don't know what it is."

Mrs. Brown reappeared and took the baby while her underlings wrestled Annie into a robe. Then, they all went for a short promenade to the nursery where the baby would stay while Annie napped.

"They look after her very well," Tillie observed as Mrs. Grant stood to leave also. "Mrs. Grant?" she added on impulse. "Did you know little George's father?"

She shook her head. "No. Annie hasn't told me who he is."

"His name was George and he vanished."

"Sadly, that is often the way of it."

"Then you think he vanished deliberately?" Tillie asked her.

"I don't know. But neither is good, is it? Either something bad happened to him, keeping him from her, or else he has simply abandoned her."

Tillie nodded, frowning, then shook herself and smiled. "Thank you for everything, Mrs. Grant, including the book."

"You're welcome. Dr. Lampton will let you know about meeting the crew tomorrow."

IN THE MORNING, after examining her, Dr. Lampton pronounced her fit to go to the vicarage. "Mrs. Grant will send her carriage for you. It isn't far to walk, but I would prefer you to rest."

"Thank you," Tillie said meekly. She suspected all this resting was about to irk her, but since she had only just apologized to Dr. Lampton for previous rudeness, she held herself in check.

"And what of your memory?" he asked her. "Have you remembered anything more?"

She shook her head, feeling again that odd, fearful tilt, as though she were about to fall back into the airless, spinning darkness. She grasped the side of the bed, as though to anchor herself there.

Dr. Lampton followed the gesture but said only, "Don't worry. It can take time. Major Doverton and Mr. Winslow, the magistrate, are trying to trace your family so you will at least have the comfort of knowing who you are. And familiar faces may well jog your memory." He stood up, and his gaze fell on the book Mrs. Grant had left for her. "Have you been reading it?"

"Yes, we began it yesterday evening," Tillie replied.

"Both of you?" As though amused, Lampton turned to include Annie, who was feeding little George.

"Oh yes," Annie said fervently. "Tillie read it aloud to me. It's *wonderful!*"

"That it is," the doctor agreed with a certain ambiguity not lost on Tillie. Some people despised such tales, though she wasn't quite sure how she knew this. Some words, some tone of voice hovered on the edge of her memory, but eluded her.

When the doctor left, Tillie found it hard to contain her excitement. She was impatient to be up and off to the vicarage, and she had actually climbed out of bed with the intention of going in search of her clothes when Mrs. Cross brought them to her.

It was only as she took off her night rail that she realized her body was covered in bruises. She paused, staring at them. She supposed such injuries were inevitable from bouncing and spinning in the box, from deliberately throwing herself against the sides...

"Goodness," Annie said, awed. "Those must be painful."

"I suppose it explains why it aches to do anything." And she was certainly relieved Mrs. Cross had brought her no stays. The chemise and gown and warm pelisse were all vaguely familiar, though only because she recalled them clinging wetly to her body, and then being wrestled off her. She had been shaking uncontrollably at the time, yet was far too numb to feel the cold.

She shivered, banishing the memory as Mrs. Cross fastened the gown.

"My, how splendid you look," Annie approved from her bed. Little George had fallen asleep in her arms. "I thought you talked all proper—now you look like a lady, too. No wonder you can read."

Tillie looked doubtfully at her sea-damaged gown and pelisse. "I won't look like a lady without a hat of some kind. Lord, and I must pin up my hair."

"Here. I'll do that for you," Annie offered. "George won't mind."

"And I'll fetch your cloak from the drying room," added Mrs.

Cross, who had become very helpful and friendly since Tillie's humble apology. "You can pull the hood over your hair while you're outside."

"You look lovely," Annie said warmly when she was ready to depart.

Tillie cast her a grateful if doubtful smile. For some reason, she wanted Major Doverton to see her as more than the half-drowned rat he'd rescued from the sea.

Stepping into the carriage seemed a quite familiar act. But then, Dr. Lampton had brought her to the hospital in a carriage. Any others were beyond the reach of her memory.

It was a short five-minute drive to the vicarage. Tillie's heart beat hard the whole way, because she might recognize the sailors from *The Phoenix*, because they might know her. Because maybe one of them had shut her in a box, leaving her to die when the ship foundered against the rocks.

And because she would see Major Doverton again. For although she was finding her feet in this strange life, she felt more *comfortable* when he was with her.

She kept her hood up inside the carriage and gazed out the window at Blackhaven. Between the buildings, she glimpsed the sea, and further round the coast, a castle perched on the cliff, looking down over the town and the coast. The town was small, but quite picturesque, although clearly growing. A large hotel took pride of place in the main street, and on the other side of the road, a coffee house, a porticoed entrance to the Assembly Rooms, and several quality shops. Wealthy people resided here.

When the carriage stopped outside the vicarage, she waited for the door to be opened for her and the steps let down. Yes, this was natural to her...

The servant who admitted her appeared to recognize her, and with a civil bow, took her cloak and conducted her to the drawing room. As she walked in, her heart lifted, because she had begun to be afraid the major wouldn't be there after all, but he sat on the sofa beside Mrs. Grant, apparently in serious conversation, though both stood as she entered.

Mrs. Grant hurried toward her, hand stretched out. "Tillie, how well you look!"

"Thank you, I feel much better," she managed. "Annie tried to hide this ugly dressing in my hair, but I'm not sure how successful she was."

"Very," Mrs. Grant assured her, and moved aside.

Major Doverton stood in front of her. Her heart gave a funny little flutter as she looked up and up. She had never stood beside him before and hadn't realized he was so tall. More than that, he overwhelmed her. The kindness and the pain in his eyes, the small scar on his cheek, the sheer character in his harsh-featured yet handsome face—all hit her in the stomach like a blow. Winded, she could not speak.

His eyes twinkled. "Miss Waif," he said, bowing. "I hope you are feeling as well as you look,"

"Miss Waif?" she managed. "Surely that cannot be my name?"

"I don't see why not," he teased. "Until we learn the truth, you are Miss Tillie Waif, a gift of the sea."

She frowned. "I think I am rather *taken* from the sea which makes me more plunder than gift."

"Miss Plunder doesn't roll off the tongue so easily."

A breath of laughter escaped her. "I didn't realize you talked so much nonsense." Of course, it had been designed to put her at her ease, and it succeeded.

"Come, sit for a moment," Mrs. Grant urged. "We'll have some refreshment in just a little, after you meet *The Phoenix* seamen."

Tillie sat on the sofa with Mrs. Grant beside her and turned earnestly toward her.

"My husband is with them just now," Mrs. Grant continued. She hesitated, then said, "The thing is, as well as hoping to jog your memory, we want to catch them unaware, see how they react when you are suddenly introduced to them."

Distress twisted through Tillie, but she would not give in to it. She lifted her chin. "Because one of them put me in the box?"

"It does seem likely," Major Doverton said quietly.

"I wonder what I did to inspire such hatred."

"The fault is not yours," he said at once. "And putting you there was not necessarily malicious. Also…one man died that night. It could have been him. But this is at least something to try if you are willing."

She nodded. "I am."

"The captain—Captain Smith—did not appear to know anything about you," Mrs. Grant added, "but he did have warning we were asking him to meet a lady we'd found in the sea."

"If you're ready," Doverton said, offering her his arm, "we could get it over with quickly."

Tillie stood at once, took his arm determinedly, and followed Mrs. Grant out of the room and across the hall to another apartment at the back of the house. Of course, they had not wanted the men to see her walking up the path.

Her stomach tightened with tension. "Will you be with me?" she blurted to the major.

"Of course. As will Mr. and Mrs. Grant. And Brent," he added, nodding to the servant, who suddenly threw open the door.

Chapter Four

H ER FINGERS TIGHTENED on the major's coat as she walked into a good-sized study. The walls were lined with books, and a large, cluttered desk clearly had pride of place in the room under normal circumstances. Right now, several ordinary seamen stood around, looking awkward. Only slightly less so were their officers, including the one who stood beside the vicar at the fireplace.

Silence fell as all heads turned toward her and Major Doverton. One of these men, probably, had nailed her into a wooden box to die in the darkness. She shivered, and Doverton's hand covered hers on his arm in an instinctive gesture of comfort. It gave her the courage to meet every gaze she encountered on her excruciating walk across the study to the vicar.

Mr. Grant smiled. "How wonderful to see you looking so well."

"I wanted to thank you in person for your hospitality," she said. "I may have seemed unappreciative at the time."

His eyes twinkled. "Let us call it shyness. And indeed, it was our pleasure. Allow me to introduce your fellow survivor, Captain Smith."

She met the captain's frowning stare, even forced herself to offer her hand. But she felt no recognition, and saw none in his unhappy face.

"No idea how you got among us," he said stiffly, as though it were her fault—which, of course, it might have been. "But very glad to see you alive and well. This is my first mate and my navigator, Mr. Yates and Mr. Wilson."

Both younger gentlemen showed a tendency to stare and blush, though Tillie put that down less to guilt than their being unused to the company of ladies. She nodded to them and to the crewmen clustered about the study gawping at her.

"I'm sorry for the loss of your fellow seaman," she said.

"I believe it's down to the major that our losses weren't greater," the captain said gruffly. "And we have recovered some of our cargo. Although, sadly, the ship is gone forever."

"I hope it does not take your livelihood with it," Tillie said. "Did you own the ship, sir?"

"I had a share in it. But at least it was insured, so I shall buy into another."

Tillie murmured something about wishing them all well and then, mercifully, Major Doverton was leading her back across the room. She felt she did not breathe until Mrs. Grant closed the door behind them all and led the way back to the drawing room.

Tillie's head, her whole body, was swirling with the memory of the rolling ship. More feeling than detailed recollection, it still shattered her all over again. Only the man beside her seemed to be holding her upright.

At last, she sank down on the sofa once more.

Doverton crouched at her feet in clear concern. "What is it? What do you remember?"

"Nothing," she whispered. "None of them seemed familiar to me. If I've met any of them, I don't recall it." She rubbed her aching forehead. "I...I just remember the weaving darkness, the sense of suffocation, of pure panic..."

She drew in a breath that was only half-sob and tried to smile. "I'm sorry. I don't seem to be as brave as I thought I was. Or as helpful."

Doverton pressed her hand and stood up. "Of course you are. More so than ever."

Forcing herself, Tillie gathered her thoughts and glanced from the major to Mrs. Grant. "Did you see any signs of recognition or guilt among them?"

"I confess, I did not," Doverton said ruefully as the door opened and Mr. Grant came in.

"Neither did I," Mrs. Grant admitted.

"Nor I," Grant said. "Thank you for putting yourself through that, Miss Tillie."

"I'm sorry it didn't help us," she said. "Though, in a way, I confess I'm glad none of them was responsible."

"Not for your ordeal, perhaps," Grant said heavily. "But if you ask me, there is something inherently dishonest in Captain Smith."

"There is," Doverton agreed. "I've set some inquiries in motion in Liverpool and in Sweden. He seems anxious to be off, and we have no reason so far to keep him here. But for now, at least, he's at the hotel and his men at the tavern."

"Still rescuing his cargo?" Mrs. Grant asked.

Doverton gave a wry smile. "I wish him joy of that. I suspect a great deal of it is already in the hands—and stomachs—of Blackhaven residents. No, I have the feeling the cargo is an excuse. He's anxious. I think he's waiting for something or someone."

Tea was brought in then, and while she drank, Tillie found herself joining with enthusiasm the speculation about *The Phoenix* and her captain.

"Perhaps they're smuggling under cover of respectable cargo," she suggested.

"The brandy we found is French," Doverton admitted. "But it's a legal export since the peace, and if it doesn't land here, it doesn't need to pay duty. I doubt he needs to be so shifty about that."

"But he was down at the beach early yesterday morning," Grant pointed out. "Recovering everything he could, as you might expect, but he seemed very nervous, almost *furtive*."

"That is true," Doverton allowed. "Perhaps he was looking for personal things."

"Perhaps he found them, and that is why he is no longer truly anxious about his cargo," Tillie said.

"You mean he was just searching for a missing, water stained portrait of his wife?" Mrs. Grant said.

"Or a secret message he was carrying between Bonapartist spies," Tillie said with enthusiasm. "He has been bullied or bribed into betraying his country."

"By Montoni himself, no doubt," Doverton said gravely.

Tillie, who at once recognized the name of the villain from *The Mysteries of Udolpho*, only laughed. Mrs. Grant or Dr. Lampton must have told him about the gift of the book "I knew you would have read it," she crowed. And then felt suddenly breathless when his eyes laughed back at her.

"Nicholas," Mrs. Grant said as Tillie finished her cup of tea, "that is, Dr. Lampton, said we were to send you back to the hospital in an hour. I never disobey him, but...are you quite *comfortable* there?"

"Why, yes, everyone is most kind—especially after I stopped being foolish and spoke to them!"

"And sharing a chamber with Annie Doone?"

"I could not have found anyone better natured. She's mesmerized by *The Mysteries of Udolpho*, too."

"You read it to her?" Mrs. Grant asked, as though surprised.

"Oh, yes." For some reason, she was aware of Major Doverton's gaze on her, too. "Why?"

"I hope you will not think me snobbish," Mrs. Grant said. "But you are clearly a lady of some education and manners. While I like Annie, she is a fisherman's daughter and an unwed mother. It is possibly not an acquaintance your family would encourage."

Tillie thought about that. "Perhaps there are advantages to re-membering nothing."

"Perhaps," Mrs. Grant agreed. "But you may have a father, a brother, or even a husband who thinks otherwise."

Tillie's eyes widened in horror. "A *husband*? Oh, good God, I hope not."

"Oh, some of us aren't so bad," Mr. Grant said in amusement.

Tillie flushed. "Of course, I did not mean...only it never entered my head that I was married." She gave a slightly nervous laugh. "Maybe my husband put me in the box to punish me for my addiction to trashy novels."

Mr. and Mrs. Grant looked appalled, though whether at her suspecting such a thing or the mere possibility that it could be true, Tilly could not tell.

"Well, if he did," Major Doverton said, "he is clearly a villain, and I shall run him through for you."

"Thank you, you are most obliging."

Everyone laughed, and the tension seemed to vanish. Tillie, deciding it was time to go, rose to her feet. "I think my hour is up," she said to the Grants. "Thank you again for your help."

"Let me ring for the carriage," Mrs. Grant said at once.

"Oh, no, please, I would rather walk. I long for some fresh air."

"I don't think Dr. Lampton would like you walking so far," Doverton said. "I could walk with you as far as the hotel, where I can hand you into a hired cab. It's only a short stroll from here."

She opened her mouth to dissuade him, then closed it again. "Thank you," she said meekly. "If you are sure I'm not taking up too much of your time."

"Not in the slightest."

At the front door, she drew the hood of her cloak over her hair before walking up the path in front of Major Doverton. Outside the garden gate, she waited for him.

"Is it much of a detour to the sea?" she asked.

"We can walk via the harbor if it wouldn't tire you."

"I think I would like to." She glanced at him. "Thank you for coming with me. I wish very much to ask a favor of you."

He glanced at her, his dark, intriguing eyes unreadable. "Please do. If it's in my power, I will."

She took a deep breath. "You seem to be man who knows who and where to ask about people and find information. You are already looking for my family and investigating *The Phoenix* and so on... I would like to ask you to find out about another man."

His eyes had grown opaque, "Who? Someone you've remembered?"

"Oh, no. I'm sure I've never met him in my life. His name is George Trent. He's a private soldier, and he's the father of Annie Doone's baby."

He blinked, and yet he was sure something had lightened in his face. "Is he one of mine?" he asked. "That is, in the 44th? If so, I'll see he does his duty by her."

Tillie shook her head. "No, but she met him in Whalen, which I believe is only a few miles from Blackhaven, in company with one of your wounded soldiers. Apparently, they'd been friends in the Peninsula. Annie stopped to talk to your man whom she knew already and ended stepping out with the other. They parted when he was, apparently, sent back to join his own regiment, only she can't tell me what that regiment was or anything else about him except his name and the fact that he was going to be a solicitor's clerk once he was free of the army. Don't think badly of her. She is an affectionate and trusting soul."

"It's hardly my place to judge her, but consider, there is probably a reason he told her no more. He could be married already. There are many men who take such advantage of trusting girls and then hide themselves so they can't be held responsible."

"I know. So does Annie. That's one reason she hasn't told anyone else who the father is, because she can't bear anyone to think badly of him. She still believes he will come back."

"I imagine it's unlikely by this stage. Does she at least have the name of his friend in the 44th?"

"She called him Gunn. I'm afraid I don't have anything else."

"I'll see what I can discover," Doverton promised.

By then, they were approaching a picturesque little harbor lined with fishing boats. The pale winter sunshine reflected in the glassy sea turning it a soft, silvery grey.

"It doesn't look the same element that battered us the night before last," Tillie observed as they paused by the harbor wall. The wind was icy on her face, but not strong.

"No," Doverton agreed. "But it will turn again at the drop of a hat."

After a few moments, she felt his gaze on her face. "Are you wondering if I am used to the sea?" she asked.

"It crossed my mind."

"I don't know. I don't feel frightened of it now. But I was when you found me."

"I would have been, too. In fact, I was!"

"You gave no sign of it."

"Of course not," he said, with mockingly blatant shock. "I am an officer and a gentleman."

"Of course." She inclined her head in similar style. "Were you in the Peninsula, too?"

"Until 1812."

"What happened in 1812? To send you home, I mean."

"The Battle of Salamanca, mainly. I was injured and sent home to—for treatment." His sudden change from what he'd been going to say was smooth, but not lost on Tillie. Intrigued, she cast him a sharp glance, but he went on at once, "And then they let me shuffle papers at headquarters while the colonel was abroad. Come, it's too cold for you to stand still. Let's walk on."

She took his offered arm, and her heart skipped a beat. She liked to be walking so close to him, to feel the hard muscle of his arm beneath his coat, and the movement of his body almost brushing against her skirts. It seemed novel and rather wonderful. Whatever her life had been, she doubted she had walked like this with a man before, certainly not a man like Major Doverton.

They strolled past some market stalls, where people of all sorts were buying meat and cheese and various household items. Two well-dressed ladies cast them blatantly curious looks. Major Doverton bowed to them, and they walked on past a tavern on the other side of the road.

"What will you do now that the war is over?" she asked him. "Will you keep your position in the 44th, or go on to half-pay?"

"Do you know someone who has already done so?" he asked.

She frowned. "I don't know. Perhaps I just read about it." She looked up at him. "You're not avoiding answering me, are you? Is it none of my business?"

His lips quirked. "Am I being grumpy? Forgive me, my future is not yet decided. I might retire altogether and cultivate roses. Or grow lemon trees somewhere near the Mediterranean, now there is no war to make travelling difficult."

"I would love to travel," she said with enthusiasm, although she frowned almost immediately afterward. "At least, I think I would. It does involve crossing the sea."

"It's only a few hours to France with a fair wind. You could spend it all on deck."

"I suppose travelling inside a box is not natural or normal," she said lightly, although she couldn't prevent the catch in her voice.

Briefly, he touched her hand on his arm. "The nightmares will go, in time," he said gently.

"I think you speak from experience," she said curiously.

"Everyone has nightmares occasionally."

"What are yours about?" She thought he would say battle, but again he surprised her.

"Failure."

She blinked. "Failure in what?"

"Keeping men alive, mostly."

She regarded his strong, handsome profile with new fascination. "The world is not *all* on your shoulders."

He glanced at her with a quick, self-deprecating shrug. "But in my dreams, I am obviously all-important. What are your nightmares about? Water?"

"Darkness." She shivered. "I made Annie leave the lamp lit all night."

"Did it help?"

Her lips twisted. "When I opened my eyes, yes. What do you do to chase the dreams away?"

He shrugged. "I think of things I can control."

For him, she mused, that would be a great deal. He was a man of strength and character, and in an important position that must affect many lives. Tillie didn't even know who she was.

They had reached the main street by then. Although quite gracious for a small-town street, it was not particularly busy.

"It's a little quiet in winter," Major Doverton observed. "Since it takes a stout heart to face Cumberland in January. But in a few weeks, there will be more visitors to take the miracle waters."

She regarded him with some doubt. "Are you joking?"

"That people come just to drink the water? No, they really do. Of course, they don't all find the miracle they're looking for, but enough seem to do so that it keeps people coming."

She frowned. "I can't imagine a drink of water bringing my memory back, but I could try. Dr. Lampton did not mention it."

"Lampton is a man of science, not faith. He is also used to the success of his own treatments being attributed to the waters instead. And so Blackhaven's health reputation thrives."

"You are a cynic," she observed, smiling.

"I confess. But I am happy to conduct you to the pump room to take the waters, should you require an escort. Providing Dr. Lampton permits you to go. Other entertainments of the town include the assembly room balls, which have been going on through the winter. That is the assembly building on your left. Also, an art gallery further down High Street, and a small theatre. There is an ice parlor to rival Gunther's, and I believe the hotel does excellent afternoon tea. And that—apart from the people—is Blackhaven in a nutshell."

"I would like to hear about the people. Mrs. Grant, for example, although most kind, does not seem to me very like a vicar's wife." Her lips twisted. "Though to be sure, I can't actually remember any others."

"Well, Grant is quite an unusual vicar, too. In a good way. I'm sure you'll get to know everyone before too long."

"Perhaps," she said doubtfully. "I think it might be difficult when I don't know who I am, which part of society I belong to. Mrs. Grant thinks I am too respectable for Annie. I suspect Annie would agree with her. But this is all based on the fact that I can read and I speak well. But I could be an actress or a courtesan."

Doverton blinked, then gazed at her, his expression unreadable. "I doubt it. You'll remember everything in time."

They had reached the hotel by then, and two waiting cabs a few yards further down the road. The drivers were chatting together in the shelter of the building, stamping their feet to keep warm. But as they approached, one man grinned and came immediately toward them, touching his hat.

"Where to, Major Dove?" he asked cheerfully.

"Morning, Colton," the major replied in unexpectedly friendly spirit. "Take the lady to the hospital, if you please."

Only then did Tillie realize her predicament. "Oh!" She stepped back. "I should have thought. I have no money to pay."

"It's a trivial amount, and you may pay me back when you're settled," Doverton said casually. He opened the door as the driver climbed up, and after a moment, she accepted his hand and stepped inside.

"Thank you," she muttered in embarrassment.

He smiled and closed the door before he moved forward to exchange a few words and some coins with the driver.

He touched his hat to her, and the horses clopped away. She had to squash her foolish sense of panic by thinking of him and everything he'd said. And when she would see him again.

Chapter Five

"KNOW A MAN called Gunn?" Dove asked his batman that night as he prepared for dinner in the officers' mess.

"In the regiment?"

"Yes. Wounded at some point but not invalided out."

Cully scratched his head. "Maybe. What's he done?"

"Nothing that I know of. Send him to see me after dinner, would you? He's not in trouble."

Dinner that evening was a bit of a trial. His abdomen was still sore from the storm rescue, and he really wanted to lie in bed and sleep instead of making civil conversation with Mrs. Gordon, the colonel's wife, and his fellow officers.

Worse, Mrs. Gordon was an inveterate gossip, and he knew the questions were coming. He didn't have long to wait.

"Tell me, Major, who is the mysterious lady I saw you with at the market this morning?"

"I'm afraid I don't know, ma'am."

She laughed heartily, drawing everyone else's attention to the conversation, too. "Oh, come, Major. You needn't be shy. You bowed to me, so you know exactly which lady I mean."

"Yes, but seriously, I don't know who she is. She's the lady we rescued in the storm. She hurt her head and remembers nothing before the storm."

"How extraordinary," Mrs. Gordon exclaimed.

"Not that extraordinary, m'dear," the colonel said casually. "We had a few men lost their memories over the years, didn't we, Dove?

Fellow at Badajoz for one."

"Yes, sir, he remembered most of his life eventually, but he never remembered how he got the injury."

"Was your injury to your head, Major?" Captain Blackshaw asked. His voice was casual, but the look in his eyes was contemptuous and challenging.

Too much wine and resentment, Dove thought with some contempt of his own. "No," he replied shortly, and turned back to Mrs. Gordon.

"I just wondered what kept you from active duty for so long," Blackshaw continued. "Injured at Salamanca back in July of 1812, and yet nearly two years later, by the time we finally defeated Bonaparte, you still hadn't rejoined the rest of your battalion."

Doverton cast him a look of lazy amusement. "Looking for easy promotion, Blackshaw? I'm not going to die yet."

There was ripple of slightly uneasy laughter which caused Black-shaw to flush with anger. Kit Grantham's lips moved under cover of the noise, clearly warning Blackshaw off. It might work for this evening, but sooner or later, there was going to be real confrontation with Blackshaw. Doverton didn't know why, and right now, didn't much care. The very thought made him weary. Maybe it was time to sell out and grow roses. Or lemon trees. It would, finally, be a peaceful end for a man who had lived for war.

An image flashed through his mind. Sitting under a lemon tree in the sunshine, with his head on Tillie's lap. She smiled down at him, stroked his hair.

He banished the picture with a curl of his lip and turned back to Mrs. Gordon, who was saying, "I expect you will go to the Assembly ball next week."

"I expect I shall," he agreed and wondered if there was a way for Tillie to go.

He had to stop thinking about her. Whatever she had wondered aloud, he was sure she was no courtesan. In a lascivious moment, he had almost wished she were. He had to remind himself he barely knew the girl. And even then, he knew about as much as she did.

"Stay for another brandy, Dove," the colonel suggested when he finally excused himself after the interminable meal.

"I won't, sir, thank you. I have someone to see."

"Not the waif with no memory?" Gordon said with a grin.

"No one half so pretty, sir, I assure you." Amid the general laughter, he left the table and returned with relief to his own rooms, where he found Cully waiting along with a good-looking young soldier.

They both leapt to their feet as Dove entered. The young soldier stood particularly straight and stiff.

"Gunn, sir," Cully said. "From Mr. Blackshaw's company."

"Of course you are," Dove murmured with an internal groan. "Thank you for your time, Gunn. I hope Cully told you you're not in trouble. I'm merely looking for someone and I believe you might know him. One George Trent? From another regiment, though I don't know which."

"Yes sir, I know Trent. He pulled me back behind the lines after I was shot at Burgos. Saved my life, I reckon."

"It sounds like it. When did you last see him?"

Gunn considered. "Must have been when he came to Blackhaven last spring, just before I went back to the war. Though it was all over by the time I got there…"

"Was he injured, too?" Dove asked.

"Lost a hand, sir. Invalided out, poor bastard. But he was coping very well."

This wasn't quite what Dove had expected to hear. Nor exactly what Tillie had told him. "Poor bastard indeed. Did he by any chance step out with a girl from Blackhaven?"

"None of my business, sir," Gunn said at once.

"Unfortunately, it has become mine."

"I don't know, sir. We met Annie Doone in Whalen and he seemed quite taken with her. Beyond that," Gurney said firmly. "I know nothing."

"But you know Annie Doone has a baby? Don't you think Trent would like to know?"

"Seems to me if he did, he'd be here," Gunn said bluntly.

"Where is he?"

"No idea, sir. He's got family somewhere near Manchester."

"Is he married, Gunn?"

"Wasn't then, to my knowledge."

"Got an address for him?"

"No, sir. He don't have mine, either. He just turned up at the barracks one day, out of the blue, asking for me."

"Don't you have any way of finding him?"

Gunn hesitated. "I know of an alehouse in Manchester."

Dove groaned inwardly. "Tell me."

APART FROM WAKING up once in the middle of the night and panicking because the lamp had gone out, Tillie slept well. On the other hand, Annie's night had been disturbed. She had been wakened by Tillie's terrified thrashing about the room to find a light and had risen to light a stub of candle for her. In the morning, she wanted to sleep longer than George would allow.

"What's the matter with him?" she demanded, frightened. "Call Mrs. Brown for me, Miss Tillie!"

"He's crying," Tillie said, gazing at her in consternation. "Isn't he meant to do that when he's hungry?"

Annie picked him up. "Well, he never has before." As soon as she put him to her breast, he stopped crying.

Since Dr. Lampton came in just then, he was quickly told the story of the crying and assured Annie that this was, in fact, a sign of improved health. "Keep feeding him," he commanded, "and I will take a look at him later, just to be sure." He turned to Tillie. "And how are you this morning?"

"I feel fine. Still a little stiff and sore, but a short walk yesterday seemed to help." She gave a tentative smile. "I should not be taking up space in your hospital, but I'm not sure where else I can go."

"I'll look into it for you," he said surprisingly. "For now, sit down so that I can examine the wound on your head."

Tillie obeyed and was gratified to hear the wound was still clean and healing well.

Mrs. Brown stuck her head around the door.

"He cried!" Annie told her triumphantly.

"Well, that is good news," Mrs. Brown said complacently. "Of course, he will plague you now that he knows how! Doctor, Major Doverton is here."

Tillie's heart lurched at mention of the major.

"I'll be down in half an hour," Dr. Lampton said irritably.

"Oh, no, he doesn't want to see *you*, but Miss Tillie."

Tillie's breath caught. She could hardly refrain from smiling.

Dr. Lampton's lips twitched as he sat back and regarded her. "Do you want to see Major Doverton?"

"I would be happy to," Tillie managed, blushing.

"I see." He stood up. "Well, get dressed while I speak to him."

As Tillie dressed in haste in her only garments, it came to her that this was not normal for her. Though she could not recall any other garments specifically, she was sure she had owned many, that it was normal to have a choice and make decisions about them. Or perhaps that was merely wishful thinking.

At any rate, with Mrs. Brown to help with fastenings, she was soon dressed with her hair brushed and pinned. She could not help hurrying downstairs to the foyer, where she discovered Dr. Lampton still in conversation with Major Doverton.

They sat on a wooden bench, leaning forward, talking quietly and intensely. It was the major who saw her first. His eyes seemed to light up immediately, his lips curving into a spontaneous smile that made butterflies soar in her stomach.

Dr. Lampton stopped talking and turned toward her. They both stood and walked to meet her. She offered Major Doverton her hand—a little shyly since she was once more overwhelmed by the sheer size and presence of the man.

He bowed over it politely. "Miss Tillie. Dr. Lampton has just given his permission for you to go to the pump room and take the waters."

Lampton shrugged. "It won't do you any harm. In fact, the fresh air and the company of people may well do you good. Forgive me, I have other patients to see. Good morning." In his abrupt way, he strode off.

The major said, "I happily offer my escort. But if you would rather go with Mrs.—"

"Thank you, you're very kind," she said, already walking toward the door.

"Your confinement to the hospital is irking you," he observed, holding the door for her.

"I have nothing to do but read and talk to Annie. They don't like me to prowl around the corridors, let alone run there. I feel I will *atrophy!*"

He grinned and followed her outside, where he offered his arm.

The hospital was an old country house built on the edges of Blackhaven. There was a pleasant path down to the road, which continued as a track running parallel to the road into town. It made for a charming walk, especially in the sharp winter sunshine with the remains of frost still glistening on the ground.

"Were you and Dr. Lampton discussing me all that time?" she blurted, watching the speckled patterns of sun on the path beneath the trees and hedges.

"Oh, no. We had moved on to the health of a friend. I understand Lampton is pleased with your recovery."

"Oh, good. I wondered if there was some secret complication he did not wish to tell me!"

Doverton blinked. "He would not tell *me*, let alone leave you in the dark! To another subject, I believe I have discovered a way to Annie's Trent."

"You have found Big George?" she exclaimed. "Already? How clever of you!"

"Hardly that clever! I spoke to his friend Gunn who only has the name of a Manchester alehouse—*The Brown Jug*—where they vaguely agreed to meet at some point in the future, although it never happened. I have written to the landlord, but I've no idea if the place has some connection to—er—Big George, or if he merely drinks in the establishment. I would go there in person, but my duties, combined with a visit from my brother, prevent me doing so this week."

"Oh, of course not, this is wonderful. Thank you."

"Gunn does not believe Trent was married when he was here last year. But... did Annie mention he had lost a hand in the war?"

Her eyes flew to his, stricken. "No. I didn't know that..."

"Are we sure it's the same man?"

"I'll ask her," Tillie said, frowning. "But you know, she is such an *accepting* creature... I can imagine that once she had got used to his injury, it would not enter her head as a means of describing him to anyone else, if you see what I mean."

"I do," Doverton said thoughtfully. "It is a pleasant trait. I think you like this Annie."

"She is quite fun and extremely kind," Tillie said enthusiastically and found herself telling him all about last night's candle incident, even though she hadn't meant to since it reflected so poorly on her.

But as she talked, the funny side of it came out, and he laughed at her description of blundering into furniture, knocking the all-important lamp onto the floor, and rousing Annie, who'd threatened the supposed intruders with blood-curdling punishments.

The major had a good laugh, deep and rich and infectious. It made her feel instantly better about everything, and she wanted to hear it again. But then, realizing she was still smiling at him, she hastily collected herself.

"And what of our mysterious sailors?" she asked. "Are they still in Blackhaven?"

"Yes. Grant cunningly organized a service of thanksgiving for them at church tomorrow, so they are really bound to stay until after that. Will you go?"

"I don't know. To be honest, I had lost track of the days of the week! Will you?"

"Perhaps. I don't go very often, but I might feel obliged to since I was involved in the rescue. As were you!"

"Yes, but who will give thanks for a waif who remembers nothing, thrust upon the community at vast expense?"

"Blackhaven." His lips curved. "It's a funny little place, full of curiosity and gossip and increasing numbers of strangers. But you'll find they accept everyone with kindness. Like your friend Annie."

"And yet, they don't accept *her* because she has a baby out of wedlock."

"Sadly, that is universal," he observed. "But when everyone is used to her again, I'm sure it will all die down."

"But no one else—no one else respectable—will marry her, will they?"

"A man who loved her would."

She frowned up at him. "Do you think Big George loves her?"

"I can't know that." He hesitated. "But it seems to me, if he did, he would have come back to her long before this."

"And if we make him come back, if we force him to marry Annie to make her respectable, and he does not love her... they will be miserable together."

"What is misery compared to respectability?" he said lightly, and yet she recognized the wryness in his voice, along with a hint of something that could have been bitterness.

She said, "If I had to choose, I think I would rather have happiness instead of the respectability." She frowned. "You know, I really might be a courtesan with morals like that."

A shout of laughter escaped the major. "Don't say so in company," he begged. "You might as well retain your respectability as long as you can."

"Are you making fun of me?" she asked with a quick smile.

"Only a little. For what it's worth, you do not behave like a courtesan."

"Truly? Have you met any, then?"

"One or two," he said gravely.

She opened her mouth to ask more questions, but he caught her gaze with mock severity.

"Don't dare ask me for details! Let me just say you seem to be a modest, educated young lady with an unruly tongue."

She frowned. "Perhaps I simply don't remember how I normally behave. I could have forgotten how to flirt and be coquettish and however else it is such women go on."

"Anyone would think you wanted to be a courtesan."

She wrinkled her nose. "No, I think I would hate it. Having to spend time with horrid men I would rather not even exchange distant bows with, just for money. Although, I have only a vague idea of how such things work. I could have forgotten that, too."

"It will be a blessing," he assured her.

"Actually, it probably would. I don't want to remember the horrid men, who are probably ugly and fat from over-indulgence, don't you think?"

"Oh, I'm sure of it," he said faintly.

She laughed. "I'm sorry. You are right about the unruly tongue. I shall be glad not to be a courtesan. I suppose I'm trying to think of the worst so I won't be disappointed when I finally remember my life."

"I don't believe you'll be disappointed," he said quietly. "And if you are...well, this is a fine opportunity for you to change things and be who you wish to be."

She liked that idea and mulled it over for the rest of their walk. In between times, she asked the major lots of questions about Black-haven, and he pointed out landmarks like the circulating library, the ice parlor, and the new theatre.

"What is that place?" she asked once as they strolled past a rather gloomy but solid old building set back from the main road. It wasn't clear whether it was one large house built around a courtyard or a smaller house with several out-buildings.

"They still call it The King's Head," Doverton replied. "It used to be an inn, but I believe it was disused even before they built the hotel."

"A hotel sounds very smart," she observed.

"Oh, it is, and very expensive, too. Between you and me, I think many visitors and travelers would welcome a respectable, reasonably priced inn. Not everyone can afford the hotel or wishes to risk the sailors' tavern by the market, which is little better than a thieves' den."

"What an exciting little town it is," Tillie observed, amused.

"You have no idea," Major Doverton murmured.

When they entered the pump room, a noticeable silence fell as everyone turned to look at them. It was only an instant before conversation started up once more, but it was enough to make her wonder what on earth everyone thought of her. They must know she was the unknown woman discovered alone at sea, unclaimed by anyone, with no business being on board the ship.

"Sit and rest here," Doverton said kindly, handing her onto one of the cushioned benches. "Make yourself comfortable while I fetch you some of this famous water."

Mrs. Grant hurried through the door before he had even left her. "Ah, there you are," she said as though delighted. "I'm sorry to be a little late! Babies do consume one's time! Major, how kind of you to escort our guest."

Although flustered, Tillie realized at once that the vicar's wife was throwing the cloak of her own respectability around her. She was touched, for Mrs. Grant had no need to do more than bow to her. But she sat beside Tillie, making civil conversation until Doverton returned with a glass of water for them each.

"I'm hoping for greater energy since my confinement," Mrs. Grant said. "Also, it brings me out every day, which Dr. Lampton approves of, even if he denounces the charlatanism of the spring water claims."

"Do you think the waters would help Annie?" Tillie asked.

"I understand it is good food and rest that will help Annie," Mrs. Grant said, "but of course, you may take her a bottle if you wish. Dr. Lampton would not object. At least it doesn't taste nasty like the Bath waters."

As Doverton sat down beside them, Tillie sipped her water. It was cool, clear, and fresh.

A little later, another beautiful young woman came to join them. She was around the same age as Mrs. Grant, spoke with an exotically foreign accent, and knew both Tillie's companions by name.

"This is Tillie," Mrs. Grant told her. "Whom Major Doverton rescued from the storm. Tillie, Princess von Rheinwald, who is engaged to marry Dr. Lampton."

Tillie, who had known nothing about the doctor's private life, was most intrigued by this information. A princess and a doctor seemed an odd match. She greeted the princess civilly and asked her about her own country—"a tiny principality in Germany which is about to vanish into the peace at Vienna," the princess said. "My son will retain some lands but no political power. It is the new Europe, and perhaps it will be better."

Like my own life, Tillie thought. *Perhaps...*

Chapter Six

"So," Major Doverton said as he escorted her back to the hospital. "What do you think of your first glimpse into Blackhaven society?"

"I found everyone very kind and friendly." Several ladies and a few gentlemen had stopped to greet her companions. Tillie had been introduced and included in the conversations. "But I rather think it is *their* thoughts of *me* that matter."

A frown tugged at his brow. "What do you mean?"

"I feel... I was being looked over, tested for basic courtesy or manners. Or grammar, for all I know."

"Perhaps, among some." He hesitated while a farmer's cart trundled past on the road. "And perhaps Mrs. Grant and the princess were trying to determine your background as a means to help you. Even to nudge your memory into something it recognizes."

"I wasn't criticizing them," she assured Doverton. "I just noticed it. Believe me, I have questioned myself in much the same way!"

"It does not make you angry?"

"How could it?" she said ruefully. "I imagine I, too, would be wary of a complete stranger thrust upon my community with no clue as to her family or character."

"It is harder for you," he pointed out.

"But I'm holding on to what you said. I can be whoever and whatever I wish to be."

"And what is that?" He drew her off the road as the distant sounds of horses and carriage wheels reached them from around the bend.

"I haven't decided yet. But I think I would like to do some good in the world."

"That is very worthy," he murmured.

She wrinkled her nose. "Yes, but I don't want to be *worthy*. In fact, I don't think I could be if I tried. I have no money to be charitable or generous, but in some way, I would just like to make people...*feel* better. As you do."

He glanced at her, clearly startled. She couldn't read his expression, yet a fleeting smile flickered across his face. "You already do. It's your gift, not mine."

An intense stab of pleasure deprived her of breath and the witty response she wanted to make. And then, distracting them both, a carriage drawn by four horses swept around the bend, followed by a gentleman on horseback, who quickened his pace to catch up with the carriage as soon as they were all on straight road.

The horseman glanced across the road at Tillie and Doverton without a great deal of curiosity and then abruptly, his head snapped back round to them again, and he reined in his horse.

"Dove!" he shouted. "By God, it *is* you!"

"Ash?" As though stunned, Doverton stopped in his tracks. The rider kicked his horse back into motion, trotting toward them. His hand was already held down to seize and grip the major's.

"Good God," Doverton said, shaking hands enthusiastically. A huge smile had formed on his face, one of rare, unmixed pleasure. "I can hardly believe my eyes! What on earth brings you to Blackhaven?"

"You do, of course! Or more precisely, your brother and sister-in-law. When I heard they were coming, I thought I might as well join them—since you were quite clearly not going to visit me in the south any time soon."

"You mean John and Ellen are in that carriage currently disappearing toward the horizon?"

"Well, toward the town," the rider corrected, his gaze at last landing on Tillie. "But forgive my rudeness! Introduce us, Dove."

"Tillie, this reprobate is my oldest friend, Mr. Robert Ashton. Ash, this is Tillie."

Since he appeared to be such a good friend of Doverton's, she smiled and gave him her hand, which he bent from the saddle to shake. "Just Tillie?" he teased.

"So far," Tillie replied. "It's a long story."

"I look forward to hearing it."

"Oh, I'm sure you have much more interesting things to discuss," Tillie said lightly. "Major, thank you for your escort, but I shall easily go the rest of the way alone and let you join your friend and your family."

"No, you won't," Doverton said firmly. "I shall escort you the rest of the way and give Ash and John a few minutes to settle in before I descend upon them. Are you all at the hotel?"

"Indeed, we are."

"Then give me half an hour," Doverton said.

Mr. Ashton tipped his hat with an engaging grin and wheeled around to gallop after the carriage.

"What a pleasant surprise for you," Tillie murmured as they walked on. "Did you not know they were coming?"

"Oh, I knew about John and Ellen, although I didn't expect them until later in the day. But I'd no idea Ash was coming, too."

However, now that they were alone and walking on, he seemed to sink into silence. When she glanced at him, a faint frown creased his brow and he seemed deep in thought.

"Go and follow them back," she said gently. "I would not for the world keep you from your family."

At once, his brow cleared and he covered her hand on his arm. "I know you would not. I have plenty of time to see them, and at this moment, I would far rather be with you."

She flushed with pleasure, hoping he could not see the heightened color in her face. But still she sensed unease. "What is wrong?" she asked curiously. "Have you quarreled with your brother?"

"No." His smile was twisted, at once rueful and amused. "Quite the opposite. Oh, don't misunderstand me, I would not swap my brother or any of them for the world. Only…families fuss so and make things more—" He broke off with a quick laugh. "Truly, I am glad to see them here."

She thought that was probably true, but his pleasure was most definitely mixed with something uneasy. She wondered if it was the fact he had been seen with her, a nameless waif without family or character, whom he did not wish to introduce to his family. The thought depressed her, made her ashamed, although there was nothing she could do about it until her memory came back.

She wanted her memory for more than familiarity and comfort now. She wanted it to make *him* comfortable, which was a confusing enough thought without the added appreciation that when her memory did return, it might not make *anyone* comfortable.

DOVE FOUND HIS waif a little too quiet and thoughtful on the second half of their journey, as though she imagined he was only there from duty. In fact, that was ridiculously far from the truth. The more he talked to her, the more he liked her. He liked her compassion and humor, her imagination, the outrageous things she said in perfect innocence, or at least he believed it was perfect innocence.

He wished John and Ellen hadn't driven down the road at that particular moment. For some reason, he'd wanted to keep his family separate from Tillie. Not because he was ashamed of either, but because they would talk to each other. Because Tillie would learn the truth and inevitably change toward him. He didn't think he could bear her pity.

But they parted on good terms in the hospital foyer. She gave him her hand and smiled in a way that melted his heart. And he walked back to town knowing that, with her, he was on dangerous ground.

As he'd promised, he went straight to the hotel and was conducted to his brother's rooms.

The door was open and the voice of Ellen, his sister-in-law, drifted out to him. "...my dear, it is good if he is out for long walks. It shows how much better he is feeling."

"Ellen, I *know* Dominic, and he would go anyway, however he was feeling! It does not make excessive exercise good for him."

"Good for whom?" Dove asked, strolling into the room.

At once, Ellen flew across to greet him, her face wreathed in genuine smiles, although her eyes were anxious as they devoured his face. John came more slowly, holding out his hand as though he expected Dove to be too weak to grip it.

"How are you?" Dove asked, smiling.

"Well, of course."

"You look it," Dove agreed. "As does Ellen! But where is your enormous family?"

"With my sister, as you very well know," Ellen scolded. "And six children is not so enormous!"

"Of course it is," Dove teased, but he could not distract them for long.

"More to the point," John said heavily, "how are you?"

"Well, as you see. Shall we dine here at the hotel this evening? They do a very tolerable dinner."

"By all means," John said. "Sit, sit, you must be exhausted."

"Not in the slightest," Dove said, although, obligingly, he sat opposite his brother.

"How far did you walk?"

"Barely any distance. I assure you it's no trouble to me. I ride, too, and row. I am perfectly well."

John sighed, misery in his eyes. "Yes, but you aren't, are you?"

Death could often be harder on those left behind. The dying, with warning, could come to terms with it or panic or rage against the Almighty. Whatever, it had an end in sight. Those who loved them merely had an extended period of grief to deal with.

"I am fine for now," Dove said patiently. "If I wasn't capable of doing my duty, the regiment would not have me here, would they? Cheery up, John, I shan't turn up my toes just yet. Ellen," he added, changing the subject with relief, "I have got vouchers for the assembly room ball next week. I thought you would like it."

"Do you go to balls?" Ellen blurted.

Dove fixed his smile determinedly. "I even dance, and I shall take no refusal from you."

ALTHOUGH THE CLOUDS had darkened, Tillie still wandered around the enclosed garden at the back of the hospital. She forced herself to remember the darkness, weaving and jolting with the movement of the ship before the waves had come crashing in. Desperately, she tried to look beyond the darkness, to how she'd come to be on the ship and why. Did she live in Liverpool? Were her family looking for her? Surely, with Major Doverton looking for them…

Dove, she remembered, smiling faintly. His friend Ashley had called him Dove. She rather liked that.

Hastily, she dragged her mind back to the darkness. How had she got there?

Tillie. What had made her latch on to that name? She had vaguely imagined a voice saying it. Her voice? Or someone calling to her. *Who?*

"Tillie!" Mrs. Cross exclaimed. "You'll catch your death of cold out here! Come in, now. Mrs. Grant would like to speak to you."

"Oh!" Hastily, Tillie turned her steps toward Mrs. Brown and the door back inside.

The door led into what once must have been a pleasant apartment. It was somewhat soulless now, with a bare wooden floor, one small table, and four aging armchairs set in a row. Convalescing patients used it sometimes. The view from the window over the cliffs and to the sea was agreeable. Only Mrs. Grant occupied the room just now, since Mrs. Cross had hurried away about her duties.

"You must feel I'm haunting you," Mrs. Grant said with a quick smile. "I hope you are not sick of the sight of me."

"Of course not! How could I be? I am always glad to see you."

"I wanted to talk to you about this earlier, but I needed to speak first to Dr. Lampton and to my husband. Which I have now done. So…would you be comfortable staying at the vicarage until we can locate your family?"

It was so totally unexpected that Tillie's jaw dropped. "At the vicarage?" she repeated, stunned.

"I know." Mrs. Grant sighed. "It's not peaceful. People come and go all the time to see Tris—or me, for I am, you know, an incorrigible social butterfly! And then there is Nichola who is not so well-mannered as little George and cries with a lot more gusto. But we do have space. There is a spare bedchamber about as far from my own and the nursery as one can get without actually leaving the house."

Tillie couldn't help smiling. "Oh, you are so kind inviting me! It seems I must either impose upon the hospital or upon you, for I have no money to stay at the hotel or anywhere else, or even to return to Liverpool." She frowned. "If that is where I came from."

"No, no, absolutely you must stay in Blackhaven, for Major Doverton and Tris and Mr. Winslow all wrote in their letters that you were here. This is where your family will come to look for you."

Not for the first time, Tillie wondered if she wanted them to come for her. What if *they* had caused her to be put in the box for some reason?

"Tillie." Mrs. Grant leaned forward, touching her hand in friendly spirit. "Leaving aside the needs of the hospital, I think we must consider yours. Wherever you came from, you were clearly brought up a lady. We must consider your reputation as well as the environment most likely to connect to your memories. Dr. Lampton is in favor of the move."

"And the vicar?"

"Of course! He's glad to welcome you to our house."

Tillie swallowed, her thoughts flitting to poor Annie and little George.

But someone else needed her bed. And in the vicarage, she would not be so confined. "I have but one sea-stained gown," she managed.

"I will disgrace you."

"Oh, nonsense. Besides, I have trunks full of clothes I have not yet given away. Are we agreed, then?"

"Thank you," Tillie said, giving in with relief. "Just until I find my family. I would be most grateful for your hospitality."

"SO, WHO'S THE girl?" Ash asked, pouring Dove a glass of wine. They sat in Ashley's rooms, which were on the other side of the passage from John and Ellen's.

Dove smiled faintly and took the glass. "A waif from the sea."

"Then it's true."

Dove raised his eyebrows. "What is?"

"The hotel porter is very talkative. When he heard John's name, he asked if he was related to you and told heroic tales of you rescuing sailors and a beautiful young lady from a storm."

"Ah, no wonder John grilled me about my health. Without mentioning the storm, of course."

Ash shrugged. "He's proud of you, but he hates to think of you risking yourself just now."

Dove's lips twisted. "I risked myself in the army for nine years, and to a far greater degree. What's the damned difference? I'm already dying."

A flash of pain struck Ashley's eyes, quickly hidden, "*That's* the damned difference. He can't help it. He wants you to live as long as possible and die gracefully in your bed, not throw yourself into the sea in a heroic gesture that deprives you of whatever time you have left."

Dove took a mouthful of brandy. "And what do you think?"

"I think it's your business and your life. But he can't help how he feels any more than you can. You're his little brother."

"I know." Dove let out a short laugh. "Damn him."

"So, what about this waif? She's extraordinarily pretty."

"I know."

"Who is she?"

"That, I don't know, and neither does she. She was injured and remembers nothing before the storm."

"What a pity. I was hoping she was someone happy to be taken advantage of."

Dove laughed more easily this time. "She did point out that she might be a courtesan. Don't tell Ellen that because I'm as sure as I can be of anything that she isn't!"

"I didn't mention her to John and Ellen at all."

"What a model of discretion you are in your old age," Dove marveled, setting his finished glass on the table. "Shall we go down for dinner? And you can tell me everything that's been happening at home."

SINCE THE VICAR did not come home for tea, Tillie spent her time getting to know Mrs. Grant and little Nichola.

"What an unusual name," she said.

"She's called after Dr. Lampton, who delivered her early on Christmas morning. My little Christmas miracle."

"More of a miracle than any other baby?" Tillie asked, gazing down at the sleeping infant.

Mrs. Grant smiled. "For me, yes. The doctors said I was barren, and certainly I never gave my first husband children."

Intrigued, Tillie would have asked more, only she was still on her best behavior and bit her tongue.

"Come," Mrs. Grant said. "Let us take advantage of my miracle's brief sleep and look at some gowns!"

In Tillie's very comfortable guest bedchamber, she rang the bell, and an instant later, a lady's maid appeared. "Little, bring some gowns that might suit Miss Tillie."

Little looked her up and down assessingly, but she seemed more resigned than disapproving. Before long, she returned with an armful of gowns.

Thus began a rather amusing hour trying on various garments, some of which swamped Tillie and others which looked far too splendid, inspiring a self-mocking strut in front of the looking glass. Mrs. Grant went off into peals of laughter, and it wasn't long before they were getting on famously.

At the end of the hour, Little went off to alter two evening gowns, a ball gown, and three morning gowns, and Tillie became the proud owner of several chemises, stockings, garters, stays, and gloves. She even had a bonnet and a red wool winter cloak.

"Do you really not need all this?"

"Lord, no. I was wantonly extravagant when I lived in London. I have given lots away, but it seems there is always more! And then, I am a slightly different shape since giving birth!"

"That is temporary, is it not? Besides, you may easily have them altered."

"Well, I might, once you are restored to your family and no longer need them. Ah, listen, I think that is Tristram home. I'll leave you for now, but come down to the drawing room whenever you wish. Dinner will be at seven...probably!"

With a quick smile, Mrs. Grant left her. Tillie sank down on the comfortable bed, feeling the fine silk embroidery of the coverlet, and beneath, cool, fine linen sheets. There was something familiar about the textures. They were not new to her. She closed her eyes, letting her mind wander, but it only came back to darkness, and then to Major Doverton.

Chapter Seven

S INCE SUNDAY'S CHURCH service was giving thanks for the survival of those who almost died in the storm, Tillie thought she should go at first.

Then, when the vicar mentioned Captain Smith's name at breakfast on Sunday morning, another idea came to her. Neither Major Doverton nor Mr. Grant seemed to trust his honesty, and if there was the smallest chance of him knowing anything about her, Tillie wanted him to tell the truth. If Doverton couldn't make him—or Mr. Grant with God behind him—then Tillie stood no chance of persuading him.

On the other hand, she knew he was staying at the hotel, and everyone seemed sure he would go to church.

And so, Tillie said casually, "I think I will go for a walk, if you don't mind. I hope I'll be back in time for church, but don't wait for me!"

After several days in the sea-stained gown and her chemise and stockings washed every night, it felt rather decadent to be wearing her third different dress in four-and-twenty hours. She had worn one of Mrs. Grant's altered evening dresses for dinner last night, when they were joined by Dr. Lampton and Princess von Rheinwald—though not, sadly, Major Doverton, since his family was in town.

"Are you acquainted with his family?" Tillie had asked them.

"No, I'm not sure they've ever been here," Mr. Grant said. "But then, I don't know the major well." He frowned. "Which I suppose is odd when he's been here as long as I have."

Dr. Lampton lifted his glass. "The man isn't sociable. Nothing wrong with that. He's always been there when it matters."

There was some mystery about Major Doverton that intrigued Tillie. She resolved to get to the bottom of it. However, the mystery of Captain Smith seemed more urgent right now.

Thanks to Little's magic, Tillie wore one of Kate Grant's day dresses and felt rather pleased with it. She was also quite pleased with her own deviousness. For, wearing the borrowed cloak and bonnet, she walked round to High Street and pretended to gaze in shop windows until she saw the man she was looking for stroll out of the hotel.

Captain Smith crossed the road, going in the direction of the church. Tillie walked to the hotel door, nodded in a superior kind of way to the doorman who opened it for her, and sailed through the foyer as if she had lived there all her life.

Of course, she had never been here before and had no idea of the arrangement of the building. She had thought about demanding to be taken to Captain Smith's rooms, but she suspected no one would obey. Worse, they would remember her.

So, she merely took in as much as she could as she crossed the foyer with the most confident demeanor she could manage. From all she could observe with secret glances, the bedchambers seemed to be upstairs. On the ground floor, she saw only a coffee room, a restaurant, and a large hall just visible through half-closed double doors. A young clerk watched her surreptitiously from behind a desk, but otherwise, there seemed to be no staff around.

She climbed the stairs without pause to the first landing. It seemed she knew something about hotels, though, for as she had guessed, the maids were taking the opportunity to clean up while guests were out. She heard two women gossiping from an open door on the left, and as she passed, she saw them making up a large bed.

"Is Captain Smith in?" she asked innocently.

The maids stopped talking at once, dropped their sheet, and curtseyed. "Captain Smith, ma'am? He's upstairs on the next floor."

"Oh, how foolish of me. Thank you."

She walked quickly upstairs to the second floor and walked along the passages until she found another half-open door. She peered inside. One girl was dusting energetically while another swept the floor. And under the window stood a large, water-stained seaman's trunk.

Tillie whisked herself out again. She took a deep breath, then knocked sharply on the door.

"Hoi!" she said stridently. "There's an angry woman in the kitchen shouting blue-murder for you two!"

"Oh, lumme!" exclaimed one of the women inside. Tillie fled around the corner, from where she watched the maids race out of the captain's room. As she'd hoped, they did not turn the key in the lock.

Tillie walked smartly back to Captain Smith's door and let herself in, leaving the door half-open so she would hear the maids' return. She doubted she would have long, so she went hastily to the trunk. It opened easily, but it was empty. She found a wardrobe with two suits of clothes and a few shirts and handkerchiefs, but after rifling them hastily for anything hidden, she turned instead to the desk.

A half-finished letter to his wife made her feel guilty for looking. Instead, she opened one of the drawers and found maps and charts and, beneath them, to her delight, a list of *The Phoenix's* cargo for Ireland and Sweden.

Cotton cloth, manufactured garments. And French cognac.

She didn't know what else she had expected, *one crate of young lady of indeterminate origin?*

Hastily, she hurried around to the other drawer. Here were more private letters from his wife and friends, it seemed, mostly stained with sea water. And then she found one in French, which she drew out, frowning. But there were footsteps in the passage outside and she froze.

At least it wasn't the maids. The steps sounded too masculine. *Go on, go on,* she prayed to whoever the feet belonged to.

They stopped at the door.

Her heart racing, Tillie slid the drawer closed and bolted through the inner door into what must have been a servant's chamber. Fortunately, there was no one in it. But the door to the passage creaked slightly, and the footsteps entered the main room.

It was a man's boots that crossed the floor unhurriedly yet relentlessly. *Captain Smith?* Drat the man, why couldn't he stay in church for an hour? What on earth could she say to him?

Nothing. Worst of all, she hadn't replaced his letter in the desk drawer.

The door to her little chamber swung open. She gasped, jumping back out of the way and snatching the purloined letter behind her back.

Major Doverton stood in the doorway, gazing at her without surprise. Or any expression at all.

Tillie sagged with relief. "Thank God. I thought you were Captain Smith."

"Fortunately not. What the devil are you doing here?"

"Oh, I must put the letter back," she exclaimed, trying to brush past him. But he didn't move, merely gazed down at her. His large, solid body barred her way. She could not read his eyes. For the first time, she felt she didn't have his approval.

Well, she'd entered a man's private room without permission and read his correspondence.

She flushed, only slightly ashamed. "It's in French," she said defensively.

Something flickered in his eyes. He stood aside, and she hastened into the main room. Feeling his eyes burning into the back of her head, she paused at the desk, scanning the words in the letter before folding it once more and replacing it in the drawer.

"Hurry," he said grimly, seizing her by the hand and pushing the drawer shut with the toe of his boot. "Someone's coming."

It was the maids returning. She could hear their voices along the passage, still wondering who on earth had called for them if it wasn't Mrs. Manners—whoever Mrs. Manners was, presumably some dragon of the kitchen.

Running, she and Doverton whisked themselves out of the room. He dragged her hand through his arm and they slowed to a walking pace for the benefit of any observers. Still talking, the maids went into Captain Smith's room. An elderly gentleman with a stick walked toward them, and they all exchanged polite nods.

Before Tillie could speak, Doverton knocked peremptorily on another door and pushed it open, pulling Tillie inside with him before kicking it shut again.

"What the devil were you about?" he demanded furiously.

"Trying to find out about Captain Smith," she retorted. "You are all convinced he is dishonest in some way. I was merely discovering *what* way. I wondered if it was to do with me, and even if it wasn't, I–I wanted to *help*."

He stared down at her, his angry frown fading. He dragged his hand through his hair. "And what if he'd come in, Tillie? What, then?"

"I thought he had," she confessed. "Only it was you, thank God. I was desperately trying to concoct a story, but nothing seemed terribly convincing. I had been going to say the maids let me in to wait for him and hope they didn't come back to give me away." She forced herself to stop talking and closed her mouth.

"Please don't take risks like that again," he said.

"Listen to who's talking," said another voice entirely. The major's friend, Mr. Ashley, walked through from the room beyond, closing the door behind him. "Miss Tillie, how delightful to see you again. You didn't tell me you were bringing her on a visit, Dove."

"I didn't know until a moment ago."

"Please, sit, Miss Tillie," Mr. Ashley invited. "While Dove fetches his sister-in-law to play propriety." He glanced from one to the other. "We are playing propriety, aren't we?"

"Yes," Doverton said.

"No," Tillie said at the same time. "I have to go to church."

"Looking bad for you, Dove," Ashely commented.

Doverton let out a hiss of laughter. "Shut up, Ash. Tillie, I'm truly grateful for your help, but please will you discuss it with me, or at least with the Grants, before you do anything else?"

"Pot," Ashley observed obscurely. "Kettle. Black."

"Will you hold your damned tongue?" Doverton demanded.

But Tillie had caught on to the thread of his friend's interruptions. Frowning at Ashley, she said, "Are you saying Major Doverton takes dangerous risks, too? You're right, of course, since he rescued me and many others during the storm." She smiled at Doverton. "I'll make a deal with you, Major. I'll tell you my risky plans if you tell me yours."

Doverton blinked, then stared at her. A breath of laughter seemed to catch in his throat.

"I'd take it, Dove," Ashley recommended.

Doverton held her gaze. "You are a minx, my waif," he said softly. "Come, I'll escort you to church."

"Don't you want to know what was in the letter first?" she blurted.

He paused, the frown back between his brows.

"It wasn't water damaged like his other documents," Tillie said. "I think he received it since being in Blackhaven. It was asking him to continue to Sweden as soon as he could find another ship."

Doverton's frown deepened. "And written in French. Together, that is…interesting."

A hurried knock at the door heralded the arrival of a well-dressed man in buff pantaloons and a blue coat. He might have been in his late thirties and was certainly a good-looking man. But what drew Tillie's attention was his resemblance to the major. He had the same bone structure, the same shape of eyes and mouth. In the newcomer, the features seemed softer, less defined, the eyes less piercing, the body rather less lean. But she had no difficulty in recognizing Major Doverton's brother, even before he spoke.

"Ashley, is Dominic—" The newcomer broke off as he took in the presence of the major and Tillie. "Ah." He opened the door wide and a lady walked in past him.

The lady paused, her nostrils flaring with distaste. Certainly, it was not good for an unmarried lady's reputation to be discovered unchaperoned with two gentlemen in private rooms. Tillie tilted her chin, refusing to admit wrongdoing.

Doverton said easily. "Excellent timing. We are about to leave.

Miss Tillie is on her way to church, so we can all walk together that far. Let me introduce her to you, Ellen. This is Miss Tillie, our waif from the sea. Tillie, my brother and sister-in-law, Mr. and Mrs. John Doverton."

Tillie curtseyed. Mrs. Doverton inclined her head very slightly, while her husband gave a rather shallow bow.

"I think you would rather walk with your family in private," Tillie said. "I shall not intrude. Mr. Ashely." She inclined her head to her host and hurried out of the room.

For an instant, it seemed the major would detain her, but she flashed him a look of pleading and he merely stood aside, his expression one of rueful understanding. Clearly, he recognized a desire to escape when he saw one.

Tillie hurried out of the hotel as fast as she could while maintaining her dignity and walked briskly toward the church. She didn't want to dwell on what Major Doverton's family thought of her. She shuddered to think of it, but she couldn't even be angry because even if her crime wasn't what they might be imagining, she had still behaved badly, shocking even the major. It made her cringe. Anxiety clawed at her stomach, because it seemed she didn't know how to go on in society after all. Either that, or her past was not a terribly moral one.

The church service had already begun. To her surprise, she had to stand at the back with several domestic servants and farmers, for the pews were all filled and must have been even before the service started. Mr. Grant, it seemed, was a popular vicar. And besides, the rescue of *The Phoenix* seamen was a great thing.

She could see the captain and his sailors toward the front of the church. She wondered if they just had an impatient importer in Sweden. Or if there was some other reason for the captain in particular to be there. Was his purpose really to transport cotton garments and brandy? Or to betray his country?

ON MONDAY, THE day before the much-anticipated ball, Tillie went sick-visiting with Mrs. Grant to various homes around the town, from a genteel lady housebound by arthritis, to a one-legged soldier who seemed to be dying, and a fishwife with a fever. They brought gifts of soup and a little company for each.

Although it was difficult to see their suffering, Tillie found her role surprisingly easy, almost familiar.

"Do you think you have made such visits before?" Mrs. Grant asked her as they walked on toward the hospital.

Tillie frowned with the effort of remembering. "I think I might. Only the illnesses were different. Infected lungs, epidemics of cholera that spread around whole neighborhoods."

"Which neighborhoods?" Mrs. Grant asked casually.

Tillie thought, then sighed. "I don't know. They're just words, names. I can't see the faces that go with the suffering people, or their houses or who I was with. But I don't feel it was I who was ill."

At the hospital, she was happy to renew her acquaintance with Annie Doone and little George. Annie exclaimed in delight to see her. "And goodness, how smart you look! Are you a great lady after all?"

"I don't know, but Mrs. Grant is! How is little George?"

"He's getting fatter," his mother said proudly. "And so am I. They might let me go soon."

Tillie sat on the edge of her bed. "Where will you go, Annie? Back to your mother?"

"They don't want to deal with crying babies no more," Annie said carelessly. "I'll find something else."

But without work, she'd have nowhere to live. And how could she work and care for little George at the same time?

"A creche," she said suddenly.

"I beg your pardon?"

Tillie rubbed the side of her head. "Children from several families looked after in one place while their mothers work. The mothers take it in turns to watch the children."

"In someone's house?" Mrs. Grant asked, arriving in time to hear the tail end of the conversation.

"No." Tillie frowned. "At their place of work. They had a room, a bit of a yard..."

"There's no employers like that around here," Annie said with certainty.

"Where did you come across this?" Mrs. Grant asked as they finally made their way out of the hospital again.

"I don't know." In frustration, Tillie bumped her fist against her forehead. "I don't remember. It just doesn't seem fair, though."

"What doesn't?" Mrs. Grant asked.

"Why, that you—" She broke off, appalled by the impossibility of saying what was truly on her mind to this woman who had been so kind to her.

But it seemed Mrs. Grant was no fool either. "That I don't need to work and yet have servants to care for my baby whenever I want to go out even on the most frivolous of pretexts. While Annie, who needs to work to live, cannot leave her child to do so."

"An accident of birth," Tillie said lightly. "We need Big George! I wonder if Major Doverton has heard anything back from Manchester."

"I think he would have told you if he had."

Everywhere they went that day, Tillie kept hoping to run into Major Doverton, but she didn't. Nor did he call at the vicarage. It was the first day since the storm that she had not seen him, and his absence depressed her.

She wondered if she had truly disgusted him by snooping in Captain Smith's rooms. Or perhaps he had simply been induced to see her through his sister-in-law's eyes. As nothing, no one. Certainly no one worthy enough to be in the same company as Major Doverton.

In all, she looked forward to the ball with a tense mixture of excitement and anxiety. Under no circumstances could she dream of not attending, and since it would go on until late, she knew she should retire early as Mrs. Grant suggested, in order to be at her best.

However, once in her own chamber, she was too restless to settle. Little had come and unlaced her gown and stays, but she could not bring herself to go to bed. She paced around the room for a while, then sat by the window gazing out at the stars. From her window, she didn't have much view of the sea, mere glimpses through the lower rooftops and between buildings, but somehow, it seemed to call to her. Which was surprising considering her recent experience at sea.

Tonight was calm and clear, though. On impulse, she rose and wrapped a shawl around her shoulders before donning her borrowed red cloak and slipping quietly out of the house. The Grants had given her a key to allow her to come and go as she pleased. In Blackhaven, it was not uncommon for respectable ladies to go out alone in daylight, but she doubted such leniency extended to nighttime. So, she pulled the hood of the cloak right over her head and hurried through the frosty streets toward the town beach.

The distinctive smell of the sea and the sound of the waves seemed deeply familiar to her. Without the lights of the town, she relied on the moon and stars to light her way. Fortunately, the beach seemed to be empty, and for several minutes, she just walked along the edge of the water, enjoying her solitude and freedom of movement. Until she saw a dark figure running along the beach toward her.

Perhaps this had not been such a wise idea. Her first instinct was to seek the shadows of the rocks, but to get there, she needed to cross a considerable expanse of open beach. In any case, she must already have been seen. If this running person meant her any ill, she could not hide from him. However, apart from his hurry, he did not appear to be threatening, making no effort to hide or to swerve from his own path into hers.

It was a tall, athletic man in shirtsleeves and pantaloons, a red coat tied around his neck by its sleeves. She kept her eyes focused straight ahead and thought she would seek out the road again, just as soon as he had passed.

But to her unease, he slowed down as he approached. She could hear his rapid breathing.

"Tillie?" he said, coming to a halt.

"Major?" If anything, even more startled than he, she veered toward him in mingled relief and guilt and sheer pleasure. "Is anything wrong?"

"Oh, no, nothing."

"Then why are you running?"

He gave a breathless laugh. "Because I can."

Intrigued, she gazed back at him, waiting for more information. But she could guess. A flash of something like memory struck her—the childhood exhilaration of running, long lost to a ladylike adulthood. For an active man, she guessed the torture of inactivity, caused by his injury, must have been severe.

He slipped back into his coat. "But I don't think you should be out alone at this time of night. Where are you going?"

"Just walking," she said with a rueful smile. "Because I can."

"Hmm." He offered his arm. "Come, I'll take you back. I presume the Grants don't know you're out."

She looked at his arm but did not take it. "No, but I'm more content now. Don't stop on my account. I can easily go back by myself."

"Funnily enough, I'm more content, too, having run into you."

"I thought you were angry with me," she blurted. Bravely, she raised her gaze to his.

The moonlight glinted on his steady eyes and emphasized the sharp lines and dark hollows of his face. Butterflies seemed to take flight in her stomach.

He didn't answer, but took a step nearer, a faint frown of confusion on his brow. "Why would I be angry?"

"I don't behave like a lady." *I'm probably not a lady.*

His lips curved. "I would hate you to change."

"Truly?" she asked with doubt.

"Truly. You are refreshingly honest and open and kind. You treat everyone as your equal. It may not be conventional, but it is most...appealing." His hand lifted, and she was afraid to breathe when he touched her cheek.

"Tillie," he said with an odd little catch in his voice. His warm fingertips were rough in texture and yet incredibly gentle as they traced a line from her cheekbone to her parted lips. As if he couldn't help it, he dipped his head, and the butterflies in her stomach soared and plunged.

And then a breath of something like laughter stirred her hair. His hand dropped, and he stepped back, taking her hand and placing it decorously on his arm. In curious silence, they walked back along the beach together.

It should have been uncomfortable, even tense, and yet it wasn't. She didn't want to break the moment. With the sound of the sea in her ears and the beauty of the moon and stars above, it was somehow enough just to have him by her side, the hint of his warmth under her fingers, brushing occasionally against her skirts. She hadn't known she could feel such peace and such excitement in one moment. One long moment that she didn't want to end.

But inevitably, he guided her back onto the road and through the streets to the vicarage. She barely noticed the people they passed on the way. For her, there was only him. Her heart galloped as she turned to face him at the gate. Slowly, he took her hand from his arm and bowed over it.

His smile melted her heart. Her lips curved in response. And then it was all too much. She longed for him to touch her again, to be closer, much, much closer. With a gasp, she almost fled down the path to the front door, slid her key into the lock, and hurried inside. Only when she turned to close the door did she see that he still stood there.

A strange, new happiness was struggling up within her, yearning for recognition. She leaned against the closed door, listening to the sound of her heart.

I love him. God help me, I love him...

Chapter Eight

S INCE TILLIE HAD much the same coloring as Mrs. Grant, the borrowed gowns suited her very well, particularly the ballgown of such a pale blue that it looked like ice, embroidered at the bust and hem in silver silk.

"It looks much better on you," Mrs. Grant approved. "It was always too modest for a wicked lady like me!"

"You're not wicked, you're regal," Tillie argued with a hint of envy. "I wish I could be."

"I imagine I am ten years older than you. Regality is a benefit of old age."

Mr. Grant complimented them both warmly, and since it was raining, the carriage was summoned to take them to the assembly rooms.

Although Mrs. Grant had warned her the ball might not be so well attended, it being a quiet and wintry time of year with few visitors, the ballroom seemed to fill up rapidly. The Grants appeared to be known to everyone, both residents and visitors alike. Tillie was introduced to so many people that her head spun and she got their names muddled. She even forgot to keep looking to the door for the sight of Major Doverton's arrival.

When the orchestra struck up for the first dance of the evening—a country dance—Mr. Grant asked Tillie to stand up with him. Since his wife had already gone off on the arm of a rather devilishly handsome young man, Tillie accepted gratefully, for the vicar was entertaining company and she was, besides, quite at ease with him.

As they danced, she noticed a smile of what seemed to be approval twinkling in his eyes.

"Have I done something clever?" she asked as they came together.

"You dance," he said.

"Well, of course I—" She broke off, her eyes widening as she understood. She remembered to step back and move forward before coming back to him. "You're right! I can dance! I never even thought about it."

"You appear to be a lady of many accomplishments."

"So I do," she said, much struck. "I speak French as well, you know, and I can play the piano a little."

"The young men will be fighting over you."

Tillie laughed, though deep in her heart she wondered if it meant she might possibly be respectable enough for Major Doverton. Exactly what this signified, she shied away from, but it did lighten her spirits. And she was more desperate than ever to see him again after last night's strange encounter on the beach and the stunning revelation of her own feelings that had followed it. She had begun to wonder what it would have felt like if he *had* kissed her. Even imagining it left her breathless. And yet, she worried that something had changed in their relationship, that the ease of friendship might have vanished, that discovering her alone on the beach at night had made him think of her without respect.

She didn't notice his arrival, in the end, but when she and the vicar made their way back to their seats, he and another officer were already with Mrs. Grant. Her heart lurched at her first glimpse of him and she blushed, although she hoped her heightened color would be put down to the exertions of her recent dance. He looked particularly handsome and dashing in his dress uniform, and somehow more distinguished than his fellow-officer.

"Miss Tillie," he said, smiling as soon as he saw her, and the relief that they were still friends almost overwhelmed her.

Smiling back, she gave him her hand, and he bowed over it punctiliously. Her fingers felt cold when he released them.

"And this is Captain Grantham," Mrs. Grant said. "Who particularly asked to be introduced to you."

"How do you do, Captain?" Tillie said civilly.

"Very well—and even better if I can persuade you to dance with me."

"The next dance, obviously," Doverton inserted. "Not this one."

"Pulling rank on me, Dove?" Grantham asked.

"Oh yes, if the lady will have me."

"Then, the one after, Captain Grantham, if you will," Tillie said gaily and gave her hand to Doverton. "Why *this* dance in particular?" she asked as they walked toward the dance floor.

Doverton snatched up a glass of lemonade from the table as they passed and presented it to her. "Because it is a waltz, of course."

Her eyes widened. "You waltz in Blackhaven? How very daring!"

He paused by a pillar, turning toward her. "Then it was not common in your own circle?"

She frowned. "I think not. A new European decadence bound to be taken up in London but not fit for decent ladies. Or something of that nature." She sipped her lemonade, hearing the disapproving voice that spoke the words, searching for the face, the name that went with it. "It is almost there," she murmured. "I glimpse fringes that are almost memory, a feeling, a familiarity, but the detail is all hidden."

As the orchestra struck up, she gasped and raised her startled gaze to the major's watchful one. "Oh dear. What if I cannot waltz?"

His eyes lit with lazy amusement. He took the glass from her hand and set it on a nearby table. "Then it is a great time to learn."

"Not if I step all over your toes and embarrass us both."

"It won't embarrass me," Doverton said, leading her onto the dance floor. His arm slipped around her waist and he took her hand. Her other hand rested on his upper arm as if of its own accord. He didn't release her gaze. "I suppose everyone has told you how especially beautiful you are tonight?"

Whether it was the compliment or the unaccustomed closeness, her breath vanished.

"It's Mrs. Grant's dress," she managed, following him as he stepped back and turned with the rhythm of the beguiling music.

"No, it isn't. The gown is merely a frame."

"Are you teasing me?"

He blinked. "No. Why would you think so? Are you not used to compliments?"

"Everyone is kind…" She frowned, with another tingle of unspecific memory. "Since I came here. I don't remember before."

"And yet it seems you waltz."

A breath of laughter shook her. "It seems I do. And I have been caught twice now in the same way."

"What way?"

"Distraction. So that I don't think about it, I just dance."

"Perhaps. But you *are* beautiful. And you should know it."

She shook her head, blushing and smiling. Whether or not it was true, she was glad he thought enough of her to say it. "I was afraid I had given you a disgust of me," she admitted. "That we were no longer friends."

"*Disgust?*" He stared at her, frowning in bafflement. "Why on earth should you have imagined that?"

She lowered her voice. "Because I walked alone on the beach at night. Because I snooped in Captain Smith's rooms."

"That wasn't disgust, you goose, it was plain, honest fear. I don't yet know how dangerous Smith is, and I do not want you caught in that kind of situation." He leaned even closer, causing her heart to gallop. "Besides, I have already been through everything recovered from the sea."

"You did not tell me that," she said with dignity.

"No, I didn't," he agreed. "And it's true the letter in French was not among his papers, then."

"So I *did* discover something!" she crowed.

"Yes, you did. You're very clever and very foolhardy, and you're *not* to do such things again."

"Unless you are with me."

His breath hitched. His deep-set blue eyes, overwhelmingly intense, seemed to swallow her. Much as they did last night. "Unless I am with you. You know Captain Smith is here at the ball?"

"Oh! No, I haven't seen him."

"He's in the card room for the moment. Now, there is another man here I think he might try to contact."

"A man of great villainy?"

"Opinions differ, and you needn't say it with such glee. Do you see Dr. Lampton and the princess?"

"I do. She is very lovely, isn't she?"

"She is. Beside her is a small lady in spectacles and a tall man."

Tillie craned her neck slightly. "Yes! Who is he?"

"That is Mr. Lamont, formerly known as Captain Alban, a man with a somewhat shadowed past, to call it no worse, who owns a fleet of ships, some of which, I suspect, are not unconnected with smuggling."

"Ah! Then you think Captain Smith might approach him to get himself and his cargo to Sweden?"

"I would certainly like to know if they converse this evening."

She glanced back to Doverton. "Is this an innocuous task to keep me out of trouble?"

He laughed. "Just something else to occupy your mind, should you get bored. I shall probably go and see Alban myself. What I really want is for you to enjoy the evening."

"Oh, I am enjoying it," she said with enthusiasm.

They danced in silence for the next few moments. Tillie allowed herself to relax into the dance, to secretly delight in his closeness. It made her heart and her stomach flutter most pleasantly. Even when she caught sight of his sister-in-law watching them, she did not feel cast down. She felt proud.

"How is your family?" she asked. "Are they enjoying Blackhaven?"

"Yes, I believe so."

"I expect your duties prevent you from going home much."

"I could go more often than I do," he said a little ruefully. "If I had gone in the autumn, it would have saved them travelling in the winter."

"Why didn't you?"

His lips parted to speak, then closed again in a slightly twisted smile. "Good question. I was wounded in the war as I told you—oh, more than two years ago—and John and Ellen fuss over me now. I am not good at being fussed over. But I do miss them."

Tillie nodded in understanding. "I expect they'll fuss less, now that they've seen you so fit and healthy."

"I expect so," he agreed.

It sounded innocuous and yet some faint, out-of-place tone in his voice made her peer at him more closely. The major *did* have a secret.

"Something has made you sad," she said.

At once his smile relaxed, lighting his eyes. "How could I be sad with you in my arms?"

"It is obviously a mystery," she said wryly. "But...you will tell me if I can help?"

His veiled eyes softened. His thumb stroked her hand, an almost involuntary gesture, she thought. "Thank you. You're very sweet."

"I don't *think* I am," she said doubtfully.

He laughed and whirled her around with rather more exuberance than was proper. Her toes barely touched the floor, but it was fun, exhilarating, and she didn't think she had ever been so happy.

DOVE HAD BEEN only too well aware of the danger since last night when the sheer strength of his emotions had taken him by surprise. He hadn't spoken as they'd walked home for the simple reason that he had no idea what to say. His desire to kiss her, and more, had been so powerful that it had not been easy to draw back. In truth, he was shocked at himself for coming so close to taking advantage.

But dear God, coming upon her at that moment, in so unlikely and so isolated a spot, he had been utterly overwhelmed by her beauty, by her sheer... *Tillieness*, for want of a better word.

She was unique, and there were so many reasons to like her and desire her. But it wasn't reason that urged him on, or made him draw back. He didn't understand what it was exactly, but he'd known he had to keep it in check.

And yet, here he was the following evening letting it all happen again, and in public. Perhaps it was the same old reckless spirit that had propelled him into battle on numerous occasions. But whatever the cause, he did not try to stop it this time. It was too sweet to hold her in his arms, to flirt and make her laugh, to watch the color heighten and fade under her skin and see her eyes soften and smile. He did not care who she was or where she came from. He did not even know when it had begun, but he was falling in love, rapidly, relentlessly, and that was rather wonderful. If he had to die, he wanted to do so loving her.

When the waltz ended, he was reluctant to give her up, deliberately taking the long way back to the Grants. It brought them up against John and Ellen, who nodded to her with distant politeness, and Ashley, who promptly asked her to dance.

"I believe I'm promised to Captain Grantham for the next dance," Tillie said apologetically. "If he remembers."

"Oh, he remembers," Dove murmured, watching Grantham scour the room.

"Then I suppose I must retreat and hold my fire for the next waltz," Ash said sardonically.

Although the night was young, Dove gave her up with reluctance to Captain Grantham. Then, catching Kate Grant's speculative gaze upon him, he bowed and strolled away before he could be catechized.

He had only gone a few steps before a voice said quietly, "Major."

Dove glanced down and saw Captain Alban sitting alone. The man hooked his foot around a chair and drew it to his table in silent invitation.

Intrigued, Dove sat. "How can I help you, Captain?"

"Smith," Alban said without preamble. "Of *The Phoenix*. He's inquired about hiring one of my ships."

"I thought he might. To Sweden?"

Alban nodded. "Via Ireland. What do you want me to do?"

Dove considered. "Keep him here a few days if you can. Have you any idea what he's up to?"

"Only that I offered to take the cargo without him and was refused. He needs to be there in person to fulfill his obligations, he tells me."

"Interesting," Dove observed.

"I thought so." Alban lifted his glass. "I hear many things on my travels. Recently, I learned of a rumor that despite joining the allies, Bernadotte is, at the least, turning a blind eye to conspiracies to free Bonaparte from Elba."

"What can they do from Sweden?"

Alban's lips twitched. "Sail. It is far enough away to make plans with impunity. No doubt the Swedes are fed up with having no real say at the Congress of Vienna. Perhaps a forgiving Bonaparte is seen as another chance for them. Or perhaps the Swedish government is not involved at all. It's an innocent-seeming place for anyone to meet and conspire if they wished."

"And Smith...merely a courier, raising money to retire in peace?" Dove suggested. He certainly gave no impression of being a rabid Bonapartist.

"It is possible."

Dove stood up. "Thank you. You'll let me know if you learn anything else?"

"Of course."

Dove went on his way, content with the knowledge that he and Alban understood each other well enough. Returning to his brother, he asked Ellen for the following dance.

"Oh, get along with you, Dominic, I'm far too old to dance!"

"Of course you're not," Dove insisted.

As he sat down. Mrs. Winslow passed, flanked by two of her daughters. "Major!" she exclaimed. "The hero of the storm! I have not seen you since to thank you for the lives you saved."

Mrs. Winslow occasionally seemed to forget that she was not responsible for every soul in the vicinity. It could be an annoying trait, but in truth, she was a kind woman.

"I just did my duty, ma'am," he said deprecatingly. "As did everyone else. Allow me to introduce my brother and sister-in-law, Mr. and Mrs. Doverton, who are visiting Blackhaven for a week or two. Ellen, Mrs. Winslow, the squire's lady."

Everyone bowed and murmured greetings, and then Mrs. Winslow presented her daughters. "My eldest, Lady Sylvester Gaunt," she said proudly, "and my second daughter, Genevra."

Dove knew and rather liked the quiet Catherine, now Lady Sylvester, but the younger daughter, her pretty face brimming with fun, looked as if she'd be rather more of a handful.

"In fact, next we are holding an impromptu party for Genevra's seventeenth birthday," Mrs. Winslow said. "I shall send you a card, Major, to include Mr. and Mrs. Doverton, of course."

Dove said all that was proper and was soon glad to see Ellen and Mrs. Winslow conversing like old friends.

"How is Trotmere?" he asked Catherine.

"Water-tight, fortunately! We have cleared lots of land, ready for spring. Sylvester is thoroughly enjoying himself."

"Who would have thought it?" Dove said in exaggerated wonder.

Catherine laughed. "Not I. He is trying his luck at cards now, which is much more natural behavior."

"Would you do me a favor if you have a moment?"

"Of course."

"Make friends with Kate Grant's new protegee."

"Oh, the girl you found in the sea?"

"Indeed. She knows virtually no one in Blackhaven and she can't remember her own people."

"I'll definitely speak to her," Catherine promised.

Shortly afterward, he danced with Ellen, and couldn't help noticing that Tillie was now dancing with Blackshaw in the same set. When it was her turn to dance down the line and she came to Dove, she gave him a conspiratorial smile that melted his heart—until Blackshaw gave him one of pure triumph.

"What is that girl to you?" Ellen asked as they came together. "Duty or pleasure?"

"Both," Dove said promptly.

"But Dominic, you've no idea who she is!"

They separated again, saving him the trouble of answering, although when they next met, she continued, "She could be pretending you know. She could know full well who she is."

"I see no point in that."

"Because if *you* knew what she was, you would not make a pet of her as you do."

Dove scowled, turning away from her once more. And the next time they met, it was he who spoke first, "I still don't see the point."

"You have considerable prize money from the war, don't you? An honorable name. Dominic, she wants to marry you."

It was so ridiculous, he laughed aloud. Ellen clearly didn't know whether to be relieved by his reaction or affronted. Fortunately, the dance ended shortly afterward, and he was able to return her to his brother without strangling her.

Glancing around the room, he found Tillie on the arm of Captain Blackshaw, walking in the opposite direction to the Grants. Even from behind them, Dove was sure he recognized a hint of tension in her, and an instinctive tug to free her hand. Blackshaw held on to it.

"Excuse me," Dove murmured and walked swiftly round other returning couples to come at Tillie and Blackshaw head-on. He saw at once his anxiety was not mistaken, for as soon as she saw him, relief lit her face. "Ah, there you are," he said amiably. "I am sent to bring you back to Mrs. Grant."

"I would like to sit down," Tillie said gratefully.

As Dove offered his arm, she again tried to free her hand, and Blackshaw clamped it against his arm.

"Blackshaw!" Dove snapped, boring his eyes into the younger

man's.

Blackshaw actually jumped, his grip loosening enough for Tillie to snatch her hand free and lay it on Dove's arm instead. He brushed past the captain, moving directly toward Kate Grant and the vicar, who had now been joined by Lord and Lady Sylvester.

"What was that all about?" Dove murmured.

"I have no idea," Tillie said. "He talked about you a lot. I think he may have had a little too much wine, but he was perfectly pleasant up until the end of the dance. I have no idea whether he wishes to please you or upset you."

"Well, he's certainly failed in the former. More to the point, has he upset *you*?"

"Oh, no. He did not hurt me. Though I admit, I am very glad to see you!"

As they passed Grantham and Green, Dove caught Green's arm. "Keep your eye on Blackshaw, would you?"

They nodded and sauntered on. Dove formally restored Tillie to Kate Grant, who introduced her to Lord and Lady Sylvester. After sitting down with them all for a little, assuring himself that the young women were getting along and amusing each other, he jumped up again with a murmured excuse and strode away.

Restlessness drove him. He couldn't be still, because his head was full of Tillie and a pointless anger he needed to walk off. But John and Ellen and Ash were here because he had invited them, and if he went back to barracks, he might take Blackshaw apart limb from limb. Which would hardly be fair when it wasn't really Blackshaw he was angry with. It was himself. Fate. Life.

He strode around the dance floor, keeping his face carefully amiable, until he couldn't bear it anymore and stepped into one of the alcoves, letting the curtain fall back behind with relief. At least now, he could relax his facial muscles.

Throwing himself into the armchair, he dropped his elbows to his knees and his face into his hands. His fingers curled into his short hair and tugged.

You're over this, Dominic Doverton. You came to terms with it two years ago. You've already had a year longer than anyone expected. Be grateful for your life.

But God help him, he didn't want this to be the end.

The music and laughing voices from the ballroom faded. All he could hear was his own panting breath as he wrestled with his fate again.

The curtain swished. Dropping his hands, he glowered up in annoyance.

"Dove," Tillie whispered, dropping the curtain behind her once more and throwing herself on her knees at his feet. "Oh, Dove, what is it?"

"Nothing," he said shakily. She'd taken both his hands, and he twisted them to hold her fingers. "Nothing at all. I merely wished for your presence, and here you are."

"Did you?" she said wistfully.

His heart thudded. "You wish me to pine for you?" he asked lightly.

Her lips quirked. "I think I want you to miss me when I'm not there," she said frankly. "Even if only half as much as I miss you."

He released one of her hands, but only to cup her cheek. "Don't say such things to me."

"Why not, if they're truth?" she whispered.

He caressed her cheek. "Oh, my waif, you are too vulnerable, too lost to make such—"

"Don't," she interrupted fiercely. "Don't dare try to make this less than it is! Do you think my lack of memory makes me invent things? On the contrary, it leaves me clear to know my own heart. I have no idea if I'm worthy of you or your family, but that doesn't change the fact that I love you."

Sweet, intense pain flooded him, and with it came a surge of desire that went far beyond mere lust.

His slid his hand around to her nape, drawing her nearer as he bent his head. Her breath came in shallow pants, but she made no effort to avoid him. Instead, she clung to his wrist and touched his cheek, her lips parting for his kiss.

He longed to taste her. It had been on his mind almost since he'd pulled her from that damned box, most certainly since he'd encountered her on the beach last night. And she loved him. She'd said she loved him, and on no account could he throw away that miracle. Her breath was warm and sweet on his lips. Her eyelids fluttered shut.

She loved him.

"Dear God, I can't let you do this," he whispered.

Her lips trembled. Her eyes flew open. But he couldn't bear her clear, loving gaze.

"Tillie," he said hoarsely. "Run from me. If you love me, I'll only bring you pain."

"It already feels like a pain," she whispered. "In my heart."

"It's all there will be, Tillie. I'm dying."

Chapter Nine

H ER WHOLE BEING seemed to freeze. She didn't even seem to breathe. Then a frown twitched her brow, and she tried to smile. "Dying? I've never met anyone so alive."

"*Carpe diem*. Live for the day. I do."

"Because each could be your last?" she whispered. "Oh, Dove, no… How? Why, what is wrong?"

"My wound at Salamanca. It was always terminal."

"But it was two and a half years ago!"

"I know. I am already a walking miracle. I should have died on the battlefield, or at the very latest, in the field hospital. Somehow, I didn't, so they sent me home in the hope I could die with my family, though they imagined the journey would kill me first. But I made it home and somehow, I began to get better. The surface wound healed, but beneath it is such a mess that the doctors all agreed I could not recover. It was only a matter of time. The most optimistic estimate was a few months."

"And yet, here you are," she said urgently. "After more than two years. Has no one else—"

"Tillie." He took her hands and kissed them one after the other. "Tillie, they were right. I always knew that. I won't be prodded and opened up any more. I will die. I cannot let you suffer that."

"You cannot stop my suffering," she said simply. "It is too late. I loved you from the moment I opened my eyes in that box and you lifted me out. No, don't tell me it was mere gratitude, though yes, that is in among it. And don't send me away. I would ease your suffering if

I can, Dove." She touched his cheek, his lips. "Dove, give me this gift."

He stared at her. "You are amazing," he whispered. "You don't know me. You don't know what you're offering."

"Everything." Tears ran heedlessly down her cheeks. "For as long as you need me."

He was only human. He meant only to kiss her tears, but her gasping mouth was too close, and he took it in a long, fiery kiss of need and gratitude and sheer, raging desire.

Since his recovery, he had held himself aloof from women. Mostly. And his lust was intense. It wouldn't have taken much more to tip him over the edge of madness and take her here and now. But he was a gentleman, and she was precious.

Somehow, he tore his mouth free and dragged them both to their feet. One more kiss, because her lips were so red and luscious from the last, and he put her from him, dragging out his handkerchief to dry her teary face. Carefully, he replaced a fallen pin in her hair and smoothed out her gown.

"It's the second waltz," he said huskily. "I suggest you dance it with me out there to prevent me from ravishing you in here."

She gave a trembling little laugh.

"I love you," he whispered in her ear, and she looked as though she would weep again even as a smile of joy trembled on her lips. It stunned him that he could have inspired such emotion in this beautiful, brave young woman, the only woman who had touched his heart since his foolish, callow youth.

And God knew the joy was not all hers. This unlooked for, unwanted gift...

He swallowed. "Discretion, my sweet. Hold on."

He took her hand, twirling her out of the alcove and along the wall to the dance floor, where he danced the most exhilarating waltz of his life. With the woman he loved. And who, for some reason, loved him.

TILLIE HAD NEVER imagined that such overwhelming joy could exist along with the devastating pain of knowing she would lose him. Yet somewhere, she could not quite believe that this strong, vital man was truly dying. His arms were too solid as they held her, his every movement as they danced too full of exuberance and sensuality.

And yet, it explained many things—his courteous aloofness from the townspeople, none of whom seemed to know him well, and the secrets she had always sensed he was keeping. Even last night when he had run the length of the beach, *"because I can."* For him, this was a miracle in itself. And it might be the last time he did so.

Involuntarily, her fingers tightened on his. *Carpe diem*, he had said, and she *would* live in this moment, bask in his love, in the kisses that had turned her to jelly. Until that first kiss, she hadn't realized that this was what she had always wanted from him. The fierce, physical delight of his mouth on hers had taken her by surprise—sweet, arousing, overwhelming. Her lips still tingled as they danced. She felt breathless, awed, madly in love.

"I have known you barely a week," she said. "How can I fall in love so fast?"

"Because you have no one to compare me with, having no memory of life before me."

"Then what is your excuse?"

"You are."

She laughed. "Then you are mine. I'm not grasping at straws, Dove," she added as her smile faded into seriousness. "I do not *wish* to be in love until I know who I am. This just *happened*."

His thumb stroked the side of her hand. "I know." His dark, steady eyes, warm and glittering in the bright candlelight, held hers. "And I think we have to be a little discreet. Until we know who you are, I doubt we can be together."

"Maybe we should run away quickly before we know. I really might be that courtesan, or someone equally un-respectable, and then you won't want me."

"I don't care about your birth, nor about anyone else who might."

She couldn't deny it delighted her, although honesty compelled her to point out, "Your family will care."

"They'll come about. I would give you my protection if you need it. And if you don't, well, you are a wonderful addition to any family. I just hate to think of you in widow's weeds."

"Then I shan't wear them."

The sudden smile died on his lips. "It isn't much of a gift."

"It is," she whispered. "For however long we have together. And then I will always have that." She wanted to throw her arms around him, hug him close, but all she could manage in the middle of the ballroom was to squeeze his fingers.

As the music came to a close, she curtseyed and took his arm to be conducted back to the Grants. She still felt as though she were floating on air and was sure everyone who glanced their way must know Dove had kissed her, that she was in love. That he was hers. Elating thought...

A low voice penetrated her thoughts, one officer speaking confidentially as he apparently imagined, to his fellows. "Looks like Dove's finally been caught."

"Nonsense, old boy. He's just remembered he's a lady's man."

"Are you?" Tillie asked him, realizing she really knew very little of his life.

"No! Well, not really. I suppose I've liked a lot of women. When I was young and foolish."

"But never loved them?"

"Not truly. Apart from Felicity, I suppose."

"Felicity?"

"We were engaged in our youth, but she had the good sense to end it and marry another, more stable man."

"Were you hurt?"

"I suppose I was." He spoke lightly, but Tillie saw deeper. He had been devastated. He was a man of deep feelings and loyalty.

But there was no time for more private conversation, for Mrs. Grant was patting the seat beside her. "Let me introduce you to Mrs.

Benedict who lives up at Haven Hall."

As Tillie said what was proper, she was aware of one of the waiters speaking to Dove. Dove's eyebrows flew up, and then he nodded before bowing to the ladies and striding off across the ballroom toward the exit.

DOVE WAS A practical man. The sudden joy in his heart served to clarify rather than blur the other things on his mind. He needed to attend to Blackshaw. Something was wrong there, something more than a man grown too fond of the bottle as he dealt with the horror of war. Also, Dove and Alban needed to form a plan to discover how far this possible conspiracy of Captain Smith's went. And if he got no word back from Liverpool concerning Tillie, then he would have to go himself, leaving John and Ellen here without him. But they could not legally marry, surely, without her true name.

There were many arguments against hasty marriage, of course, not least his own views up until Tillie's passionate plea. If she still wanted it when marriage was possible, it was not a gift he could deny her.

In the meantime, he was content to lounge around the Grant's group of friends and simply enjoy Tillie's presence. It was the supper dance getting underway now.

"Major Doverton," a waiter said respectfully.

"Yes?"

"There are two gentlemen in the foyer asking for you."

"Can't you bring them in to the ballroom?" Dove asked.

"Oh, no, sir, they don't have vouchers. And they wish to speak to you in private."

Dove turned to go with him. "Who the devil are they?"

The waiter presented a card. "The older gentleman gave me this."

Dove glanced at it, but it didn't give much away.

Mr. Matthew Dawlish
Linley House
Lancashire.

In the foyer, which was markedly quiet after the noise of the ball-room, he discovered two gentlemen waiting in the chairs near the door. They rose as he strode toward them, one of late middle years, stocky of build, short-necked but well-dressed. The other had the same build but with greater height.

"I'm Doverton," Dove said briskly. "How might I assist you, gentlemen?"

The older man bowed. "Thank you for meeting us. We called at your barracks and they told us you were here. I apologize for interrupting your evening, but I'm afraid our business will not wait. Forgive me, where are my manners? My name is Dawlish, Matthew Dawlish. This is my son, Luke. We own the Linley Mill, near Liverpool."

Dove's eyebrows snapped together. He began to have an inkling of who they were and why they were here.

"Colonel Farnsworth approached me," Mr. Dawlish said. "And I'm dashed glad he did. I think you might have found my niece."

This was not quite how Dove had imagined the discovery would go, and now the possibility was upon him, he was unsure what to do. Glancing around, he saw one of the young lieutenants emerging from the men's cloakroom.

"Heath," he called. "Send Dr. Lampton out to me, if you please."

While Heath bolted to obey, Dove turned back to the men who were most probably Tillie's family. "Did the colonel explain the situation? That the young lady we found has lost her memory? Most probably due to a head injury. It is possible, even if she is your niece, that she will not know you. In fact, before we decide how best to introduce you, perhaps you can provide some kind of evidence that your missing niece is the lady we found?"

The younger man, Luke Dawlish, scowled as if offended to have his word doubted. But his father put his hand in his coat pocket and brought out a miniature portrait which he passed wordlessly to Dove.

A young, black-haired girl with large, laughing grey eyes and a wide smile. His stomach clenched, for it could not be anyone but Tillie. She was younger in the picture, perhaps only fifteen or sixteen, but she had changed little in basic appearance.

"What?" Dr. Lampton said brusquely, joining them.

Dove showed him the portrait. "We seem to have found Tillie's family. Mr. Dawlish is her uncle."

"And guardian," Mr. Dawlish said, "since the death of her father a year ago."

"What is best?" Dove demanded of the doctor. "To wait until tomorrow and warn her in the hope her memory returns steadily? Or shock her with a meeting tonight?"

"Best for her memory, or for her person?" Lampton asked.

"I'm afraid," Mr. Dawlish said firmly, "that I insist on seeing my niece tonight."

Dove glanced at Lampton, who shrugged. "The shock may work best to bring back her memory."

There was something about this that he did not like. Unease twisted through him. But he had no reason to keep her from them. He nodded once.

"I'll bring her to you," Lampton said abruptly. "And I'll bring Kate for familiarity. You stay there, too, Major. We don't want her frightened.

"She is here?" Dawlish said, brows raised. "She has made friends in your community?"

"Several," Dove said. "You seem surprised."

Dawlish pursed his lips. His son shook his head in a sorrowful kind of way.

"Alas," Dawlish said, "although my niece has a good heart, she does not make friends easily. She is not terribly...*stable*."

"She does not sound at all like the lady I know, who has dealt with the most frightening adversity with spirit and calmness. After the initial terror, but then she was pulled out of a wooden box in the sea. During a storm."

Mr. Dawlish looked genuinely shocked.

His son blurted, "She's afraid of the dark."

Dove's fist clenched in renewed fury at whoever had shut her in that box. Had they known of her fear when they did it? Was it these men, her own family, who had done it? He could see no reason as yet, and besides, he could swear the older man at least was taken by surprise.

"How did she even get aboard the ship that went down?" Dawlish demanded.

"We don't know," Dove said distractedly, for a positive deputation was emerging from the ballroom—Dr. Lampton, the Grants, and Tillie—and walking across the floor.

Tillie saw him first, and her face lit with pleasure even before the quizzical expression dawned in her eyes. He moved aside, allowing her a clear look at the men. Her gaze merely flickered over them and back to Dove.

He took her hand. "This is Mr. Matthew Dawlish and Mr. Luke Dawlish."

"How do you do?" she said politely.

"Don't you know us, Matilda?" the older man said sadly.

"Matilda?" she repeated, as though startled. A frown formed between her brows as she stared at them more closely.

"We believe," Dove said, "that this is your uncle and cousin."

Her breath came in pants, though whether because she couldn't remember or because she could, wasn't very clear.

Her cousin took a step toward her, holding out his hand. "Come, Matilda."

At once, she fell back, almost falling against Dove in her panic. Her fingers clung to his so fiercely it hurt.

"Matilda," Luke said, apparently both shocked and hurt. "You *must* remember me. I'm your husband."

Chapter Ten

"*H*USBAND? OH NO, no!" Blood sang in Tillie's ears. If it hadn't been for the sure grip of Dove's fingers, she would have fainted. As it was, this felt like some pleasurable dream turned suddenly into a nightmare.

Dove was to be her husband, her lover. Not this affronted stranger, whose hand fell at her hoarse exclamation.

"She doesn't remember you," Dr. Lampton said calmly. "She doesn't remember anything before the storm."

"She does!" Luke burst out. "She's just pretending!"

"Luke!" his father admonished. "Don't let your disappointment make you say unbecoming things that you will regret."

"Why would she pretend?" Dove asked quietly.

"She wouldn't," Dawlish said firmly. "My son is young and in love. He has been crazy with worry about her and now with disappointment that she does not remember."

Even in her agitation, Tillie thought he looked more peeved than crazed with love and anxiety. More than that, though she remembered nothing about him—and didn't want to—she had a strong feeling of revulsion, of some connection that made her fear she truly did know him. And the older man who claimed to be her uncle.

Raising one trembling hand to her forehead, she stared from her uncle to her cousin, searching for something that would unlock her memory, that would bring sense to the nightmare.

"Come with us," the older Dawlish said gently. "We'll look after you, now."

Her fingers convulsed on Dove's hand. She could not look at him, knew only that she could not go with these strangers. *Would* not go. Every instinct shrieked against it.

"Might I suggest," Dove said, "that for the lady's sake, you move a little more slowly? Allow her at least one more night with Mrs. Grant while she absorbs the new shock."

"That would be best," Lampton said, nodding wisely. "I believe she will remember now in her own time. Call at the vicarage, perhaps, let her familiarity with you grow until it connects with her memory."

"How long will that take?" Luke demanded.

Dr. Lampton shrugged. "Who knows? I believe you have set something in motion, so I suspect it will not be long at all before all becomes clear."

"We do need to return," Mr. Dawlish said. He tugged at his lower lip. "But we can certainly wait until tomorrow." With a kindly smile, he held out his hand.

Hesitantly, Tillie took it for the briefest moment and slipped free. Luke made the same gesture. She had to force herself rather harder, but she managed to shake hands with him, too, however briefly. As they walked away to the door, she stared after them in silence.

"Oh, Dove," she said brokenly as the door swung closed behind them. "I cannot be married to that man!"

His tightening fingers were his only answer. He was not looking at her, but she knew he would not desert her, whatever the pain. He looked sick, as if he had been punched in the stomach.

"We will find out," Lampton said firmly. "Don't worry. We won't desert you yet. Go back with Kate and rest."

Mr. Grant called to the doorman to send round their carriage. At Mrs. Grant's encouragement, she forced herself to let go of Dove's hand and walk with her to the cloakroom which was, fortunately, empty.

"Is it true?" Tillie blurted, dropping onto a chair and kicking off her dancing slippers. "Do I look like them?"

"Not really," Mrs. Grant admitted. "But that means very little."

She reached out and caught Tillie's hand as she picked up her slippers, spreading it on her lap. "More significant *might* be that you never wore a ring. Nor is there a mark where one would have been. But again, that means little. You could have lost the ring at sea, or not worn it the day you boarded the ship. And the wedding could have been too recent for any mark of a ring to show."

"I have to remember." She squeezed her eyes shut. "But God help me, I don't want to now. I don't want to know if I'm my cousin's wife."

"Because of Major Doverton?"

She nodded once. There was no point in denying it, and she didn't want to. "If I have hurt him again, if he loves me and I am that man's wife…"

"Hush." Mrs. Grant's arm came around her. "Be strong, my dear. You will remember, and then we will know what to do. You have friends."

"Thank you," she whispered, giving the vicar's wife a quick hug in return. She dashed her hand across her eyes before donning her outdoor shoes and reaching for her cloak.

There was only time for one brief moment with Dove as he handed her into the carriage outside the assembly rooms.

He held her hand in both of his and then kissed it. "Sleep well, my love," he breathed, and she wanted to laugh because she knew she would not sleep at all. She clung to his hand a moment too long. Although she could not speak, she was sure he knew what she was trying to say.

And then her hand was cold. She sat in the carriage beside Mrs. Grant, and the door closed with a bump before the horses moved off.

As it turned out, Tillie was wrong. She *did* sleep, a strange light sleep by the glow of the lamp, hovering on the verge of knowledge and memory. As before, she was flooded only by feelings, and yet when she awoke, the memories crowded in and she remembered every-thing.

Afterward, she never knew how long she lay there, battered by her own life, by the awfulness that had come just before the storm, and the happiness of what had come after. Her first new thought was that she had to tell Dove, and with that she sprang up, washed and dressed as best she could without a maid to lace her up.

She knew she should take Mrs. Grant with her for propriety, but as she passed the main bedchamber, she heard Kate cooing to the baby and knew she was feeding her. Tillie couldn't wait. She hurried downstairs and left the house, all but running around to the hotel in the relentless rain. There, she instructed the first cab driver to take her to the barracks and jumped in before she remembered she had no money to pay him.

Blushing, she hoped Dove would not mind paying for her.

An officer strode out the front door as she stepped down from the cab. He glanced at her and then, eyes widening, he came straight to her.

"Miss Tillie," Captain Grantham said in clear surprise. "May I assist you?"

"Could you please find Major Doverton? It is really quite urgent I speak with him."

"Dove isn't here," Grantham said.

She blinked. "Isn't here?" Why had she not considered that? She swallowed. "Do you know when he will be back?"

"Not until tomorrow, I'm afraid."

For some reason, that floored her as none of her memories had managed to. Of course, Dove had every right to go wherever he wished, or wherever he was sent by his commander. But she could not help feeling very alone, and more than a little hurt that he had gone the very morning after she had been discovered by her family.

It was a lesson in self-reliance.

"Can I help?" Grantham asked.

"Thank you," Tillie said firmly, "but no. I shall speak to Major

Doverton when he returns." She turned back to the cab, then paused to say over her shoulder. "Perhaps you'd tell him I called?"

"Of course." The captain handed her in and closed the door. "Send for me if you need to," he urged.

"Thank you." But in truth, there was only one person she felt could help her.

Only as they drove back down to Blackhaven did it strike her that if she told the truth, she might not be believed. Her breath seemed to vanish. Worse than that, it might well put her in danger. And everyone else who knew. Including Dove...

DOVE HAD RETURNED from the ball rather earlier than his comrades, for it seemed to him suddenly there was no time to waste. And his first priority had been to get some sleep. However, striding past the officers' mess, which at first glance was empty, he'd caught sight of a solitary figure with a glass in front of him. *Blackshaw.*

Other matters closer to his heart clamored for attention instead, but he had never shirked his duty. After only a moment's hesitation, he walked in and poured himself a glass of brandy before he crossed the room and sat down opposite Blackshaw.

"Good health," he said, raising his glass.

Blackshaw toasted him back somewhat sardonically, but he did not appear to be so drunk or pugnacious. All the same, Dove wouldn't know how to proceed until the other man spoke.

Blackshaw played with the stem of his glass. Slowly, he raised his blood-shot eyes to Dove's, a desperate challenge in them, along with a huge dose of misery. "I should sell out, shouldn't I?"

"Do you want to?" Dove asked.

"It would only be fair. I'm not the officer I wanted to be."

Dove shrugged. "Neither am I."

Blackshaw's lips twisted. "But you're the hero of the regiment, everything we all aspire to."

Dove lifted his glass and drank. "It gets out of proportion. The truth is, we act and react in the moment. I could just as easily have legged it."

"But you didn't."

"Not that day." Dove looked at him. "I took part in many engagements, many battles. I did not always cover myself in glory. No one does. You, I think, are hampered in that you only fought in one. And it was a big one. The next time will be different—better or worse, who knows? But it will be different. The question isn't about the past but the future. Do you want to remain in the army? You will be a baron one day, I gather. You can choose. But make sure you do it for the right reasons. It will make you a better soldier." He smiled. "Or a better baron."

Blackshaw thought about that for a little until his eyes came back into focus on Dove. "You're not really a stuffed shirt, are you?"

Dove grimaced. "No. I'm just a soldier like you wondering what the future holds."

Blackshaw reached out and they clinked glasses.

AFTER BARELY TWO hours of disturbed sleep, Dove rose in the dark, and by the light of a single candle, scribbled hasty notes to John, Colonel Gordon, and Dr. Lampton. After which, he saddled his own horse and rode for Manchester. Changing horses frequently, he arrived in Manchester not long after midday, and by asking directions several times, found his way to a rough back street alehouse called *The Brown Jug*.

A few men sat drinking and smoking pipes, but it was not a lively establishment—at least not at this hour. The floor had been recently swept and in all, it was not as bad a place as Dove had expected.

No one paid him much attention as he wandered up to the counter, behind which, a man was rolling an ale cask into place.

"What can I get you?" the man asked, straightening.

He was unexpectedly young and good looking, although he seemed very weary and his hair was too long. More interestingly, his hand had been amputated at the wrist.

"A pint of ale, if you please," Dove said.

While the man poured it, Dove watched him. He hadn't expected to find Trent this easily.

"I don't suppose," Dove said, "that you know where I could find one George Trent?"

"Depends who's asking."

"I am," Doverton said, swinging off his cloak to reveal his uniform. "I wrote you a letter. Major Doverton of the 44th."

The man glanced at him with only a shade more interest and pushed his beer across the counter. "I can't read."

He was silent a little longer. Dove chose not to help him. After a moment, the man said, "I knew a man in the 44th. Tom Gunn."

"You saved his life as I understand it."

George Trent blinked. "You been talking to him?"

"A little. I understand you have a mutual friend in Annie Doone."

Trent's gaze fell. "You got some odd friends for an officer."

Doverton said nothing, just took a long draught of ale. After several seconds, Trent's eyes lifted reluctantly. "She keeping well?"

"Not really, no."

The man scowled. "Why not? You ain't taken advantage of her, have you?"

Doverton lifted one disbelieving eyebrow. "*I* have not, no."

"What's that supposed to mean?" Trent demanded, bristling.

"It means she bore your son a couple of weeks ago and the pair of them barely survived."

"Oh, Jesus." Trent sat down abruptly on a cask, his face changing color. "I didn't know. God, I didn't know. Is she doing better?"

"Apparently. But her future is hardly rosy."

Trent gave an unamused laugh. "Neither is mine."

Dove looked around. "Have you worked here long?"

"Since I was a nipper, off and on." Trent sighed. "It was my da's. I took the king's shilling to get away from it, but I always knew it would suck me back in. And it did. About as soon as I got home, the old man up and died, leaving me to support my old mum with one hand. Nothing to do except keep this place going,"

"And Annie?"

Trent flushed. "Couldn't bring her here, could I? Besides, I told her a lot of nonsense about getting taken on as a solicitor's clerk and earning good money. Made myself sound respectable and prosperous to impress her." He grimaced, curling his lip in self-deprecation.

Dove set down his half-empty mug. "With respect, Trent, Annie has a few more serious issues than your self-importance. Her family don't want her, since she's disgraced. What do you think happens to girls like Annie when they have no respectable way of earning enough for her and the child to eat?"

Trent whitened. "I don't want that for her. Or the baby."

Dove picked up the mug and took another drink. "Then you'd better decide what to do about it." He set the mug down again, delved into his pocket for a few coins, which he dropped on the counter. "She's staying at the hospital in Blackhaven for the next couple of days at least. You can find me at regimental headquarters."

"I can't leave this place," Trent said as Dove made for the door.

Dove ignored him.

"Sir?" Trent said desperately.

Dove glanced back at him.

"Tell Annie she's the best girl I ever had."

"Tell her yourself," Dove said.

Outside, he untied his horse, which was attracting rather too much interest from some street urchins, mounted up, and rode away. He wanted to be in Liverpool by tea time.

"THERE YOU ARE!" the vicar said in relief. Dressed to go out in his great coat and hat, he had opened the front door just as Tillie walked up the garden path to the vicarage. His keen eyes searched her face. "I thought I had failed at the first asking."

"Failed to do what?" Tillie asked, walking past him into the house.

He closed the door behind her. "Look after you. You haven't been to see your uncle and cousin, have you?"

"God, no," she said with an involuntary shudder. "Though I suppose I could have run into them. Would you mind very much paying the cab?"

When the vicar returned, she was still standing where he'd left her, deep in thought. He took her cloak and bonnet and hung them up with his own. "I think meeting your family alone would have made you uncomfortable. Come into the breakfast parlor."

She followed him somewhat lethargically and was surprised to see not only Mrs. Grant but Dr. Lampton, both of whom greeted her with smiles of relief. Amidst the confusion of her own thoughts and fears, their concern touched her.

"Were you worried about me?" she asked, forcing a smile. "Thank you, but there is no need. I only went to find Major Doverton. He's away for a few days."

"That's why we were worried about you," Mrs. Grant said. "He left in the middle of the night, in a great hurry, apparently, not even taking his batman with him, but he took the trouble to write to both Tristram and Nicholas here to ask them and me to look after you while he was gone."

"And not to let you go with the Dawlishes," Grant added, "unless you specifically asked to, and remembered everything before the storm."

"I'm afraid that isn't the case," Tillie said. She didn't want to lie more than necessary to these people who had treated her with such kindness, knowing nothing about her. She swallowed. "Did Major Doverton not write to me?"

Grant urged her into the chair beside his wife and helped her to some eggs and ham. "No, and I expect that was deliberate. The thing is, just about everyone must have noticed that he has been …courting you, for want of a better expression. And so, the revelation that you are married puts you both in a rather awkward position with regard to propriety and reputation."

She stared at him. "But I don't *remember* marrying Luke!"

"What exactly *do* you remember?" Dr. Lampton asked. His sharp gaze was unblinking.

Tillie shook her head. Tears started to her eyes because she was lying to them. "Nothing," she whispered.

"Then you don't know who hurt you, who put you in that box on board *The Phoenix*?"

She shook her head.

"Then that will be our line of defense," said Grant, who had once been a soldier. "Surely it would not be good for her to be sent to them, remembering nothing?"

"As her doctor, I would strongly advise against it," Lampton said, rising to his feet. "And since we don't actually *know* that they're Tillie's family, we'd all be failing in our duties if we gave her up to them without more proof than a miniature portrait which could, after all, have come from anywhere. I have to go over to Henrit later, so I'll have a word with Winslow while I'm there. It would do no harm to have him on our side."

Tillie gazed at him in wonder. She was right to protect them, for they were protecting her.

"But you must cooperate with us, Tillie," Mrs. Grant said urgently. "No more wandering on your own. And if Tris and I are not in, you must not receive them here."

"That will not be a problem," Tillie assured her. And then the tears prickled again. "I do so appreciate your kindness to me."

"Oh, you are now our favorite mystery of the winter," Mrs. Grant said lightly. "Surpassing even that of Elizabeth's governess before Christmas."

"Kate," Lampton objected from the door.

Mrs. Grant laughed. "There is always something going on in Blackhaven."

"That much is true," Dr. Lampton said, with a brief bow to the room. "I'll call back in the evening."

"Wait, are we not all dining with Elizabeth at the hotel this evening?" Mrs. Grant said.

"Is that a good idea?" Grant asked doubtfully. "The Dawlishes are staying there."

Lampton's gaze fell on Tillie. "A little cooperation goes a long way. She should meet them, in the safe company of her friends. Until she remembers. Are you agreeable, Tillie?"

Tillie nodded. If her uncle and cousin saw and heard that she still remembered nothing, then her friends would be safe, at least while she worked out what on earth to do.

Lampton frowned. "In fact, I have to see one of the hotel maids who's sickly. I think I'll call on Mr. Dawlish while I'm there and explain the situation. Until this evening!" He left abruptly enough to leave a swirl of air behind him.

Tillie returned to chasing pieces of egg around her plate without a great deal of enthusiasm. "Where has Major Doverton gone?" she asked.

"He didn't say in his note," Grant replied. "Just that he would be away for a couple of days. I assume it's duty because he's left his brother here, too, and Colonel Gordon must be aware of his absence."

Mrs. Grant reached for the coffee pot. "Yes, but what duty would require him to start in the middle of the night when he clearly wasn't planning such a thing when we last spoke to him? It's a bit of a coincidence, isn't it? I think it has something to do with Tillie and the Dawlishes."

At that, a stream of warmth tricked through Tillie's heart. Of course, he would not have abandoned her to her fate. After all, he had warned the Grants and Dr. Lampton to look after her. He just hadn't realized that someone needed to look after *them*.

Chapter Eleven

TILLIE SPENT THE rest of the day helping the Grants in their charitable works. They ran a kitchen twice a week to feed homeless and injured soldiers, and Tillie helped cook and serve the soup. Besides which, she listened to their unlikely stories, laughed at their jokes, and even broke up a fight before Grant could get there and bell the protagonists off in no uncertain terms.

As well as keeping her occupied, the work brought its own rewards, and Tillie walked back to the vicarage with Mrs. Grant in a happier frame of mind.

"You have a natural way with them that they like," Mrs. Grant said. "I think you must have done this kind of thing before."

"I might," Tillie agreed. "Equally, I might have been on the receiving end of such charity."

"I doubt it." Mrs. Grant cast her a quick glance. "Do you think Mr. Dawlish could be your uncle? A wealthy mill-owner? It would explain your education and the good clothes you were wearing when you were found."

"I suppose it would."

"You don't sound happy about it."

"I suppose I thought I would remember family," she said evasively.

"Or were you wishing you were a gently-born lady to be a suitable match for Major Doverton?"

Tillie flushed. "Am I so obvious?"

Mrs. Grant took her arm. "For what it's worth, I don't think he cares what your origins are. He has been around the world enough to value people for who they are and what they do."

"But he would care about me being married to my cousin. You don't think that's why he bolted, do you?"

"No," Mrs. Grant said firmly. "And he didn't bolt. He hastened."

Tillie couldn't help frowning in worry. "I hope his journey was not too arduous... Did you know him before he was wounded?"

Mrs. Grant shook her head. "By the time I had settled in Blackhaven, he was recovered and put in charge of the second battalion. I gather he never speaks of it, but I believe he was wounded while saving his men. Tris says he was awarded the Army Gold Medal and the Peninsular Cross during the conflict. I don't think he finds many things too arduous!"

Not then, perhaps. But he was still dying of that wound, and no one seemed to know it.

THEY MET BEFORE dinner in Princess von Rheinwald's rooms at the hotel, and Tillie was introduced to her four-year-old son, who was protesting loudly about going to bed—until Dr. Lampton came in. The child rushed at him with unexpected joy. And Tillie saw quite another side to the grumpy doctor, who threw the boy up into the air and let him ride on his foot into his bedchamber, escorted tolerantly by his nurse.

When he came back, he accepted a glass of sherry from the princess with a quick, tender smile. This was, decidedly, a town of odd marriages. The doctor and the princess, the vicar and the wicked lady...for that was how the infamous Lady Crowmore had been known before she had married Tristram Grant, then merely a country curate. Perhaps there was hope for the major and the mill-owner's daughter, too.

"You go ahead," Dr. Lampton said. "I'll just have a look at Tillie's wound and then we'll join you."

While she sat in an armchair, he removed the dressing—artfully hidden in her hair—and pronounced it healing very well.

"I'll take the stitches out in the next day or so," he said. "For now, we'll let the fresh air get to it." He sat down on the nearby chair and held her gaze. "Is there anything else you would like to tell me? About what or who you remember?"

She almost told him, for he gave a strong impression of kindness and utter efficiency, as though he could take care of everything. But he couldn't. Even Dove couldn't.

She shook her head. "There is nothing. But... I did want to ask you something else. Are you Major Doverton's doctor?"

To her disappointment, he shook his head. "Most of the military men have gone back to Dr. Morton since he came home from the Peninsula. I never saw the major before that either. Why?"

"If a man was badly wounded—oh, say two and a half years ago—so that no one thought he would survive, only he did... Would you think it possible he could *still* die of that wound?"

"Of course. But without details or examination, it is impossible to say. A wound could be the cause of death in days or in fifty years. Are you trying not to break confidences?"

She nodded once.

"Military doctors are more familiar with those kinds of wounds than I," Lampton said. "But, have him come and see me." He paused in the act of rising. "In fact, where battle wounds are concerned, there is another physician of my acquaintance who might be more help. I'll see if I can arrange it."

"Thank you." The greater problem might well be getting Dove to cooperate with such an arrangement, but she clung to the hope.

"I spoke to Mr. Dawlish this morning," Dr. Lampton said as they walked toward the door. "And explained the harm it could do to remove you at this moment from your comfortable surroundings. He has agreed to wait another couple of days while meeting with you occasionally in the hope of finally jolting your memory. I also told him both the magistrate and I would need proof of the relationship before we could formally release you from our care."

"Oh, well done, sir, thank you!"

"Mr. Dawlish did tell me that you had had problems with nerves before. That you could be unstable and unreasonable. Is that something you *feel*?"

"No," Tillie said indignantly. Then, swallowing, she added with difficulty. "That is, I don't remember. I could have been. But I don't *feel* I'm of a nervous disposition. Perhaps I've changed."

"It's an odd thing," Lampton observed after a moment. "I can see no reason for pretending they are your family. If you are *not* their niece and wife, respectively, why would they want to claim you were?"

"I have no answer for you," Tillie said with difficulty.

"Of course you don't." He closed the door behind them and offered his arm. "Let us join the others."

Dinner was a pleasant meal, with plenty of interesting conversation as well as laughter and banter, for they were all clearly clever and well-read people. Tillie was quite quiet, not because she felt overawed but because her mind kept slipping to other matters—Dove. Her family. Captain Smith. But mostly Dove.

"Will you read the banns for us on Sunday?" Dr. Lampton said once with his usual abruptness.

"Since it is the only way to get you in my church, yes," Grant said at once. "Then you have set a date for the wedding?"

"Three weeks on Monday," Lampton said, "if you can oblige us. We have found a house in Blackhaven that suits Elizabeth, and I have arranged with an old friend to take care of my patients during our wedding trip."

"Where will you go?" Mrs. Grant asked eagerly.

"Italy. Perhaps Greece."

"With the war over, we may go where we like," Elizabeth said happily. "And it will be so wonderful to come back to Blackhaven."

"What will you do with Andreas?" Mr. Grant asked.

"Leave him here with his nurse and governess," Elizabeth said. "A hostage for the townspeople so they know Nicholas will come back!"

To Tillie, it all sounded rather wonderful. She thought wistfully of her own marriage to Dove. Such an event seemed a lifetime away. And Dove didn't really have a lifetime… Unless Dr. Lampton or his friend could work another miracle. Tillie would be happy to nurse him devotedly until his last breath. But she would far rather he lived to travel and give her children, and enjoy *life* with her…

"Here comes your uncle," Grant warned, a smile still on his face, no doubt for her uncle's benefit.

Tillie's heart gave an unpleasant lurch, jerking her back to reality. She did not turn her head but only a moment later, her uncle walked into view. Luke was with him. They bowed civilly to everyone, and with equal politeness, Kate introduced the Princess of Rheinwald. Her uncle's eyes widened with awe. It seemed he actually had to drag his gaze away from her after another, much lower bow, in order to look at Tillie.

"Matilda, how are you?" he asked unthreateningly.

"I feel well, thank you," Tillie said, allowing a shade of nervousness into her voice. In the circumstances, it wasn't difficult. Inside, she shook with anger and all the residual fears of what they'd done to her. "I simply don't remember anything. I'm sorry, but you are strangers to me."

"And yet *these* strangers are your friends," her uncle said sadly.

"And your husband has to make an appointment just to exchange passing pleasantries," Luke said resentfully—and a shade too loudly. Several people at the next table looked toward them with interest.

"Luke," her uncle scolded, and yet Tillie thought it was deliberate. So there would be no fuss when they took her away. *Oh, he was her husband. I expect he was just tired of waiting for her to remember. One can't blame him.* Only her friends would make a fuss. Whether or not it made any difference in the end.

"I'm sorry," Tilly said again. "This is difficult for me, too."

"It must be," Dr. Lampton said. "Mr. Dawlish, what did you do today?"

They made polite conversation for about five minutes. Tillie did not join in, but kept her gaze demurely low, which was difficult when Luke stared at her like a cat with a mouse. She wanted to glare back to prove she wasn't afraid of such a cruel, vile bully. Yet, she had to remind herself that she didn't remember such behavior, that she didn't remember anything or anyone before Dove and the people now seated beside her.

"Perhaps we could call on you tomorrow, Mrs. Grant?" her uncle suggested.

"I have a better idea," the vicar's wife said at once. "We have tickets for the theatre tomorrow evening. Perhaps you would like to join us during one of the intervals?"

Another meeting in public. Her uncle's eyes narrowed as though recognizing what she was up to and wondering why.

"I've never been to the theatre before," Tillie said, as though eager to try the experience.

"Of course you have," Luke said. "We've been many times."

Tillie rubbed her forehead. "Oh, dear, this is so distressing, so disorienting. Where did I go to the theatre?"

"In Liverpool, of course, and in London."

"I've been to London?"

"Only last year," her uncle said.

She cast him a quick smile. "I will keep trying to remember."

"That is all we ask," her uncle said, smiling back.

But of course, it wasn't true. The last thing he wanted was for her to remember and make accusations among people who could hurt him. Which was why he would be quite capable of hurting them first.

TILLIE LAY AWAKE most of the night trying to think of ways of stopping her uncle and cousin before they could hurt anyone. However, her solutions became increasingly fanciful, and by the time she rose, she had achieved little but a pale and wan look, with dark circles beginning to form under her eyes.

"At least I look ill," she muttered to the glass.

Mrs. Grant obviously thought the same, for there was a concerned look in her eyes over breakfast and she suggested a visit to the pump room to take the waters. Tillie hesitated, for if Dove came back today and called at the vicarage, she wanted to be there to greet him. On the other hand, she knew she would drive herself mad pacing the house until she had to face her uncle again at the theatre, so she fetched her cloak and accompanied Mrs. Grant.

They walked to the pump room with James, a large footman trailing behind them. Although Tillie was glad of him, she wondered what had possessed her hostess to bring him, for she didn't normally go out in this manner. In fact, Tillie was sure the vicarage hadn't employed any footmen at all when she had first come.

This morning, the pump room contained mostly elderly ladies, although Tillie's heart beat a touch faster when she glimpsed Captain Smith among them. He rose and bowed as they passed him with their glasses of water, and on impulse, Tillie paused to speak to him.

"I hope you suffer no ill effects from the late storm," she said.

"Indeed, I don't believe so. At my age, I merely seek to stave off the inevitable. And if I remain healthy with a glass of water..."

"I'm not sure it works that way," Tillie said doubtfully. "Otherwise, the population of Blackhaven would be incredibly old."

Captain Smith cast a significant glance around the other clientele, and Tillie laughed. "Well, perhaps you are right. How long will you remain in Blackhaven, sir?"

"Until I can board another ship."

"Is there one to be had in Blackhaven?"

"Several, if you know the right man to ask."

Alban. He meant Captain Alban. "Then I hope you are successful."

"I'm just awaiting the arrival of my vessel in Whalen. I hope to be gone the day after tomorrow."

"Then I wish you well, Captain."

"And I you, ma'am." He frowned as though just recalling the oddity. "Though I still wonder what on earth you were doing aboard my ship."

"We all wonder that," she said sardonically.

At that moment, someone else walked in. Her uncle and cousin. She was sure their feet faltered as they caught sight of her in cozy conversation with Smith.

Mrs. Grant, who had stopped some distance away to talk to a group of ladies, began to extricate herself. "Come, let's sit, Tillie."

But her uncle and cousin stood on either side of her, hemming her in. For an instant, she could not breathe, for the memory of the darkness and the terror. But she forced it down and merely stepped back to give herself space.

"I see you've made the acquaintance of my niece, Captain," her uncle said.

Smith's jaw dropped. *"Your niece?"* he uttered in astonishment that came close to fear.

"How do you do, Mr. Dawlish?" Mrs. Grant said civilly, taking Tillie's arm. "Sit over here, my dear. You'll never get well if you don't rest... Interesting," she added as soon as they were sitting with a modicum of privacy. "They know each other, but Smith does not know you."

DOVE HAD NOT called by the time they returned from the pump room. Nor had there been any sign of him before they left. So, once more with James, the large footman, she went to the hospital to visit Annie.

She found her friend a little less cheerful than usual. In fact, she seemed almost tearful, though this may have been due to the fact that as little George's health improved, so did his appetite. She got little sleep from having to feed him so often.

"We can't stay here forever," she said once. "And George—Big George—he isn't coming back, is he?"

"Don't worry about that just now," Mrs. Grant said. "Dr. Lampton wants to be sure both of you are well before he lets you go."

"What *can* we do for her?" Tillie asked as they walked home in the winter sunshine.

"Not much," Mrs. Grant admitted. "Even if I could persuade one of the landowners to let her have a cottage rent-free, there would be talk. And she still would have the problem of working and caring for the baby at the same time." She frowned. "I've been thinking about your creche idea, though. I wonder if it's possible at the vicarage?"

"It would be a lot of noise," Tillie said doubtfully.

"Hmm. And poor Tris trying to write sermons and discuss people's bereavements and spiritual problems. Perhaps it is not such a great idea. Not at the vicarage anyway. But there may be a solution in there." She glanced at Tillie. "You remember the noise? Or you just know babies cry?"

"I think I remember the noise," Tillie muttered. It was difficult to keep straight in her mind the things she could and couldn't know, and she felt increasingly uncomfortable about lying to her friends.

"Did you work there, then? Forgive me, you seem to speak too well to be a mere nurse, but perhaps you are a governess?"

"They could not afford the services of governesses! These places were not schools, but cooperatives, run by the women themselves. Blackhaven is different. You have no large concentration of workers in one place. Everything is scattered."

"And yet, it seems there is the need of something."

"It seems there is," Tillie agreed thoughtfully.

BLACKHAVEN'S THEATRE WAS not large by London, or even Liverpool, standards. But it gave a pleasant atmosphere of coziness, almost as if the actors on stage were playing in a private drawing room. The Grants had their own box from where Tillie could see the rest of the audience as well as the stage. She could easily have lost herself in the plays, almost feeling herself to be part of the action, except she could not quite lose awareness of her uncle and cousin in the box directly opposite. Just wondering when they would descend upon her kept her sitting on the edge of her seat.

They did not come until the end of the pantomime, and even then, seemed to be in such good humor from the hilarity of the performance that Tillie was almost soothed. They mostly discussed the comedy of the pantomime, and the possibilities of the tragedy to come, impersonal topics that didn't strain Tillie's nerves too far. Besides, they were diluted for part of the time by other visitors to the box.

In all, their visit was so innocuous that Mrs. Grant invited them to return in one of the subsequent intervals. Tillie understood her purpose was to imply some improvement in their relationship with Tillie, to keep them hanging, as it were, until her memory returned to make everyone comfortable.

Only it wouldn't. It didn't.

At least they did not come in the next interval, although Tillie saw their box was empty. She hoped they had gone home, for she couldn't see them in her sweeping glances around the other boxes. And so, she flirted with Captain Grantham, since he seemed so inclined, and deflected the curious questions of some of the Grants' friends who had clearly heard some kind of rumor of her connection to the Dawlish men.

"Oh dear," twittered a rather deaf lady as the play began again. "I have talked so much I did not notice…"

"See the next act with us, Miss Muir," Mr. Grant said kindly.

"But I have taken Miss Tillie's chair." She began to stand, but Tillie waved her back down.

"I can see perfectly well from here, ma'am," Tillie assured her. "Sit and be comfortable." She moved her chair back to get the cooling draught from the passage outside. Even on this wintry day, the sheer number of candles made the theatre over-warm.

Tillie tried hard to concentrate on the play, but in truth, her mind wandered all over the place, seeking solutions and wandering down paths that led nowhere. Only curtains separated the boxes from the passage, and when the one beside her gave a little swish, she welcomed the cool air.

Until a gloved hand closed over her mouth and she was yanked suddenly out of her chair and straight into the passage.

Chapter Twelve

TILLIE TWISTED AND wriggled, trying to lash out, but her hands were trapped by one of her captor's arms, and she couldn't scream for his hand over her mouth. She could not even get a decent bite at his gloved hand, for it was too hard against her teeth. All she could do was kick.

He grunted as she connected with his knee and shin, but it didn't slow him up. He simply dragged her along the empty passage and through the door to the back stairs.

She knew who he was, just by his smell. Luke Dawlish, her cousin.

"Stop it!" he said fiercely. "Don't make me hit you."

Tillie was beyond caring whether or not he hit her. Under no circumstances would she go anywhere with him if she could possibly avoid it and she meant to. It was a deadly struggle on the stairs, with her doing her best to trip him, push him or otherwise injure him to make him let go. But he was bigger and stronger, and even though she managed to slow him up and annoy him, their progress was inexorable.

Eventually, when she got in a particularly vicious kick to his shin and then hooked her foot around his ankle to trip him, he lost patience.

"Damn it, woman," he muttered savagely. For an instant, her body was freed as he reached upward, but before she could take advantage, he simply pinched out the candles in the wall sconces above his head and the stairwell was plunged into darkness.

Her breath escaped on a sob, muffled in his hand as the terror flooded her, paralyzed her. Hours of hellish darkness, still and dreadful or spinning and heaving. She couldn't stand it again. She would lose her mind.

But she could not give in to this, not again. Dove needed her. She *would* be with him and she would not let *them* win, these vile creatures who called themselves her protectors. It took her until she made out the glimpse of light through the door at the bottom of the steps, but this time, she did manage to think through the terror.

She went limp in his hold, as if she had finally succumbed. He grunted with relief, although she made herself as heavy and floppy as possible.

Only when he hauled her through the door into the main foyer— no doubt he meant to tell the doorman and anyone else who happened to be there that she was ill—did she spring up again.

Wrenching her mouth free of his mercifully slackened hand, she cried, "Help me!" and lashed out with her fists, twisting violently.

"My wife is having a turn!" he said grimly. "Please hold the door. My father is waiting outside with the carriage."

Tillie stamped hard on his foot, forcing him to let out a howl of pain, and then suddenly, he was torn away from her and she was free. Someone had Luke by the collar and struck him hard, sending him sprawling back against the wall.

As his attacker turned, the blurry light resolved, and she saw that it was Dove, his fist still clenched and poised.

She smiled tremulously. "It's you," she said happily, and then his arms were around her, safe, secure, and wonderful.

But only for a moment, for this was a public place. The doorman stood in the middle of the foyer, as if he'd skidded to a halt there when Dove had hit Luke. And her uncle walked through the door from the street, stopping dead when he saw his son staggering to his feet, and a no doubt badly tousled Tillie clinging to Major Doverton's arm.

"What the devil?" Mr. Dawlish exclaimed. "Sir, what have you done to my niece?"

"Unhand my wife, sir!" Luke panted, holding on to his jaw. "I swear I shall challenge you for this!"

"Forget duels," his father said impatiently. "Call the Watch!"

"With pleasure," said the doorman. "They'll have the young gentleman clapped up in no time. Major, perhaps you'd like to take the young lady into the office."

"The man is mishandling my sick wife!" Luke raged.

"The only mishandling I saw was yours," the doorman retorted. "I knows the major very well, and I'm glad to see he still plants a decent facer."

"Thank you, Watson," Dove said mildly. "Perhaps you'd show these gentlemen out." He turned his kindling gaze on Luke. "I'll give you a hand if you like. Or a boot."

Luke glared, though he gave Dove and Tillie a noticeably wide berth as he made his way to his father. "My challenge stands!"

"On what grounds?"

"Trying to steal my wife!"

Dove laughed. "Then send your seconds if you must. I'm sure Captain Grantham will act for me. Watson, can you find me a cab? And then send word to Mr. Grant's box that I've taken the young lady back to the vicarage?"

There was so much Tillie wanted to say, *needed* to say, but first she had to stop the trembling of her limbs. It almost felt like the night he'd plucked her from the box in the sea when she'd thought she'd never stop shaking again.

The cloakroom maid handed over her cloak, and Dove placed it tenderly round her shoulders before ushering her outside and into the waiting cab.

She clung to his hand, resting her head on his shoulder as it moved off.

"How much are you hurt?" he asked. His voice shook.

"I'm not, not really. Except when he doused the lights. I've always been afraid of the dark and he knows it, uses it. I couldn't let him do it again. I couldn't let them take me away from you."

He lifted their joined hands to his lips and kissed her knuckles.

"Forgive me for not being there. It just seemed suddenly urgent that we find out the truth."

"I came to tell you the morning after the ball, but you'd gone."

"Tell me what?"

"That I remembered everything during that night. That I know the truth."

He stared at her, frowning. The lamplight flickered over the planes and hollows of his face, casting shadows that reminded her how little she truly knew him. Although she had always, instinctively trusted in his protection, she'd never imagined him hitting Luke like that. Not that she was sorry.

"Then Grant knows?" he said with odd grimness, perhaps because Grant had taken her to the theater and exposed her to her cousin's villainy.

"No, none of them know anything," Tillie said, giving his hand a little shake so he would pay serious attention. "In fact, once I thought about it, I wasn't sure I should even tell you. Only now that you've hit Luke, they'll suspect you know anyway. But you mustn't tell the Grants, Dove, not even Dr. Lampton."

"Mustn't tell them what? That that blackguard offered you violence, tried to abduct you?"

She plucked at her lip with her free hand. "I suppose we must tell them that. The story will be all over town by tomorrow anyway."

"You misjudge Watson."

"Perhaps. At any rate, it will be put down to a husband's impatience or jealousy or something. What you mustn't tell them is that I remember, that I have my memories back."

"Why the devil not?" He put his arm around her. "My waif, have you done something bad?"

For no reason, she wanted to cry. Because she knew from his voice that even if she had committed some crime, he would still look after her, still love her.

She shook her head wordlessly. "No, it's not for me, but for their own safety."

Any further confidences were curtailed as the carriage halted at the vicarage. Hastily, she pulled the hood of her cloak over her head to hide the disarray of her hair, and Dove handed her down. He paid the driver while she walked down the path to the front door.

In no time, they sat together before the drawing room fire. At Dove's request, the maid brought her a cup of tea.

"Look," Tillie said, stretching one arm out with pride. "I'm not shaking."

"I would have spared you that if I could," he said hoarsely. "I should have been there."

She shook her head, and without a word, he began to pin up her hair, using only the pins that still clung to it by some accident.

"Tell me," he said. "Quickly, if you don't want the Grants to know."

She took a deep breath. "My name is Matilda Dawlish. My mother was Matilda, too, but everyone called her Tillie, which must be why the name clung to my mind when nothing else did. My father was Francis Dawlish who made a fortune from cotton mills in and around Liverpool, and then another by wise investments on the London exchange. Or something. I don't really understand that part. When he died a year ago, I inherited most of his fortune in trust until my marriage."

She looked at him. "Matthew Dawlish is my uncle. He was left one of the mills near Liverpool. He and his wife and son were my only family, since my mother's side would have nothing to do with us."

"Why not?" Dove interjected.

Tillie shrugged. "Snobbery. My father was a weaver's son, and they thought he wasn't good enough for her. Her father disowned her, and she had no contact with him or her brother or sister from the day she married my father. Even when she died, they ignored us."

She waved that away with angry impatience. She didn't want to go over all that again. "So, when my father died, I went to live with Uncle Matthew. He is my guardian until I am one-and-twenty, but he shares control of my fortune with a whole board of trustees."

She gave a shaky laugh. "I know this sounds like a melodrama that Mrs. Radcliffe might have written, but they really did want me to marry Luke so they would have my fortune."

"I ran out of time," Dove said with difficulty. "I could find no trace of your marriage in the parish church records, but I couldn't look further afield if I wanted to be back in Blackhaven tonight. If you were forced to marry him, we'll have it annulled. Or I could just shoot him," he finished with savage satisfaction.

"You don't want to be imprisoned for murder," she said seriously. "Which reminds me, Dove, you mustn't meet him in a duel under any circumstances. He will cheat—he'll shoot early, or my uncle will have someone else kill you first. There is nothing they will not do to achieve their aims, and they have an army of servants to do their bidding."

"I have a bit of experience with armies. What I want to know is how you ended up in the sea, in a box. Do they inherit the money if you die?"

She shook her head. "No, it will go to a charitable foundation. Um... I'm afraid I put myself in the box."

Dove closed his mouth. "That, I did not expect. Why? How?"

She closed her eyes. This was the difficult bit. "I'm afraid of the dark."

"I know," he said gently, smoothing her hair. "Everyone's afraid of something."

"They're my family, so they always knew. Luke shut me in a cupboard when I was six and wouldn't let me out. I screamed for hours, even after they let me out. My mother eviscerated Luke, verbally. My father beat him. His own father said he did, but I doubt it ever happened. In any case, he never did it again...while my parents were alive. But he remembered. They *all* did."

Dove's arms came around her. "Dear God," he whispered. "They locked you up to persuade you to marry Luke?"

She nodded, clinging to him. "In the townhouse in Liverpool. Which is mine. For nearly three days, I think. They even sent the domestic servants away so no one would hear me scream and let me out. I think... I think I went a little insane."

"Dear God, anyone would, even if they hadn't begun with a fear of the dark." He kissed her hair, holding her close, and she had never felt so safe. And yet during the time she was describing, she thought she would never be safe again. "How did you get out?"

"My aunt. I told her I was really sick and afraid of dying. And when she opened the door, I threw my chamber pot at her and ran."

She gave a hiccough of laughter. "That was funny, looking back. But at the time, I didn't notice. I jumped over her, into the first room I came to, and jumped out of the window. My uncle's servants pursued me. One of them had a dog. I felt like a hunted animal."

She hugged Dove tighter. "Eventually, I found myself at the docks. I had this idea of boarding a ship, going anywhere that would take me away from them. But I wasn't thinking straight. I just recognized the name of *The Phoenix* for some reason."

"You own it," Dove said. "That's one of the things I found out in Liverpool."

She stared at him in shock. "I do?"

"Go on," he urged.

"My uncle's men were still chasing me. Or at least I think they were. As I said, I was a bit mad just then. I could have been running from strangers by then, or from shadows. At any rate, I thought they were close, and I hid in an empty crate."

Dove frowned. "Even though you're afraid of the dark?"

"I could see the sky and the stars, so I wasn't afraid to be there. I was just terrified of my uncle's servants finding me. I heard them walk past. And then someone else, talking all the time, shoved a lid over the top and nailed it shut, and I was in darkness again. I don't think he even saw me there, and I was too shocked to cry out. I couldn't believe I'd been so idiotic."

"And your crate was put on board *The Phoenix* with the brandy. Sweet Jesus."

"I think I slept for most of it. I was exhausted with fear, and I'd had no food and very little water. And then I was in the water and drowning…" She trailed off, shuddering.

"Don't," he said, stroking her hair, kissing her cheeks, her lips. "Don't. I know the rest. You are such a strong, brave girl coming through all of this, not only sane but sweet and compassionate. I love you even more."

"Oh, I was hoping you would, because my family is not gently born. My father began as a weaver."

"A respectable trade."

"Not to a gentleman!"

He kissed her mouth with passion, effectively silencing her, and it struck her that everything she'd suffered had been worth it just to know this man's kisses.

"I hear the Grants outside," she said breathlessly against his lips. "Quick, tell me what else you discovered in Liverpool."

"I might as well tell you altogether. And seriously, I think you are being overcautious. Even your uncle cannot go about murdering entire communities of people—including vicars—with impunity. You are the only proof of the story, and they can't kill you or they'll lose all hope of your fortune." He released her with reluctance and stood as the Grants all burst into the room, along with Dr. Lampton.

"Tillie, are you hurt?" Mrs. Grant exclaimed, rushing to her.

"No, no, I'm fine," Tillie assured them. "I merely got a fright, but Dove appeared from nowhere and struck Luke *such* a blow that he positively flew across the floor! It was wonderful."

"Hitherto unsuspected blood lust," Dr. Lampton observed, crouching down in front of her to inspect her head and peer into her face.

"Understandable blood lust in the circumstances," Dove insisted.

Lampton grunted. "How often, exactly, did you hit him? Do I have to save his life?"

"No," Dove said regretfully.

"I'm so sorry, we didn't see anything at the time," Grant said, a frown of worry between his brows. "We only noticed your chair was empty, and then I went running all over the theatre to find you. Fortunately, I ran into the cloakroom maid who was on her way to our box, and she said Dove had taken you home. I have been a poor protector."

"No, no," Tillie said in distress. "It never entered your head that they would be capable of such a thing. Especially when they have been so reasonable since coming to Blackhaven."

Dove caught her eyes, and she took a deep breath. "Also, you could not be expected to know, because I did not tell you. I have not been honest with you. Since the night of the ball, when I first saw them, I began to remember. I remember everything. I didn't want to tell you because...because, well, I thought it would put you in danger. But I'm sure now Dove is right. You have to know."

"I thought you remembered more than you were admitting," Dr. Lampton remarked without obvious anger.

"I suppose it's actually in my favor if I'm a worse liar than I imagined," Tillie said ruefully.

"Well, you didn't actually lie much," he excused her. "It was just that you said, *But I don't remember marrying Luke.* You called him by name with familiarity, and it did imply you remembered other things. So, I'm guessing Luke Dawlish is not your husband?"

She shuddered. "God, no." And she quickly repeated what she had just told Dove, reducing her listeners to appalled silence.

"And *The Phoenix*," Dove added, "belonged to Tillie."

"Which is odd in more ways than one," Tillie said. "For I was talking to Captain Smith in the pump room when my uncle came in, calling me his niece, and I could swear this was a shock to the captain."

Grant rubbed his chin. "I suppose it's astonishing enough to have a waif amongst one's cargo, without that waif being your employer. And he doesn't mix much with the townspeople, so he wouldn't pick up the gossip."

"What else did you learn in Liverpool, Dove?" Tillie asked him eagerly.

"That your uncle has been throwing his weight around, using his connection to your late father to influence decisions he has no real say in—where ships go, what they carry, who captains them, who gets what positions in the mills. There is some unease, not only among the workforce—several long-term managers, foremen, captains, have been replaced—but among some of the board members who run these enterprises."

"Well, I shall have Mr. Hatton reinstate everyone," Tillie said indignantly. "Unless they are guilty of some crime, of course. But… Smith is one of theirs?" Tillie said at once. "My uncle is behind this betrayal?"

"If betrayal it is," Dove warned. "We are only guessing. I'm hoping Alban can get to the truth of that,"

"But can we trust Captain Alban?" Tillie said doubtfully. "You said he had a checkered past."

"He will do nothing to make Lady Bella, his wife, uncomfortable," Mrs. Grant stated. "And in any case, he is quite the hero nowadays. You may trust him to do what is right, in his own inimitable fashion."

Tillie nodded, accepting this as fair. "But what could be my uncle's aim? I always thought it merely to get his hands on my father's money. Why on earth would he get involved with Bonapartists?"

"If money is his primary motivation, that is probably the answer," Dove said. "Perhaps he needs an alternative source of income until he can marry you to Luke. But it means there is someone dangerous behind them."

"The Frenchman who wrote the letter to Smith?" Tillie guessed.

"Possibly," Dove allowed. He smoothed out his frowning brow. "In the meantime, I think we have to preserve the fiction of your lost memories… You didn't say anything to Luke that would betray you knew him?"

"No, I was too busy kicking him and trying to trip him up. He was always a nasty bully."

"I think it's your best protection. That and keeping you always in company when you are out. If they imagine you've told anyone what they did, they'll have nothing to lose and may try to abduct you even more blatantly."

Tillie scowled. "Whatever they did, I would never make vows to

Luke."

"You might not need to," Grant said. "There are unscrupulous men among the clergy, as in any profession."

Tillie's eyes widened. "You mean they could get such a clergyman to ignore my protests and pronounce us married?"

"No," Dove said firmly. "It will not happen. Tillie, how much did you have to do with the business? Do you know who they trade with, partner with?"

"Not really," Tillie admitted. "In my father's day, I had some care of the mill workforce—he let me introduce the creche there, for one thing. But my uncle is not so indulgent. He kept me away from everything, and in any case, most of the boards cannot be bothered with a mere female interfering in men's work! So, I don't see who they do business with."

"Colonel Fredericks," Mrs. Grant said suddenly.

Dove blinked. "Our retired colonel? What of him? He still lives in Blackhaven."

"Yes, but he has some military intelligence role, does he not?"

Dove hesitated. "Yes, but it is not generally known."

Mrs. Grant raised an amused eyebrow. "My dear, sir, one cannot keep secrets in Blackhaven."

Actually, you could, Tillie thought, stricken all over again by the knowledge. No one knew that Major Doverton was dying.

Chapter Thirteen

DOVE WAS KEPT busy for most of the next day, catching up with his normal duties as well as keeping Colonel Gordon apprised of his suspicions of Captain Smith.

"Better report to Colonel Fredericks," Gordon advised that morning. He peered more closely at Dove. "You rode to Liverpool and back in two days?"

Dove thought it prudent not to mention his detour to Manchester. "Yes, sir. I knew you'd given me my head to investigate the matter, but I didn't want to neglect my other duties for too long."

"How are you bearing up?" Gordon asked gruffly.

"Well, sir," Dove replied with patience. In truth, his abdomen ached, and he would have liked a few more hours rest, but he would neither admit it nor give into it. He never had.

"Good, good. Well, delegate your other duties—Kit Grantham is proving useful there. Unless you prefer Blackshaw?"

"No, I don't prefer Blackshaw at this moment. Maybe later, but for now, I think he has difficulty...adjusting to being home."

Gordon cocked an intelligent eyebrow. "Still? Do I need to have a word?"

"No, sir, I believe he's coming back into line. He's a good man underneath it all."

"Good, good. But Dove?" he added as Dove turned to go. "Remember he has friends in high places. He's heir to a barony, and his godfather's an earl."

"Doesn't change his ability as an officer, sir."

"No, it doesn't," the colonel agreed with regret. "I rely on you to do that!"

RETURNING SOMEWHAT WEARILY to his quarters for a short rest before calling on Colonel Fredericks, he was surprised to find Kit Grantham waiting for him.

"Hope you don't mind," Grantham said. "Cully let me in."

"Of course I don't." Dove sank into the battered chair opposite him. "In fact, it saves me the trouble of looking for you. I wanted to discuss something with you." Dove frowned. "Two things, now I think about it, but first, what can I do for you?"

"Blackshaw just called on me."

"Did he? What for?"

"To arrange a duel," Grantham said steadily, "between you and Miss Tillie's husband."

Dove swore. "Damn the man." He had thought their talk after the ball had begun something, a mutual respect, a new start, even, for Blackshaw. But apparently not. The hate was still there. "Does no one have any discretion? What the devil is Blackshaw doing acting for Luke Dawlish?"

"I presume Dawlish sensed an ally." Grantham caught his gaze. "Blackshaw complains about you quite a lot."

"Why?" Dove asked. "I had nothing to do with him until the regiment came home."

"That's the trouble. When he first joined us in Spain, all the talk in the battalion was about you. Sorry to say it, Dove, but you were held up as a bit of a hero."

Dove snorted. He'd never done anything that felt heroic to him. He'd only ever done what he could—his best.

"To be frank," Grantham said uneasily, "I think he was jealous, tended to belittle the hero-worshippers. And then he saw action himself. Between you, me, and the gatepost, he didn't distinguish himself. He's not a great officer, in battle or out."

"And he knows it," Dove said. "Knows *I* know it, too. Interesting."

"Not sure he's savable, Dove. He's too privileged, too entitled."

And too eaten up by knowledge of his own inadequacies. But Dove never gave up on anyone. "Oh well, at least he's only *acting* for Dawlish and we don't have to shoot each other. Yet."

"Well, there's another issue, Dove. I'm sure you don't want this bandied about, but if you fight a duel, Tillie's name *will* be involved."

"I suspect it already is. Luke Dawlish is no more her husband than you are. But he is her cousin, and if I back out or apologize, it will be taken as a sign of guilt. I don't see a way out of fighting."

"There is one," Grantham said, shifting in his chair. "But you aren't going to like it."

"What?"

"He ain't a gentleman, Dove," Grantham said bluntly.

Dove's lips twisted. "And if I refuse to fight him on those grounds, I insult Tillie as well."

"Well, try not to kill him, for he's a civilian and it wouldn't look good."

"I'll hit him where I mean to," Dove said. "But...I'd be obliged if you'd look out for any tricks or cheating. His birth doesn't bother me, but he's a nasty piece of work, and that does." He gave a short laugh. "I suppose that's one way of seeing what Blackshaw is actually made of—whether or not he turns a blind eye."

"Well, I'd rather you didn't die finding that out," Grantham said grimly.

"So would I. When have you arranged it for?"

"Day after tomorrow. Braithwaite Cove at dawn since no one's in residence at the castle. The tide will be out. I suppose I'd better get Dr. Morton to come, but he won't like it."

That was putting it mildly. "Not Morton," Dove said quickly. "And not Lampton, either. Bad enough having to fight without enduring one of Lampton's tongue-lashings, too. There's a new doctor in town—Bellamy, is it? Try him."

HAVING LEFT THE matter of Captain Smith and his French correspondent in the amiable hands of Colonel Fredericks, Dove walked his horse around to the vicarage. His aim was to take Tillie and Kate Grant to tea at the hotel and hope to see John and Ellen at the same time. Even Ash, if he was lucky.

However, it seemed Mrs. Grant already had visitors. As he walked into the house, he heard his brother's voice and Ellen's rare laughter. He grinned, for he wanted Tillie to get to know his family. And it was good to hear Ellen laugh. It meant she had relaxed and was enjoying herself. Of course, Kate was excellent company, but Dove dared to hope Tillie had something to do with it, too.

"Major Doverton, ma'am," the maid announced, and as he strolled in behind her, everyone turned to look at him. Tillie, her lovely face lit with a spontaneous smile of welcome. Kate, looking uncharacteristically nervous. So did John, for some reason, and Ellen was flushed with a gleam of something very like triumph in her expression. The reason sat beside her in widow's weeds.

Dove recognized her immediately. Felicity, to whom he had once been engaged, his lost first love.

Just for an instant, he remembered that and smiled into her eyes.

THAT SMILE WAS like a dagger in Tillie's heart.

It wasn't even simple jealousy or hurt that he could look so at another woman. It was understanding, crowding in on her from all sides.

John and Ellen Doverton hadn't come to be friends, either with her or with Mrs. Grant. They had come to thrust Lady Lawrence in her face. And Lady Lawrence was clearly the first love Dove had once told her of, the lady who had broken his heart by marrying another. Tillie hadn't realized it upon introduction, but that one smile of

Dove's told her everything as surely as if he'd spoken the words.

Her world reeled. It seemed to be doing that a lot recently, only never before with this kind of pain. By the time she managed to right it enough to keep an amiable expression pinned to her face, Dove had turned to greet her.

"How are you, Tillie?"

"Oh, quite well." But piercing her own hurt, she saw that he looked tired. There were lines of strain around his mouth, dark shadows beneath his eyes. His mad dash to Liverpool and back had clearly caught up with him. Helplessly, she wondered how to persuade him to see Dr. Lampton. Or even if she should. Perhaps it was his determination to ignore his condition that kept him going.

"I'm pleased to hear it," he said, walking toward her. "And I forgot to give you some other news."

As he came and sat with her on the window seat, she was conscious of a surge of triumph and hope. "What is that?" she managed.

"I found Private Trent."

"Big George?" she exclaimed with immediate delight. "Oh, well done, sir!"

"Not *so* well done. He didn't exactly pack up and come with me, so don't say anything to Annie. He didn't know anything about the child. I do think he meant to go back to Annie, only he got stuck in Manchester looking after his father's tavern to provide for his mother."

Tillie frowned. "There must be a solution to that, but I can't think right now."

He leaned around to look into her face. "Are you truly well, Tillie? Is this all weighing you down?"

Of course, he meant the matter of her uncle and cousin. She could not say to him, *I'd care nothing for any of it, if only you had not smiled at that woman.* It was ridiculous. *She* was ridiculous.

The care in his eyes spread a tinge of warmth back into her heart. Maybe it was not over yet. Maybe she still had a chance. She forced a tremulous smile to her lips which had the effect of tugging down Dove's brows.

But then Ellen's voice said, "Oh, we must go. Lady Lawrence is eager to try the waters. Dove, will you accompany us, or does duty still keep you?"

It was a masterstroke, at once claiming Dove's escort and reducing to mere duty his visit to the vicarage and to Tillie.

Dove understood it, too, for his lips tightened, though he spoke mildly enough. "I am not on duty right now. And of course, I shall be happy to escort you, since John has clearly forgotten the way."

Ellen colored slightly and gave a tinkling little laugh. "Of course, I did not mean that! I merely meant we shall be glad of your company since you have been absent these last few days."

"I hope you will all dine with us tomorrow evening," Mrs. Grant said in the flurry of departures. "Mr. Ashley, too, if he's free."

Tillie, who had been so looking forward to seeing Dove again, was left feeling deflated and empty. She sat back on the window seat, watching the visitors walk down the garden path. Dove offered his arm to Lady Lawrence, his head attentively inclined to her as she spoke. Tillie's heart twisted, for despite the widow's weeds, they looked a perfect couple, both tall and handsome, and of the same world.

He had wanted to marry her once. Now, she was widowed. She was free. And Dove, loyal man that he was, clearly still loved her. Tillie had seen it in that first smile as soon as he'd looked at Lady Lawrence. It was an older, far more suitable love than that he bore for Tillie.

And then she realized something else. Dove had never spoken of marriage to her. Except that one mention of widow's weeds, which could just have been his way of referring to mourning. It was Tillie who had put the interpretation of marriage on his words. But men of his class married within their own social circle. Women of lesser degree were their playthings and mistresses.

She had misunderstood his kindness. He had misunderstood her kisses.

And now, with that one smile, she had nothing.

THE NEXT DAY, Lady Sylvester Gaunt called on Tillie to propose a walk and a look in at the art gallery. Tillie hesitated, for both the Grants were occupied on other matters, and to take James the footman on such an expedition seemed to be putting on airs. After all, Lady Sylvester was the squire's daughter, married to a marquis's son, and she came without servants of any kind. But after Luke's blatant attack at the theatre, Tillie was reluctant to go anywhere unprotected by a repellingly large male.

Fortunately, they were saved by the arrival of Mr. Ashely, who pronounced himself delighted to escort them to the art gallery.

"Dove is a bit entangled with family today," he said easily. "So, he asked me to call and be useful if I can."

For the first time, Tillie knew a spurt of anger against Dove. How dare he send his friend to her while spending his time with the Lawrence woman? But at least it revived her spirit.

"Useful and *most* pleasant company," she insisted. And, in fact, he was. Amusing, quick-witted, and perceptive, he kept Tillie and Lady Sylvester—whom she quickly learned to call Catherine—well entertained.

"It's upside down," he insisted of one of the gallery's less-pleasing paintings of a rather flat looking basket of fruit.

"No, it isn't," Tillie argued.

"Yes, it is—look." And he took the picture off the wall and hung it the other way around, which at least gave the fruit some life, as if they were falling out of the upturned basket.

Tillie laughed.

"I believe I shall buy it," Ashley said.

"No, don't!" Catherine insisted. "If you truly wish to buy a picture, you should look first at my brother-in-law's."

"Your brother-in-law paints?" Tillie asked, intrigued as Catherine pulled her by the arm across the gallery.

"Very well. He has become quite in demand in London."

"I'm not surprised," Tillie said a moment later, gazing at a spectacular scene of the stormy sea. It was so realistic she could almost imagine herself once more in the heaving little boat after Dove had rescued her, drifting in and out of consciousness. The painting captured the sheer, terrifying power of the sea, as well as its spellbinding beauty. "I would buy that in a heartbeat."

"Well, you wouldn't get it for this price in London," Catherine encouraged her.

But of course, she had no access to her own money. Catherine seemed to realize this after she'd spoken, for she hastily drew Tillie's attention to a sculpture instead.

But Tillie's gaze kept drifting back to the seascape.

"It's certainly apt for a waif from a shipwreck," Mr. Ashley observed.

"Does he live here?" Tillie asked Catherine.

"Tamar? No. He did for a while, but he lives down in Devon now, on the family estates. We're going to visit in the spring."

The conversation moved on, but Tillie was aware of Ashley's gaze on her.

When they left the gallery, they walked slowly, gazing in shop windows on their way back to the vicarage. There, Lord Sylvester was waiting with an old-fashioned gig he drove for himself. Greeting everyone with casual good nature, he handed his wife up into the gig and drove off.

"I believe the whole family's eccentric," Ashley commented. "I didn't know about their connection to Blackhaven."

"I think Blackhaven is connected to just about everyone," Tillie said. "Thank you for your escort, sir. Will you come in and have tea?"

He hesitated. "No, tempting as it is, I won't. You'd be sick of the sight of me, since I believe we dine with you tonight."

AFTER A GOOD night's sleep, Dove's aching body felt much easier.

However, the whole situation with Felicity being in town as his brother's guest still seemed unreal, agitating his mind.

When he had come face to face with Felicity in the vicarage yesterday, there had been a moment when the years had slipped away, leaving nothing but all his old feelings for her. And then he'd all but forgotten her again in his anxiety over the stricken look in Tillie's eyes, which he was at a loss to account for.

It was Ash, oddly, who explained that. "She knows about your late engagement," he said wryly. "And according to both Ellen and John, you just goggled at Felicity as though she was your dinner and you hadn't eaten for four years."

"No, I didn't," Dove protested. "Though I'll own you could have knocked me down with a feather when I first saw her sitting there."

"And now?"

But Dove did not want to talk about this. Something about it all bothered him too much. "What's it to you, you gossiping old woman?" he asked lightly.

"Oh, nothing," Ash retorted. "Merely, if you're hesitating, I might try to cut you out with the divine Tillie."

"Leave Tillie alone," Dove said irritably. "She's been through too much already." He caught Ashley's significant glance. "I have no intention of hurting her!"

"Too late, my friend."

"Ah." Dove sat down. "Felicity." Now that he was forced to confront the issue, he realized his instinct was right. Her being here was decidedly odd. "I never knew Ellen and Felicity were close. In fact, I thought Ellen didn't care for her."

"She didn't, until Tillie."

Dove blinked. "Seriously?"

"Seriously, Dove. Can't you see what's under your nose?"

"Tillie. I can only think of Tillie."

"Then perhaps you should make that plain to her. And to Lady Lawrence."

"Certainly to Ellen," Dove said grimly. "Though perhaps after dinner. There's nothing worse than an awkward meal."

Although he was rather touched to think Tillie could be jealous of Felicity, Dove had no wish to hurt her further and resolved to give her all the attention he could over dinner at the vicarage. In this, however, he was frustrated, not so much by Ellen, let alone by Felicity, but by Tillie herself.

When they were shown into the vicarage drawing room, he saw that there were other guests who had already arrived—Colonel and Mrs. Benedict from Haven Hall. Tillie was deep in laughing conversation with Colonel Benedict, and although she glanced up and smiled in general at the newcomers, she did not rush to meet Dove as she usually did. Instead, she returned at once to her conversation with Benedict.

Somewhat piqued, he sat beside Kate. "No further adventures?" he asked.

Understanding at once, Kate shook her head. "No, the Dawlishes have not come near us. But they are still in Blackhaven, spreading the lie that Tillie is Luke's wife. As though if they say it often enough it will be true."

"It won't," Dove said flatly.

At last, when there was a quiet moment, he strolled across the room to Tillie. She smiled in friendly welcome, but something was missing. Something he couldn't quite put his finger on.

"Is everything well?" he asked her.

"Oh, yes, of course. I have just been talking to Colonel Benedict about his book. Did you know he had published a book on botany?"

"Yes. I did know that. I believe I have a copy."

"One of the five sold," Benedict said with a deprecating grin.

"Nonsense," his wife reproved. "It has done very well!"

"Oh, Mr. Ashely," Tillie said and fluttered across the room to Ash, clearly with something else on her mind.

And Dove finally realized what he had missed in her greeting. Openness. As if she no longer trusted him. Something twisted painfully inside him. He had been too used to being a hero to her.

Although he'd denied it, he'd also taken it for granted that she would continue to think so.

At dinner, he was glad to be placed beside her, but again, she was off-hand, like some amiable social butterfly who liked him no more and no less than she liked anyone else. In fact, she spent most of her time talking to Ash on her other side. Which left him giving attention largely to Felicity Lawrence on his other side—the opposite of what he'd intended.

However, he had to admit there was no hardship in conversing with Felicity. Since her appearance in Blackhaven, there had been little opportunity to do more than offer his condolences on the loss of her husband. Now, despite her widow's weeds, she did not dwell on sad things but seemed to enjoy reminiscing about their shared youth in Shropshire, especially that summer's leave he had spent there when she had been nineteen and he a mere three-and-twenty.

"We were so young," she said after they had laughed over some prank of her little brothers' that Dove and she had got the blame of. "It seemed as if the jollity would never end."

"It can't go on, unchanging. Life has to have its up and downs, but never think that happiness is over for you."

"I confess, I have been very low," she acknowledged with a quick smile. "I do not even have the blessing of children, and it sometimes feels as if I have had my chance at happiness and lost it."

"That is silly. You are not yet five-and-twenty years old. I am sure you will marry again one day."

Her eyes were wide and limpid just as he remembered them. She was probably even prettier than she had been before, and yet she no longer moved him. In fact, the knowledge that he could be married to her horrified him. For the first time that he could recall, he was actually grateful to her for jilting him.

"Do you really think so?" she murmured, dragging him back to the present conversation.

"I know so." He refilled her wine glass and smiled encouragingly.

Beside him, Tillie and Ash were laughing at something he hadn't heard. An unworthy pang of jealousy slid through him. Had Ash been serious about trying to cut him out with Tillie? Dove was sure she was not so changeable in her affections and yet...

And yet, was Ash not a better man for her? He and Dove had been friends since their shared school days at Harrow. A respectable and charming landowner of excellent family, Ash could live into old age with her, give her children and grandchildren, and a happy life. With Dove, what did she have to look forward to? A few months, no more, with the pall of death hanging over both of them. If there was time for one child before he died, they would be blessed. And so, she would be left a widow, like Felicity. He could insure there was enough for her and any child to live on, and of course she was wealthy in her own right. But he had no land, no home to give her. And his family had already shown they thoroughly disapproved of her.

With a hint of panic, he rose to watch her and the other women follow Kate from the dining room. Tomorrow morning at dawn, he fought a duel with Tillie's despicable cousin. Although the odds were in Dove's favor, he had to face the chance that he could die. There was no provision in his current will for her. He could fix that with a letter explaining his wishes. John would see it carried out. But he did not want to part from Tillie in misunderstanding, not if it was to be their last.

"Looking a bit grim," Ash said, pushing the port toward him.

Dove helped himself. "Not I." He pushed the bottle across the table to his brother. "I just have a lot on my mind."

"Like making a choice?" John said.

Dove held his gaze. "I have made my choice. And it is not your place or Ellen's to interfere with that."

John flung up both his hands. "Acquit me. Acquit us both. Ellen merely wanted you to be aware of the current situation."

"It changes nothing."

"Of course not," John soothed. "Oh, stop glaring daggers at me, Dominic, we both just want someone—" He broke off, remembering a little late, clearly, that there were others present who could not know what they were talking about. But Dove knew.

Someone to take care of him on his death bed. They imagined Tillie, with no "breeding", would be useless at such a task. But Dove didn't desire a nurse. He desired a wife, and that only because Tillie had made it obvious she wanted *him*, whatever the state of his health.

The gentleman did not linger long over their port, all anxious for different reasons to rejoin the ladies in the drawing room.

Here, Tillie and Kate were entertaining the other ladies with some comic duet at the pianoforte. Dove stopped beside them, unable to help smiling as he listened. For the first time that evening, he saw that his presence affected Tillie. Color mounted into her neck and face, and she stopped playing with an embarrassed laugh.

Kate laughed, too, and rose to her feet. "There, I think we've tortured everyone enough."

"Hardly torture," Caroline Benedict protested. "You are both talented, and very funny together!"

As Kate left, Dove sank into her place beside Tillie. "Another accomplishment discovered," he said lightly.

"Hardly. Just a little fun."

He depressed one key and glanced round at her. "Are you avoiding me, Tillie?"

Her flush deepened. She shook her head, then met his gaze with conscious bravery. "No. Just giving you the opportunity to avoid *me*."

A frown tugged at his brow. "Why on earth would I do that?"

"Because you deserve it," she blurted.

"Deserve what?" he asked, bewildered.

"Happiness." With a gasp, she rose, and he stood, too, blocking her from the rest of the room.

"Tillie. *You* are my happiness. If I am not yours, you have only to tell me."

Something flared in her eyes, sweet and exciting and passionate, and then her lashes swept down, veiling it. "I don't change, Dove." And she slipped past him.

After a moment, he strolled after her, but since she was sitting by

Colonel Benedict, he took the place on the sofa beside Felicity.

"You are kind to that child," she said warmly.

Dove's lips twisted. "I'm not sure I am."

"I've noticed the kindness with which you treat her—a girl alone without family and out of her own class. You have a generous spirit, Dominic. You always did."

Her use of his Christian name was not lost on him. It was as if they had gone back to their childhood friendship, in the days before it was complicated by romantic love. He was glad to think that was the case.

She smiled deprecatingly, "Do you know, when Ellen invited me to join her in Blackhaven, I was nervous of seeing you again? I wondered if you would hate me for...for what I did."

"For marrying another?" Dove said lightly. "Of course not. Though I'll not deny I was disappointed at the time. I never hated you, Felicity, how could I?"

She cast him a quick, upward glance. "Then there is a chance we can be friends?"

"It has nothing to do with chance. We *are* friends."

This time, her smile was dazzling, and he wondered what on earth he'd said to inspire it. But then Tillie was presenting Felicity with a cup of tea.

"Thank you, my dear," Felicity said kindly, and Dove found his hackles rising in irritation, because her whole manner was so patronizing. But Tilly merely smiled and returned to Kate to receive the next cup and take it to Caroline Benedict.

It seemed no time at all from then until it was time to say goodnight. Deliberately, Dove took Tillie's hand and kissed it. He thought a tremulous smile hovered on her lips, and then John was dragging him out the door and away.

Chapter Fourteen

DAWN BROKE BITTERLY cold as Dove and Grantham strode along the dark beach to Braithwaite Cove. The cove was more isolated than the town beach, and more sheltered beneath the cliff and the castle that rose up from it. In the poor light, a couple of lanterns guided them to the spot where Blackshaw stood with Luke Dawlish and Dr. Bellamy.

The doctor in a heavy grey greatcoat was stamping his feet and clapping his gloved hands together for warmth.

"Bitter morning, gentlemen," he greeted them. "Bitter! Not a good spot for wheeled vehicles either, so it will be difficult to transport a wounded man off the beach to the carriages waiting above. Bear it in mind, gentlemen!"

Dove grunted. In the grey light, Blackshaw looked almost as white as Dawlish, though he was smirking and making jokes with Grantham as they compared the loaded weapons. Dawlish avoided his gaze as was only proper. It was, after all, hard to shoot a man when you looked him in the face. Or perhaps, he was simply miffed because there was nowhere for his father or some hireling to hide and shoot Dove for him.

"Your first affair of honor, gentlemen?" Dr. Bellamy asked cheerfully.

"Hardly," Dawlish muttered.

"Can we just get on with it?" Dove said.

But before they could, the seconds made one last attempt to get either party to apologize.

"Never!" said Dawlish.

"For what?" Dove asked.

Blackshaw and Grantham exchanged resigned shrugs.

"Then," Grantham said. "Will the principals please stand back to back in front of me here. When I give the word, you must walk fifteen paces to my count, then turn and fire on my command. Do you understand?"

"Of course," Dawlish said haughtily. He had his dark coat buttoned up to his chin in best duelers' tradition.

Dove merely nodded and accepted the pistol from Grantham. Although it was several years since he'd felt compelled to defend his honor in a duel, he was not afraid. He'd faced worse fire in battle more often than he could count, and his contempt for Luke Dawlish was matched only by his determination that Tillie's name would never be disparaged. And if he died now, well, he'd already had almost two years longer than he should. It might even be better for Tillie. Grant and Lampton would take care of her. And Winslow, Fredericks, and Alban between them would take care of the Dawlishes...

Focusing on his body, he began to pace with Grantham's count. "Twelve, thirteen, fourteen—"

"Too early!" Blackshaw called sharply. "Hold your fire, Dawlish!"

But his final words were lost in the explosion of a pistol.

Forcing himself, Dove had taken the last pace, his skin crawling as he knew Dawlish would shoot. His left arm jerked with the pistol's report, but he ignored it, turning to face his opponent.

Dawlish stared at him, the empty pistol falling from his hands. "It went off on its own!" he cried. "I never touched it!"

"You turned early, and you fired!" Grantham retorted. "Now, you stand. Take your shot, Dove."

"He can't! He's wounded!" Dawlish exclaimed. "Doctor, stop this!"

"You started it, my friend," Bellamy said with distaste. "Don't worry, I'll patch you both up if necessary."

Without warning, Dawlish fell to his knees.

Dove's left arm began to sting. He knew from experience it was the prelude to a lot of pain. But still, he dropped his aim with Luke's body and scowled. "How the devil am I supposed to shoot an unarmed man kneeling?" he demanded.

"He just shot you in the back," Blackshaw said, staring at him. "Kill the bastard."

"Try *not* to kill him," Grantham amended. "Makes it difficult with the law."

"God damn it," Dove exploded as the pain intensified. He strode across the sand, leaving a trail of blood. Dawlish knelt there, his eyes squeezed tightly shut. "What a pathetic specimen of humanity you are. You're not married to Tillie at all, are you?"

"No," Luke whispered. He shook like a leaf in the wind.

"In fact, you locked her in a dark cupboard for three days and she still wouldn't marry you, would she?" Dove pursued.

"No!" Luke wailed.

Dove let out a scornful laugh. Then he turned his back on Luke and walked away. Grantham and Blackshaw caught up with him just as he fainted away into darkness.

"Miss!"

Dragging herself out of uncomfortable dreams, Tillie found herself staring at a candle flame, and behind it, the anxious face of Janie, the vicarage chambermaid who slipped in and lit the fire every morning at dawn.

"What?" Tillie mumbled, baffled and still half-asleep. "What's happening?"

"I was told to give you this, miss." The girl pushed something into her hand—a folded paper—and Tillie pushed herself up against the pillows, still bewildered. And yet, sudden excitement began to grow, because who but Dove would send her secret messages at dawn?

"Light the other candle, would you?" Tillie said, unfolding the paper in her hand. She had never seen Dove's handwriting, so she couldn't tell who it was from until she began to read. It was terse.

Maj. Doverton in duel, dawn, Braithwaite Cove.

She blinked, reading it again until it made sense. Then she exploded out of bed so quickly that Janie nearly dropped her candle.

How could she have been so foolish? How could she not have imagined this scenario? She had heard Luke's challenge, the night of the theatre. She had even told Dove not to fight because Luke would cheat. It had seemed so sensible to her—it *was* sensible—that it had never entered her head an intelligent man would ignore her advice. And because Dove had never mentioned it again, she had not even thought of it.

But then gentlemen probably didn't discuss such things in front of ladies. And now, Dove would either die for nothing or he'd kill her cousin and, at the very least, rot in prison.

"How light is it, Janie?" she demanded, reaching for her clothes. *Am I too late? Is it done?*

"Not very," Janie said, pulling back the curtains. "Dawn is just breaking."

"Quick, help me dress," Tillie pleaded. She had already flung on her chemise and seized the warmer of the day dresses, which she didn't even wait for Janie to fasten properly before she simply grabbed a shawl and her old hooded cloak. She thrust her bare feet into her boots and bolted out of the bedchamber.

She could hear little Nichola crying, and then Kate's soft voice soothing the baby as she ran past their chamber. By the time she was running downstairs, the crying had stopped, presumably because Kate was now feeding her.

Thinking furiously, Tillie decided what to do. Although all her instincts urged her to get to Braithwaite Cove as quickly as possible, she had to face the possibility that the duel was already over. It would almost certainly be so before she could reach them. Dove could already be dead... But she would not let him be.

"Don't worry Mr. or Mrs. Grant with this just now," she flung at the bewildered Janie as she hurried across the hall.

Rushing from the house, she ran not in the direction of the beach, but into the next street and around the corner to Dr. Lampton's house.

His servant, clearly, was wearily used to being wakened at ridiculous hours, for Tillie had not been knocking for long—however furiously—before the door opened to reveal a yawning man, half-dressed.

"I need the doctor, urgently," Tillie told him.

The man continued to yawn prodigiously but opened the door further to admit her. He pointed to the table with one hand, scratching his uncombed head with the other. "Write down your name and direction, and he'll be there soon as he can."

"No, no, you don't understand," Tillie exclaimed. "I need him *now*! *Right* now!"

The man sighed. "I'll go and speak to him. What's the problem?"

"A man is shot and dying! Tell him Tillie says so."

"Tillie who?" the servant asked, climbing the stairs.

"Dawlish," Tillie replied, for the time for any pretense was long passed.

She waited anxiously, tapping her foot on the wooden floor and trying not to think of Dove lying bleeding and dying from such an avoidable situation. How stupid would that be after surviving such an awful war wound? Surely, even if a new wound was not so serious, it could weaken him enough to kill him?

"Tillie?" Dr. Lampton ran downstairs, still thrusting his arms into his coat. Beneath it, she glimpsed a rumpled shirt and no tie, but now was hardly the time to worry about correct dress. "What the devil are you about?"

"It's Dove," she blurted. "He's fighting a duel with my cousin Luke."

Dr. Lampton's scowl was black. "Where?"

"Braithwaite Cove."

The doctor swore under his breath. "Barnes, my horse."

As the servant hurried off, Lampton seized his bag. "Go back to the vicarage," he said abruptly. "I'll send you word."

"Oh, no," Tillie said grimly. "I should have known this was happening. I'm coming, too."

"On one horse?"

"Wouldn't we better with a carriage for bringing him back if he's wounded?"

"There will be a carriage there and a doctor."

Tillie's eyes widened. "They already have a doctor? Sir, I beg your pardon."

"No need," Lampton said, opening the front door once more. "I have to be there anyhow to shout at them."

"I've never heard you shout," Tillie said uncertainly.

"Then your life is sadly lacking." He strode up to meet the horse Barnes was leading at a trot from around the lane.

Tillie followed him, hastily gripping the horse's bridle. "I want to be there when you shout at him," she said firmly. She swallowed. "Please, Dr. Lampton."

The doctor swore under his breath once more. He leaned down, offering his hand. "Come, then."

With relief, she gripped his hand and was hauled up into the saddle in front of Lampton, who shifted behind and urged the horse forward.

They left the town at a gallop, heading not to the beach but uphill to the castle where, Dr. Lampton prophesied, there would be a carriage. Urgency and dread kept Tillie silent for most of the short ride.

Despite none of the family being in residence at the moment, the smaller gate into the castle grounds was left open to allow a longstanding right of way. Lampton barely slowed the horse as they galloped through and then veered off the main drive onto a track that led to the cliff and a path down to the cove.

Not one carriage but two waited at the top of the path, the cold horses pawing the ground. One coachman began to lead his up and down the edge of the track.

Lampton reined in and dismounted before lifting Tillie down without fuss. He abandoned the panting horse with a careless pat on its nose and strode toward the head of the path. Tillie hurried after him, her heart in her mouth. She managed a nod to the coachman leading the horses—he was the hired cab driver who had once taken her to the hospital. Dove had called him by name. *Colton?*

The second carriage seemed about to leave, for the driver was gathering up his reins and whip. Lampton cast a cursory glance through its window and kept moving, Tillie close on his heels. But abruptly, the carriage door opened, blocking her way, separating her from the doctor.

She blinked with shock. Her uncle's face loomed above her, and a large hand closed on the collar of her cloak.

She jerked back instinctively, or at least tried to, but her uncle's grip was strong. More furious than frightened—he was stopping her from getting to Dove—she brought up her fists to strike. And then another hand clamped down on the first, breaking its hold.

"I don't think so," Lampton said shortly. "Do you, Dawlish?" And he pulled Tillie with him around the carriage to the path.

Two officers in overcoats labored over the edge, all but dragging someone with them. Someone with his coat half off and his arm bandaged. She knew who it was.

With a cry, she ran to him. "Dove!"

"On the devil!" Captain Grantham exclaimed. "Lampton, very glad to see you, but why the devil did you bring the lady?"

Lampton shrugged, summoning the hired cab with a flick of his fingers. "It was quicker. Put him in there. Where is he shot?"

"Upper arm," said the other officer, who was, surprisingly, Captain Blackshaw.

Another figure lumbered off the cliff path, panting, though he drew himself up to his full height.

"Dr. Lampton," he said distantly. "I'm always delighted to see you, of course, but you are not needed here. *I* am attending Major Doverton."

"Lampton's his usual doctor though," Grantham said with scant regard for the truth. "Don't worry, Bellamy, you'll still be paid. Appreciate your time."

Tillie's face tingled icily as if all the blood had left it. Wrenching open the carriage door, she stared at Dove's still face as the officers wrestled him inside and onto the seat.

"Oh, God, is he dead?" she whispered.

Dove's eyes flew open. "Tillie? Of course I'm not dead."

With a sob, she threw herself into the carriage and onto the floor by his head. "Oh Dove, Dove, you idiot! Why did you fight him? I told you he would cheat!"

"Well, he did," Blackshaw said grimly. "Turned early and fired. Damned if I'll ever second anyone else who ain't a gentleman."

Tears trickled down Tillie's face as she stroked the hair back from Dove's forehead. "Oh, you fool," she whispered. "Why did you meet him?"

"Had to, really," Dove said. His bandaged arm lay across his chest, but with his other hand, he grasped hers. "Why did you come? How did you know?"

"I had a note," she said, even more bewildered now she thought about it.

"Ah," Lampton said, climbing into the coach. "Sit over there, Tillie. The note, I suspect, was from your uncle to entice you up here alone. If all had gone according to plan, I daresay you and Luke would be off in his carriage." Unwrapping the bandage, he glanced at Dove's face. "Did you kill him?"

From the other carriage, her uncle's voice could be heard demanding, "Where is my son? You are his second. Why are you not looking after him?"

"Because he's a blackguard and a coward," Blackshaw's voice replied with contempt. "He ran away along the beach. Better get him out of town because if any of the 44th get hold of him…"

"He's on my side now?" Dove murmured.

"Hit with a large dose of sense," Grantham remarked. "He warned his man not to shoot."

"I know. I heard him."

"Which," Lampton said grimly, "only emphasized your criminal stupidity in this entire venture. Congratulations on another hole in your body. What in God's name is the matter with you? I took you for a sensible man."

"No idea why," Dove said vaguely. "Is the ball still in there?"

"No, looks like you're lucky. It passed straight through the fleshy part of your arm. Destroyed some muscle, no doubt, but no bone." He delved into his bag. "Hold on to something," he added, unscrewing the top of a bottle. "This will hurt." With no more warning, he poured something on the wound.

Breath hissed from Dove's lips but he didn't make any other sound, even when Lampton shifted him and did the same with the exit wound on the other side of his arm. "A clean bandage, if you please, Tillie," he said briskly.

Tillie reached into his bag and produced a roll of linen which the doctor used quickly and efficiently to bind the wound once more.

"To the barracks!" Lampton called out. Then he frowned at Tilly. "Damn, we should drop you off on the way."

"No, you shouldn't," Tillie said, glaring at him.

Dove laughed and squeezed her hand.

THERE WAS MOVEMENT at the barracks, though not yet enough to worry Grantham and Blackshaw, who had squashed into the carriage in order to smooth the way. Dueling was officially forbidden in the army, and they didn't want to force their colonel into having to deal with it.

Fortunately, Dove seemed to have recovered his strength, and by the time everyone else had spilled out of the carriage, he was able to climb out unaided. They all entered the building together. A passing officer even held the door most courteously for Tillie, although his expression was one of surprised curiosity.

"Er... am I allowed to be here?" she asked nervously.

"We have married quarters here, too," Grantham said cheerfully. "A few wives, including the colonel's, live here, so you won't stand out just for being female."

"You all know I'm perfectly fine?" Dove said. "Lampton, you should take Tillie home, and Grantham, you and Blackshaw leave me with Cully and bu—" He broke off with a quick, apologetic glance at Tillie. "And go away," he finished.

"Yes, sir," Blackshaw said insolently. "In a little."

After a long, winding walk up staircases and along various passages, Grantham threw open a door at the end of a corridor and led the way in.

"Please, come in," Dove said sarcastically.

A soldier was pacing up and down within a slightly tatty siting room. With an exclamation, he came straight toward them. "Sir! Where the devil have you been?"

"Getting shot," Dove said. "Sorry, Cully. This is Dr. Lampton. And you may remember Miss Tillie from the sea."

Distracted, the man's worried gaze shifted to her. "God bless my soul."

"*I* certainly do," Tillie said. "I haven't been able to thank you in person for what you did, but know that I am extremely grateful."

"Happy to help, miss," Cully muttered, blushing. He turned to Dove almost with relief. "I'll help you into bed, sir."

"No, you won't," Dove said irritably. "I'm not going to bed."

"Yes, you are," Lampton interjected.

Cully peered at him, then shrugged and took Dove's arm. "Come on, sir. Captain, will you report him sick?"

"I will," Grantham said. "If you need anything, come directly to me." He nodded to Tillie and ushered Blackshaw out in front of him.

From the bedchamber came no noise, as if Dove had given in, which was somehow more frightening than having to fight with him to make him rest.

"How bad is it?" she asked Dr. Lampton anxiously.

"As wounds go, it's not too serious. If it's kept clean and there is no fever."

"But for *him*?" Tillie pressed. "With his old wound?"

"I don't know," Lampton said. "I have not examined him or even talked to him on the subject."

Tillie held his gaze, silently pleading.

Muttering something, Lampton snatched up his bag and strode into the bedchamber.

A moment later, Cully came out and picked up the large washing jug. "Been sent for hot water, miss. Make yourself comfortable."

"Thank you," Tillie said politely. "I will."

When Cully had gone, she took off her cloak and lowered it slowly to a chair while she stared at the closed door to the bedchamber. She could hear their voices, but not what they were saying. And she had the feeling neither of them would tell her. Yet, she had to know. For Dove's sake.

Although eavesdropping went against the grain, she refused to apologize, even to herself, as she walked across the room and stood in front of the bedchamber door, leaning closer.

Dr. Lampton's voice was saying, "...bit more comfortable. I'll leave you some laudanum for the pain."

"I won't take it, Lampton," Dove said. "They dosed me with so much of that damned stuff at one time, I couldn't think. And then it hurt when I stopped."

"This was when you were injured before? When you came home from the Peninsula?"

"Yes."

"May I see?" Lampton asked with surprising civility.

There was a pause. "I'd rather not. The wound was so poked and prodded for months, I'm weary of it."

Dove, you idiot, she thought in frustration.

"Very well, I shan't touch it, but I would like to see the scar."

"It's healed," Dove said impatiently. "And quite clean."

"Yes," Lampton agreed after a moment, when clearly, he looked at the wound. "It is. Does it hurt, still? Internally?"

"Not now," Dove answered after a moment. "Or at least, only when I exert myself."

"Like rescuing men from shipwreck and riding to Manchester and back?" Lampton said wryly.

"That kind of thing. I scarcely feel it now."

"Does eating give you problems?" the doctor asked.

"Not anymore. In the beginning…I couldn't. I lived on water and thin gruel. Now it doesn't even hurt."

"How long did they give you?" Lampton asked casually.

There was silence. "Have you been speaking to my brother?" Dove asked.

"About this? No. Answer the question."

"Hours, days, weeks. At the last examination, six months. That's when I returned to the regiment to duties here."

"That was nearly two years ago." After another short silence, Lampton said, "I won't examine it. Despite the outrageous number of gunshot wounds I've had to deal with since coming to Blackhaven, I am not an expert in such injuries. However, I do know another physician who is."

"I've seen quite enough of Dr. Morton, thank you, excellent as he is!"

"Not Dr. Morton. He's a very different man, spends most of his life at sea. With your permission, I'd like to arrange for him to—"

"No," Dove interrupted. "I don't want any more damned doctors. With respect."

"Doverton. You have a lot to look forward to. Don't you owe this to *her* as well as yourself?"

There was a pregnant pause. The outer door snapped open, making her jump. As Cully strode in, she hurried guiltily across the room, wishing he'd stayed away just thirty seconds longer.

Chapter Fifteen

"HE IS NOT a weak man," Dr. Lampton said abruptly. "At the moment, I see no reason why this new wound should kill him."

Tillie sat down in sheer relief.

"Come, now, come back to the vicarage with me," Lampton said.

She shook her head. "I'll stay with him, but if you could let Mrs. Grant know, I would be grateful."

This did not please the doctor, but Tillie was adamant. When she had finally persuaded him to leave without her, Tillie returned to the bedchamber door and knocked.

"Come in, damn it, Cully," Dove said irritably.

Tillie entered to see him propped up in bed against many pillows. "I'm not Cully," she apologized. "He's gone to fetch you some breakfast."

Dove almost goggled at her. "Good God, Tillie, you can't be here!"

Deliberately, she pinched the skin of her wrist. "Yes. Apparently, I can."

Dove scowled. "You know what I mean and why."

Why he would bother with the reputation of his proposed mistress was something of a mystery to her, so she ignored his comment, merely sitting on the edge of the bed. "I want you to know that it was I who told Dr. Lampton about the severity of your old wound. I want him to give you his opinion and his treatment."

His eyes narrowed. But he deliberately veiled his feelings, giving her no clue. "Why?"

"Because I want you to live!" she whispered.

A hint of pity spilled from his eyes. He reached out and took her hand. "I don't think any of us, even Lampton, have much say in that, Tillie. I would not build your hopes or mine only to have them come crashing down. I've learned to live with this knowledge, to live for every day I have."

Tillie held his gaze, understanding and yet refusing to give in. "If people weren't waiting for you to die any day," she said, with deliberate brutality, "they would not keep fussing about you every time you stay up late or ride a horse. Personally, I cannot see that you have anything to lose."

He narrowed his eyes. "Did I tell you that you were a minx?"

"Think about it," she said. He kissed her hand, and she rose from the bed. "While you sleep."

FOR MOST OF the day, Tillie and Cully took it in turns to stay with Dove. He slept quite a lot and ate, then slept again. Secretly, Tilly loved the intimacy of watching him sleep, especially since he did not appear to be disturbed by pain or fever. Instead, he looked peaceful, almost boyish. *Almost.* But Tillie was too aware of the manly body beneath the covers, distracting her from inevitable anxiety.

Otherwise, she occupied herself in examining the books on his shelf—an eclectic mixture of military treatises, history, and science, with a few novels thrown in. She spotted Colonel Benedict's botanical book and drew it off the shelf to read.

In the late afternoon, Dr. Lampton returned with Kate Grant. While the doctor changed Dove's dressing, Kate told her she had to come back with her.

"You are neither his family nor his wife," she said firmly. "In the eyes of the world, you should not be here, and your reputation will suffer should this get out. Besides, Cully is more than capable of looking after him,"

"I am, miss," Cully agreed. "And what Mrs. Grant says is true. It ain't right for you to stay tonight. In fact, he don't know you're still here now and will whip me when he finds out."

"No he won't!" Tillie said, shocked.

"No, he won't," Cully agreed. "But he won't be pleased. Come and visit tomorrow with Mrs. Grant! Though chances are, he'll be right as rain by then."

THE FOLLOWING MORNING, Dove awoke feeling well but restless. Dr. Lampton pronounced himself pleased with the wound, which was healing with unusual rapidity, thanks, Dove suspected, to the vile-looking ointment the doctor had slathered on it before bandaging it.

"You should do," Lampton said. "So long as you commit no further folly to aggravate it. Cully tells me you are on leave of absence for another couple of days, so make the most of them and rest."

"I'll try," Dove said placatingly, although Lampton had found him beginning to climb into his clothes.

Lampton grunted, but helped him back into his shirt before he stood to go. But inevitably, word of Dove's duel had got out, and Dr. Morton chose that moment to visit. He frowned at the sight of Lampton who said without embarrassment, "Forgive me trampling on your toes, sir. I happened to be there, and so I am following my handiwork. But I shan't poach your patient."

Morton's brow relaxed. "I'm sure we need not worry about such things. On the other hand, Dove, I have just met Mr. and Mrs. Doverton, who are now in your sitting room."

"Oh, damn, do they know?"

"About the duel? Of course. This is Blackhaven."

"Bear up, my friend," Lampton said wryly. "You've suffered worse. Good morning, gentlemen. I'll find my own way out."

"Anyone would think he was pleased," Dove observed, allowing Cully to help him into his coat.

"Like me," Morton said with dignity, "he disapproves of duels."

"Well, I tend to agree. Waste of good powder." His coat fastened, Dove took a deep breath and strolled into the sitting room. "Good morning," he said. "You did not need to come here, you know, I was going to call on you later."

"Is it true?" John demanded. "Were you dueling?"

"Well, I tried, but truth be told, I doubt anyone would grace that debacle by such a term."

Frowning, Ellen stepped out from behind John. "Then you were not shot?" she asked hopefully.

It was tempting, but he could not bring himself to lie. "It's only a scratch."

"Then what was Dr. Lampton *and* Dr, Morton doing here?" John demanded.

"Making sure it became no more than a scratch," Morton said jovially. "The wound is already healing, and he'll be right as rain in no time. If you'll excuse me, I have other duties."

At least Ellen waited until he departed before she burst out, "But Dominic, this was so foolish of you! Is it true you fought some *tradesman*? That girl's husband?"

"Goof grief, Ellen, I can't discuss such matters with you," Dove said firmly. "Though I will say, if you are referring to Miss Dawlish, she is not married."

Ellen, clearly, had more to say, but for once, John interrupted her. "Come back with us to the hotel and we'll have a pleasant, lazy day."

"Then give me two minutes."

"Can Cully not bring your things over later?" Ellen suggested.

Dove blinked. "No. I am not *staying* at the hotel, Ellen. I have perfectly good quarters here."

There was silence as he returned to gather his hat and overcoat from the other room. He suspected John had once again obliged Ellen to hold her tongue.

One of the things he had long ago accepted, along with the knowledge of his own inevitably early death, was that he needed to make it easier for his family. He couldn't take away their grief, but he could avoid thrusting it under their noses. This was one reason he had insisted on returning to the regiment rather than living quietly with John and Ellen. The other reason, of course, was that *he* didn't wish to be constantly reminded of his imminent demise by the watchful, worried faces of his family. Now he had to remind himself of the patience he had promised, and let them fuss even while he laughed at them for it.

"You never did like to be treated as an invalid, did you?" Felicity said as they sat by the window of John and Ellen's sitting room. "I remember you escaping your sick room as a boy and everyone out looking for you."

Dove laughed. "I only had a cold."

"I believe it was influenza!"

"At any rate, I was better."

Felicity smiled. "Life was simpler then, wasn't it? Do you never wish you could go back?"

Dove thought about it. "No. Do you?"

"To childhood, sometimes. And to other periods in my life when I believe I would do things differently."

"Such as what?" Dove asked. He wasn't paying a great deal of attention, for he had just glimpsed Tillie hurrying along the street below with Catherine Gaunt and Ash. His heart gave its usual leap, eagerly hoping she was coming here.

"Breaking off our engagement."

That got his attention. He stared at her.

She gave an embarrassed little laugh. "I'm sorry. Perhaps I shouldn't have said that, but I wanted you to know."

"Thank you," he managed, pulling himself together. "It's all water under the bridge now."

He was relieved when John interrupted their *tete a tete*. But when he glanced down at the street once more, he saw Tillie and Catherine turning the corner toward the vicarage. Lord Sylvester had joined them. And only Ash visited the sitting room.

"You can't stay out of trouble, can you?" Ash said, his anxious gaze belying his casual tone. "Glad to see you looking so well."

"It was only a scratch," Dove repeated for the umpteenth time. Impatiently, he waited for Ash to mention Tillie, but he didn't. An unworthy pang of jealousy had him wondering if his friend had actually put Tillie off calling on him.

IN FACT, THE decision had been Tillie's. Because she'd glanced up to the second floor, instinctively looking for Dove's brother's room, and she'd found it. Dove sat very close to it, gazing at Lady Lawrence as though enraptured. The lady was looking down as though over-whelmed by whatever amorous words he'd just spoken.

Of course, she had no idea what those words were, or even if there were any at all. The little scene could have betokened anything. But that unblinking attention, that was something she had known directed at herself, and to see it now with another woman—one, moreover, to whom he had previously been engaged—devastated her. More even than driving up to the barracks with Kate and discovering him gone. She already knew from Dr. Lampton that he was well, and his wound healing, and she could not face meeting him just then, not with her present agitation, for she didn't think she could hide her feelings well enough.

"Do you think," she asked Catherine as they walked back to the vicarage, "that a man can love his wife and his mistress at the same time?"

"Tillie!" Catherine explained. "You aren't supposed to know about such things, let alone talk about them."

"But do you think so?" Tillie insisted.

"I have no idea."

Tillie glanced at Lord Sylvester, who seemed lost in his own thoughts. "Would you mind if *he* had a mistress?"

"Yes, she would," Lord Sylvester said, scowling. "And I don't.

Neither does Doverton, to my knowledge."

Tillie flushed, finding it impossible to explain that *she* was the mistress she had been thinking about. And wondering if she could really share him with a wife. She didn't think she could, even for however long he had left. And in fact, her imagination balked at Dove deceiving his wife. On the other hand, men were strange. Women always said so.

More likely was the scenario that he would simply marry the Lawrence woman, once Tillie's troubles with her uncle and cousin had been dealt with. Tillie thought she could even bow out gracefully, if Lady Lawrence would only make him comfortable and happy.

"She wouldn't," Tillie said decisively.

"I beg your pardon?" Catherine said.

"Oh, nothing. I was thinking aloud. Do you mind if I ask you both something?"

"If it's about mistresses, I do mind," Lord Sylvester said severely. "Even *I* know it ain't a proper subject!"

"No, no, nothing like that," Tillie assured him. "I was just wondering…which of you wanted to marry the other first?"

"I did," Sylvester said at once with no embarrassment whatsoever.

"Were Mr. and Mrs. Winslow amenable?" Tillie asked.

"Not exactly," Sylvester said cautiously. "I was a penniless younger son with no prospects and a shocking reputation."

In some ways, Tillie thought ruefully, his position matched her own. She might not be penniless, but she was certainly deemed too unsuitable, if not downright wicked, to wed a Doverton. "Then how did you win her?"

Catherine laughed. "He abducted me. But don't tell anyone."

Tillie glanced from one to the other. Clearly it was a joke between them, but one with a modicum of truth. Discreetly, she asked for no more details, but her brain was galloping ahead and forming a daring plan that was—*probably*—too mad, even for her.

THE FOLLOWING MORNING, she received a slightly bizarre letter from her father's old friend, Mr. Hatton, asking her to do nothing until she received a visit from her trustees and another important personage. Since her only communication with Mr. Hatton since she'd come to Blackhaven was to inform him of her whereabouts, she was at a loss to understand what he meant.

Still mulling it over, she walked up to the hospital to see Annie. James, the Grants' large footman, trailed behind her. She would rather have walked beside him and chatted about his life and his work, but she suspected that if she did so, he would be even more shocked than anyone else who saw them together. *Perhaps I am an inappropriate wife for a Doverton*, she thought ruefully.

She found Annie dressed and in the sun room downstairs, little George asleep in her arms. She looked much healthier, a tinge of color in her cheeks and a less cadaverous look about her. On the other hand, she seemed more worried. The time was fast approaching when she would have to leave the hospital and find some way to support herself and her son.

"Peggy told me there's a vacancy at the tavern, but I couldn't take little George there, could I?"

"The hotel would be better for you."

"Yes, but they only take girls of good character."

The monstrous unfairness of that silenced Tillie.

But Annie gave her a brave grin. "I'll manage! But I hear you've remembered your name and your husband! Do you have children, Miss Tillie? That is, ma'am."

"No, I don't have children and I am not married! That was my cousin's silly joke."

"Oh. Seems a funny kind of—" She broke off, staring at the doorway.

Major Doverton had just walked in, looking large and handsome, causing Tillie's heart to bump and race. With him was a thinner man in shabby clothes, twisting a cap in his hands.

"Oh, sweet Jesus," Annie whispered, all the pretty new color draining from her face.

Tillie frowned at her in incomprehension.

"I have a visitor for you, Annie," Dove said mildly.

The other man was staring at Annie as though he would devour her, and then his eyes dropped to the baby and he fell to his knees. "Annie," he said hoarsely. "Oh, Annie."

Suspicion finally dawned. Wide-eyed, Tillie sought Dove's gaze. "Is it...is it Big George?"

Dove nodded once.

Big George had hold of Annie's hand. "I am so sorry," he muttered. "I had no idea about the baby, none at all. I thought losing you was just one more regret, more bad luck in my life. My da died almost as soon as I went home from seeing you last, and I couldn't get away. And then there seemed no point because I couldn't bring you to a place like *The Brown Jug* anyhow. I lied about my position to impress you, to see... And then the major came and told me about little George, and I didn't know what I could do about it. But I couldn't leave you alone now, I couldn't."

Slowly, Annie's gaze lifted to Tillie's. Understanding, Tillie rose, took Dove's arm, and walked out of the room, leaving them alone.

"This is wonderful!" Tillie said with enthusiasm when they were in the passage. "How did you persuade him to come?"

"He just seems to have thought about it, realized whatever life he was taking her to in Manchester was better for her than being alone here. I believe he's a good man."

Tillie glanced back through the door. Big George was holding little George in his good arm, gazing down at him. His face looked decidedly damp. Annie was staring at him, her lips trembling.

"I don't think we need to stay, do you?" Tillie said. "Oh, where is Big George going to sleep? He's not going to dash back to Manchester, is he?"

"Cully will find him a bed."

"He's very useful, your Cully." By that time, they were crossing the foyer to the front door, and Tillie had begun to remember how she had last seen him, gazing so fixedly at Lady Lawrence. Jealousy and not a little anger clawed at her stomach. But then, so did anxiety. "How is your arm?"

"It's fine. It was only a scratch. Cully said you came to the barracks yesterday. I'm sorry. I didn't know you would do that. I'd already gone into Blackhaven with John and Ellen."

The Grants' large footman sprang up from his seat and opened the front door.

"I was just glad you were well enough," Tillie said carelessly. The cold air outside took her breath away. "I think it might snow… Major?"

His gaze swung on her. "*Major?* What happened to *Dove?*"

She waved that aside. "Your duel. I think you fought it for me because you thought admitting guilt would be worse for me."

"It may have been part of my reasoning."

"While I'm very grateful for the thought…" She met his gaze determinedly. "Please don't do anything so foolish again. I warned you he would cheat, and my reputation is not your concern. More importantly, I refuse to be responsible for your death."

Not surprisingly, he blinked. "I had no intention of dying."

"I imagine you had no intention of getting shot either," she retorted.

His lips tugged into a quizzical smile. "I had no idea you could scold so effectively."

"Oh, I have many talents you know nothing about."

"That is probably true."

They walked on in silence for several minutes, the Grants' footman still lumbering after them at a discreet distance. Tillie grew increasingly furious that Dove neither fought back nor explained anything about Lady Lawrence. Was she truly going to have to ask?

Dove said thoughtfully, "You know, the best thing for George would probably be to sell *The Brown Jug* and buy something a bit more—"

Tilly halted in her tracks. "That's it!" She stared across the road to the disused inn he had once pointed out to her. "They should run *this* place!"

Dove blinked. "Not sure the proceeds of *The Brown Jug* would run to something of that size, let alone the cost of repairs."

"Of course it wouldn't," she said impatiently. "*I* shall buy it. As an investment. Everyone agrees Blackhaven needs a respectable inn that costs a lot less than the hotel, and I'm sure many people would prefer to drink their ale somewhere that was not a thieves' den like the tavern. George and Annie will run it for me. There will be space for George's mother to come, too, if she wishes to, and I expect she will now she has a grandson. We can even find the space for a small creche if there is the interest. Then—"

"Slow down," Dove interrupted, amused. "I'm sure it's an excellent idea, but I think you really need to consult Annie and George first. Besides, you know, they need something *now*, not whenever you gain access to your funds."

"I think Mr. Hatton may come to see me soon. I'll get him to do it, then. Otherwise, I suppose I shall have to go home and...do you suppose my uncle and cousin have gone back to Liverpool?"

"I doubt they stayed here."

"Cully said the whole regiment was out for Luke's blood."

Dove flushed slightly, as though touched, and yet surprised by such universal support. "You don't seem distressed by their blood lust."

"I'm not. Blood may be thicker than water, but I'm not a good enough person to forgive my uncle and Luke for what they did to me, or to you."

He put her hand back on his arm and walked on. "I can't make up my mind whether or not we are friends anymore."

"I know you can't."

He frowned at her. "What have I done to make you angry with me?"

"I don't think I *am* angry with you. Just with me." She took a deep breath and looked him in the eyes. "How is Lady Lawrence?"

His gaze fell, and so did her heart. This was something he would not discuss with her. "She is well."

Damn you, damn you. "Then I trust I'll see her tonight at the Winslows' party," she managed.

"I believe you will. Tillie—"

"Goodness, it's cold. Shall we walk more quickly?"

Chapter Sixteen

T ILLIE'S PLANS WERE made. She just had to decide whether or not to act upon them. And that rather depended on Dove.

It had come to her during the afternoon as she tried to write a long letter to Mr. Hatton, that she was making a lot of assumptions from little or no evidence. In truth, her feelings for Dove had tied her in foolish knots and deprived her of the good sense she had always prided herself upon.

On the other hand, what harm was there in a little adventure? She suspected Dove had been missing those since his days on the Peninsula.

Regardless, she needed an honest conversation with him before she decided irrevocably. In fact, the closer she got to the party, the more she thought she had been a little hasty, even foolish. Not for the first time, she acknowledged ruefully, as Little finished pinning up her hair in a rather elegant knot that left a lock of hair trailing over her bare shoulder.

The maid nodded with satisfaction. "The pearls will set you off a treat."

"Oh, no, I couldn't wear Mrs. Grant's jewels. She has been too kind to me already." Which was something else she should have thought of before—how her behavior would reflect on the kind hosts who had taken her in and supported her. "Where is James?" she asked abruptly.

"Gone out, miss. It's his night off."

Drat the man, he'd left already. She couldn't stop him setting her plan in motion. Oh, well, it didn't matter. She didn't need to do anything, after all. She could just send him home again later.

Henrit House was not a long drive from Blackhaven, even in the flurries of snow that had been falling occasionally since the afternoon. The snow was light and wispy, and there was not enough of it to lie on the ground, but it seemed to freeze the air, adding to Tillie's sense of unreality, of being in an isolated world somewhere between fantasy and reality. Almost like the days after the shipwreck when she could remember nothing.

"You're very quiet." Kate observed once. "Is everything well with you, Tillie?"

"I think I need to go back to Liverpool."

"But you have nowhere to go in Liverpool." Kate objected. "You cannot live with your aunt and uncle any longer, and you cannot live alone."

"Stupid convention. I could live alone perfectly well. Besides, who's alone with a house full of servants?"

"Please consider staying with us for a few more weeks," Mr. Grant said. "If you can bear us."

"*Bear* you?" Tillie exclaimed. "You have been wonderful to me! But you know I cannot intrude upon your hospitality indefinitely. Besides, I think I am too wicked to live with a vicar."

"Nonsense," Kate said. "I live with him, after all."

Tillie couldn't help laughing. "There is nothing wicked about you, ma'am. I've no idea why anyone ever called you that."

"Well, I have no idea why anyone would call you wicked either."

Tillie sighed. "Well, perhaps I am not wicked, precisely. Perhaps mischievous is more apt. Either way, I have been good too long, and I should go before I erupt."

"And Major Doverton?" the vicar asked bluntly.

Tillie looked out the window, her heart twisting. "I am not of his class."

Kate took her hand. "If he loves you, Tillie, he will not care."

If he loves me. "The world will care."

"In Blackhaven," Grant observed, "we get used to the...the *unconventional* very quickly."

Tillie smiled with difficulty. "I know."

Mr. and Mrs. Winslow and Genevra welcomed them at the drawing room door. They had hired a trio of musicians who played quietly in the corner, and one half of the gracious room had been cleared to use as a dance floor.

Beside her, Kate said, "This is where I first realized I belonged in Blackhaven and that the good people here were my friends."

Tillie glanced at her with quick curiosity, but Kate only smiled and moved away to talk to Mrs. Muir. As Tillie walked further into the room, acknowledging acquaintances and trying not to search constantly for Dove, she saw that two farther rooms off the drawing room had been set aside for refreshment and cards, respectively.

"He isn't here yet," Catherine Gaunt murmured, coming up behind her.

"Who?" Tillie asked defiantly.

Catherine laughed. "I always liked him. Most of us did, to be honest. But I don't believe he ever looked at any of us in more than a friendly kind of way. Not as he looks at you. In fact, here he is."

Although she didn't mean to, Tillie jerked her head around to the door in time to see all three Dovertons arriving with Lady Lawrence and Mr. Ashley. Dove's gaze found her at once, and his face lit in a spontaneous smile.

"You see?" Catherine said smugly and passed on.

Tillie didn't know whether to laugh or cry with the sudden happiness that surged up from her toes and curled warmly about her heart. She had been foolish, suspicious, a little crazy in her schemes, when all she had really needed to do was to trust Dove as she had since he'd lifted her from that box at sea.

But a country dance set was forming, and Lord Sylvester asked her to dance. Tillie was happy to. She could wait for her time with Dove now that the silly mists of jealousy had cleared from her eyes. She gave herself up to the energetic dance, and as she did, she reflected that Kate was right. Blackhaven was an easy town to belong to.

After the dance, Lord Sylvester left her with Catherine and went off to fetch them lemonade. Catherine was talking quite intensely to a young man called Bernard Muir, so with a moment to herself, Tillie glanced around the room in search of Dove. She found him standing near the card room doorway with another officer and an unknown lady. He was smiling faintly, and love surged in Tillie, making her smile even while the emotion caught at her breath.

Someone sat down on Tillie's other side, and she turned with something of a start to see Lady Lawrence.

The lady smiled kindly. "Good evening, Miss… Do you know, if I ever heard your surname, I have foolishly forgotten it?"

"Dawlish," Tillie said. "Good evening, ma'am." She had no desire to talk to this woman, but for Dove's sake, she meant to be civil, even when the condescension frayed her temper, as she was sure it would.

"I saw you looking at Major Doverton. You must be glad to see him recovering so well."

"Of course," Tillie acknowledged.

"He is a man of great kindness, with a rather over-developed sense of responsibility," Lady Lawrence said. "Having rescued you from your predicament at sea, it was inevitable that he would feel compelled to look after you. But Miss—Dawlish, did you say?"

"I did," Tillie said patiently. In her lap, she clasped her fingers tightly together.

"Miss Dawlish, it is quite unsuitable for him to be fighting duels in your name. I understand society is new to you, so you will not mind my hinting to you, but such duels are not romantic or exciting. They are quite vulgar and dangerous, and you must not look for anything similar to happen again."

Tillie dug her nails into her palm. "Must I not?" she managed. Damn the woman's insolence. Did she imagine Tillie had put him up to it? "Do tell me why."

For an instant, intense dislike spat out of Lady Lawrence's eyes, before she veiled it in a smile. "Because I shall not allow it, of course," she said gently. "I have been married before. I know how to keep a husband in line."

Tillie's lips fell apart. "H-husband?" she repeated.

"Did you not know? We are not announcing it yet, of course, because I am still in mourning, but I thought he might have told you, just to prevent any further misunderstandings. We will wait probably until the end of the year, but he proposed marriage to me yesterday, and I accepted."

Stunned, Tillie felt the blood rush into her face and then drain so quickly that her ears sang. *Yesterday.* He had proposed yesterday, perhaps when she had seen them at the window? And her own conversation with him today, which had so comforted her and given her hope? She could not imagine him courting two women at once, even if he wanted one for his wife and the other for his mistress. That was simply not *Dove.*

Somehow, she forced her lips to curve into a smile. "I wish you both very happy. You will excuse me, ma'am. Mrs. Grant will be looking for me."

She rose and walked away, forcing her hands to unclench, her body to relax. But there was nothing she could do about the misery. She had thought…What had she thought? That he would truly marry the weaver's daughter? That if he didn't, she could share him with a wife? She doubted now she could ever have done that, but most certainly she couldn't share him with *that* wife.

I know how to keep a husband in line.

No and no and no. Felicity Lawrence was not for Dove, so calculating and cold and deliberate in her warning off of the ridiculous upstart. Lady Lawrence would stifle him, make him miserable. However well they'd been acquainted in their youth, she did not know him now, did not love him, would not care for him should the worst…

Her furious train of thought stumbled. *We will wait probably until the end of the year.* Perhaps she had the same doubts as Tillie about the amount of time left to Dove.

Or perhaps she simply did not know he was dying.

Under no circumstances would Dove engage himself without revealing such information.

Relief surged up from her toes. Lady Lawrence had lied, and Tillie should have known it at once. They were *not* engaged. Not yet. But the woman had most definitely been warning Tillie off, which meant she was sliding her claws into Dove, and Tillie would not have that. Rage flooded her, against Lady Lawrence, against Dove for allowing things to get to this stage. Well, it would have to be now. Tillie would force the issue, because she could make him happy. She *would* make him happy, and if the worst happened...

Angrily, she dashed a hand over her face. She could not cry in public. Worse, Dove was coming toward her. In panic, she swerved away and came face to face with Captain Blackshaw.

"Ah, Captain," she said hastily, "Do walk with me a moment." Obligingly, he turned to walk beside her, though he looked somewhat apprehensive. "I wanted to say...about the late duel. I think it must have taken a lot of courage to do the right thing and act against my cousin in the end. I want to thank you."

Blackshaw blinked. "You do?"

"I do. Thank you, sir." Since they were now passing the drawing door, she took the opportunity to excuse herself and dash in the direction of the cloakroom. There, she hid behind the rail of cloaks and sat on the end of the shoe ledge to shake out her reticule which contained her father's watch, a handkerchief, and a folded-up note. According to the clock, it still lacked five minutes until the carriage would be waiting.

So, she should hide in here for five minutes and then set her plan in motion.

DOVE SEARCHED FOR Tillie with some anxiety. He had been looking forward to spending some time with her at the party, talking, and dancing with her—mostly to enjoy her company, but also to discover, if he could, whether she still wished to marry him. And if she did, how she wished to proceed. A dying man was not the sort of husband most girls dreamed of, but he had known from the beginning that Tillie was far from being *most girls*. On the other hand, she had seemed nervous and changeable of late, being distant or even avoiding him one moment, and the next, nursing him as if his life was all that mattered to her.

He had been biding his time as she danced with Sylvester Gaunt and had already begun to extricate himself from his current conversation in order to go to her when he had seen Felicity Lawrence with her.

That had rung definite alarm bells for him, bells which had, in fact, been pealing furiously since she'd mentioned her regret at ending their engagement. Felicity, he remembered, had been a manipulative and selfish child, inclined to temper and determined to get her own way. In adulthood, sheer beauty and a new gentleness of character had won his heart, but now he remembered that their engagement had come about quickly—of necessity since his leave had been limited and he needed to return to the Peninsula.

But now that he no longer looked at her through the misty lens of desire and a boyish love closer to infatuation, he understood her character had not changed so very much. It had merely been polished slightly by an adult's appreciation of reality. And he did not like her seeking out Tillie.

Nor did he like the way Tillie had bolted away from him. Felicity had clearly said something to upset her, something malicious, and that, he would not forgive. When she did not immediately return to the drawing room, he cornered Blackshaw.

"What did Miss Dawlish say to you?" he demanded.

Blackshaw scratched his head. "I'm not quite sure. I believe she was thanking me for turning on her cousin, or for helping to preserve you. It was hard to tell. She seemed more eager to be gone."

"Where did she go?"

"I have no idea."

Kate Grant and Catherine Gaunt were both in the drawing room. As far as Dove knew, she had no other particular friends in Blackhaven. He glanced in the other rooms opened up for the party, including one where some girls were showing off their accomplishment—or lack of it—on the pianoforte. But there was no sign of Tillie. Crossing the hall, he came across Mrs. Winslow at the top of the stairs talking to a tall, distinguished old gentleman in evening dress and someone who looked like a man of business, very out-of-place in the current company.

"Forgive the interruption, ma'am," he said to his hostess. "Mrs. Grant is looking for Miss Dawlish. Perhaps you have seen her?"

The tall, old gentleman stared at him from beneath glowering brows.

"Why, no," Mrs. Winslow said, worriedly. "Truth be told, we're looking for her, too."

Dove frowned. "Is something wrong?"

"Oh, I'm sure not," Mrs. Winslow said. "I'll just have a quick look in the cloakroom…"

As she walked across the hall and into the room being used for ladies' cloaks, Dove turned aside with a quick nod to the two men and made to go downstairs.

A maid on her way up the staircase stopped beside him and said breathlessly. "Major Doverton, sir." And when he glanced at her, she pushed a folded paper into his hand and ran on.

Dove blinked after her, already unfolding the paper. Impatiently, he glanced at it and read: *If you wish to see Matilda Dawlish again, come immediately. A carriage awaits you on the path from the stables.*

Dove didn't hesitate. Crumpling the paper in his fist, he bolted down the stairs in three strides and under the open-mouthed gaze of a footman, threw open the front door and ran outside. At full tilt, he rounded the side of the house onto the stable path. It was well lit for the evening's comings and goings, and he was in time to see a female in a red cloak leap up the steps of the carriage facing him. A coachman huddled inside an overcoat and muffler sat on the box, his whip raised.

Dove sprinted to the carriage, arriving just as it began to move. He hurled himself inside, knocking his injured arm and all but fell onto the seat as the coach sped up. With an exclamation of distress, someone reached past from the opposite seat and slammed the door.

"Oh, no," Tillie's voice cried. "Your poor arm!"

Yes, it was undoubtedly Tillie, frowning with concern in the flickering light from the coach lanterns.

"Let me see," she demanded, throwing herself beside him with a bump and reaching for his arm.

"It's fine," Dove said, staring at her. "Believe me, it's so well padded you could poke it with sticks and I wouldn't feel a thing. What the devil is going on, Tillie?"

Reluctantly, it seemed, she released his arm and met his gaze with what looked like very conscious courage. A funny little smile curved her lips. Her eyes glittered with defiance as she tilted her chin.

"I'm abducting you," she said clearly.

He stilled. "I beg your pardon?"

"I'm abducting you," she repeated.

He couldn't help it. He laughed.

"I'm serious!" she said furiously. "I sent the note to you. I arranged with James to hire the coach and to drive it!"

That sobered him. An involuntary frown dragged down his brows. "James?" he repeated. "The Grants' footman?"

She nodded with an air of triumph.

"Well, I'm not sure how to break the news," Dove said, leaning forward to peer out the window, "but whoever is driving this carriage—at break-neck speed if you haven't noticed—it is certainly not James."

Chapter Seventeen

T ILLIE STARED AT him. "Not James?" she repeated stupidly. "What do you mean?"

"I mean the man is huddled into his coat with a muffler almost up to his eyes, but his hair is grey and he looks to me to be roughly twice James's age, besides being decidedly smaller."

"But...but that's impossible. I even called him by name as I got in."

"Didn't you look at him?"

"No! I just got in as fast as I could. I needed you to follow me and not have to be manhandled inside, because of your wound, and...and, no, I didn't look. I just assumed." She gazed at him, uncomprehending. "But if it isn't James, why on earth is he driving us? Shouldn't he be waiting for someone else?"

"One would think so," Dove murmured. Reaching up, he rapped loudly and peremptorily on the coach ceiling. Nothing happened. The horses didn't slow, merely took a corner at such high speed that Tillie fell against Dove before she could prevent it.

"Either he can't control the horses," Tillie said shakily. "Or he is deliberately abducting both of us. I don't know which frightens me more."

"Frightened?" Dove grinned at her. "Not you. I wonder where they're going with us."

His careless curiosity had its effect on her. She peered out of the window. They were travelling far too fast to jump out without severe injury. "It's certainly not the north road, is it?"

He glanced at her over his shoulder. Catching the lantern light, his eyes glittered. "The north road? Were you planning to abduct me to Gretna Green?"

She flushed, nodding, and he sat back on the seat beside her. "I'm very flattered," he assured her. "Only…why?"

"To be sure."

"Of what?" He actually sounded baffled. "Of me?"

"Yes," She lifted her chin. "I know I'm beneath you in birth, but I also know I can make you happy. I didn't want to push you into marrying me, but it seemed to be the only way. I almost gave up the idea as silly, but I can't let you fall into marriage with *her*."

"With whom?" he demanded.

"Lady Lawrence."

He blinked. "I have no intention of marrying Lady Lawrence."

"I had the feeling she was lying," Tillie said, gratified for an instant. "But if she had her claws into you—and she has—I knew she would find a way."

"So, you came up with abducting me?" The laughter was back in his voice.

"Catherine came up with it. It was how Lord Sylvester persuaded her to notice him. Or something."

His shoulders shook—with more laughter, she could only assume with some wrath—until he took her hand in his. "For future reference, my sweet, modelling your behavior on Sylvester Gaunt, or indeed on any member of his family, is not very proper."

"I know," she said miserably. "But I don't care about convention, and I was *desperate*."

His hand tightened. "For what?"

"For you," she whispered.

She couldn't look at him. In any case, silly tears were blinding her. His hand touched her chin, turning her face up to his. His eyes searched, then slowly, his frown smoothed out and he bent his head.

His mouth closed on hers, and she gasped. Released, the tears gushed down her face, splashing on her cheeks, his hand, their lips. But his kiss was firm and possessive and tender, and it seemed to melt every bone in her body. She forgot where she was in the sheer wonder of his kiss.

"Did I not say that I loved you, little waif?" he whispered against her lips. "Why would you imagine I would then marry another woman?"

"Because you do not need to marry me."

He drew back, staring down at her. The frown was back. "You thought...after everything, that I would take you as my mistress?"

Beginning to see the truth, she smiled and nodded.

"Would you have done it?" he asked unexpectedly. She let out a choke of mingled laughter and outrage, and he dragged her across his chest and kissed her again, a little more roughly, a little more deeply. "Well? Would you?"

"I would do anything for you, Dove, I—" The rest was lost in his mouth as he kissed her again with great thoroughness. She lost her train of thought, forgot even where they were, until, with an obvious effort, he drew back.

An unsteady breath of laughter shook him. "I'm glad we have finally reached this understanding. You will marry me, Tillie Dawlish, and not at the border. But first, we have to establish where we're going and how to get back to Henrit before you are ruined."

"You seem to take abduction very lightly," she observed.

"I learned from you." He looked out of the window. "We're coming into Whalen... Interesting."

"Why, what is in Whalen?"

"A deeper water harbor than in Blackhaven," he said thoughtfully. "Among other things."

Tillie caught her galloping breath. "Could it be Captain Smith? Making sure you don't find out any more about him?"

"Perhaps," Dove said, as though unconvinced. "Though it was noticeable the carriage moved forward as soon as you were inside. It didn't exactly wait for me."

"I thought it was James misjudging, because he was nervous."

"So he should have been," Dove said, delving beneath the seats. "I don't know what he was thinking of, or how you persuaded him—"

"What are you looking for?" she interrupted.

"Something to use as a weapon. Look in the pockets."

Tillie obeyed, searching the pockets at the corners of the carriage, but she discovered no useful pistols. Nor did Dove appear to find anything weapon-like. "Don't you have something with you?" Tillie asked in frustration.

"It's not customary to go to a civilized party armed to the teeth," he observed.

"That was my other worry," she confided. "I didn't want you to hurt James either."

"Well, when we get out of this mess, he'll have to have a dashed good reason to prevent it."

"I told him it was a prank," she said anxiously. "A joke that you would laugh about. I assured him no harm would be done. I think he assumed we were going to marry anyway."

"Well, at least he got something right." Dove sat back, flexing his arms and fingers. The carriage was slowing. "It will have to be the old-fashioned way. When he opens the door, I'll rush him. You jump out the other side and run."

"But Dove, your arm—"

"It will have to do." He grinned. "Hopefully, I'll only need one hand."

Anxiously, she peered out the window. Lights from the harbor, and from a large ship, reflected on the sea.

"You might be right," Dove said, "about Captain Smith."

"Dove," she said urgently as the carriage slowed to a halt. "Please don't be hurt…"

She caught the end of his smile as he reached for the door.

But their abductors were prepared, and someone else opened it first. Dove flew at him, and too late, Tillie saw that their opponent was armed. Dove, fortunately, must have been aware, for the pistol was knocked into the air in a flying arc.

Relieved, Tillie yanked open her own door—and came face to face with another armed man who, however, was a little more circumspect, standing well back. She paused.

"Out," he said levelling the pistol at her. "Round to the other side. Quickly."

She needed no second urging, for she knew she could not fight him and she needed to know that Dove was safe.

In fact, he was rolling on the ground with his attacker, while the coachman lumbered down to join in.

"Enough!" ordered an impatient voice—and one Tillie recognized. Captain Smith had come round from the horses' heads. His command halted the coachman, but there was little the other man could do when Dove had him locked on the ground, his fist raised threateningly. "Major," Smith said sharply. "We have your companion in custody."

At once, Dove's fist unclenched. He released his man and stood up slowly. Tillie couldn't see if had reopened his wound.

"Don't aim at her," he said. "I'll be good."

"Then be so obliging as to follow me on board," Smith said, with a curt nod to his underlings.

Tillie all but tripped over her feet in her urgency to get to Dove. "Are you hurt?" she demanded.

"Devil a bit," he said cheerfully. "Which is interesting."

"Is it?" she asked, inclined to be outraged. "Dove, are you *enjoying* this?"

"I might be," he admitted. "If it weren't for someone pointing a pistol at you."

Side by side, they followed Smith up the gangway. Tillie touched Dove's fingers for comfort, and they immediately curled around hers—large, warm, and reassuring. But as soon as they were on deck, the captain began issuing orders for the gangway to be pulled up and the ship to get under way.

"You can't do this!" Tillie exclaimed. "You can't take us abroad!"

"I apologize for the inconvenience," Smith said with something approaching sincerity. "It is not my choice."

"One last task for my uncle?" Tillie guessed with contempt. "Are you to throw me overboard?"

"I am not an assassin," Captain Smith snapped. "Follow me to the cabin, if you please."

"There's nothing to gain by throwing me overboard," Tillie allowed. "They wouldn't get the fortune in any case."

"I believe your uncle means to meet us in Ireland," Smith said, opening the door to the cabin.

"Looks like they still want to marry you to Luke," Dove observed.

Reluctantly, Tillie walked into the cabin, heartily glad of Dove behind her. The room's sole current occupant turned from the table.

"Ah, Miss Dawlish," Captain Alban greeted her. "And Major Doverton, too. What an unexpected pleasure."

Tillie glared at him. To think they had relied on his help. "You, sir, are a traitor!" she cried.

Alban did not appear to be put out. "It depends on your point of view," he said. He had, apparently, been pouring brandy. He pushed one glass across the table to Smith and lifted his own. "To partnership," he said mildly and drank.

Smith took a mouthful, more dutifully that anything else. "I still don't see why you needed to come with us," he said pettishly. "I manage much better alone."

"Well, there is the example of *The Phoenix* to dispute that," Alban argued. "I prefer to keep my eye on my investments. And do we still sail to Sweden after Ireland?"

Smith hesitated. "No," he said. "Not necessarily. If all our cargo unloads at Larne." He took another nervous drink. "Plans change."

"According to whose whims?" Dove asked with a hint of contempt. "The Dawlishes?"

"Sadly, yes," Smith snapped. "They are aware of information that could do harm to myself and my family."

"Indeed," Alban said, clinking his glass against Smith's in an encouraging kind of way. "Your family's health, Captain."

"And *your* family's, sir?" Tillie said furiously to Alban. "Do you not have a wife and child?"

"I do, and a second on the way," Alban replied without shame. He raised his glass again. "To *my* family's health."

Tillie curled her lip as they both drank. "They would be ashamed of you. Sir, do we *need* to stand here and watch the pair of you become intoxicated?"

"Why not?" said Alban. "It might amuse you. But, do please sit. Forgive my manners."

He held a chair for her, and as she sat with as much dignity as she could muster, she looked anxiously at Dove for signs of bleeding or weakness. But he, as upright as usual, was gazing at Smith, who was, somewhat owlishly, staring at Tillie.

Dove said, "Are you quite well, Captain Smith?"

"Quite," Smith said. His eyes suddenly rolled upward, and Alban and Dove were only just in time to catch him.

"What's the matter with him?" Dove demanded.

"Here, drop him on the bed through here. It seems he can't take his brandy."

It struck Tillie as they half-carried the man into the inner cabin that even *she* could manage three sips of brandy. On the other hand, she had no idea what he'd been drinking before. He and Alban could have been at this since the afternoon.

A moment later, Dove and Alban returned, the captain closing the door on the inebriated Smith.

"How much has he had?" Tillie asked.

"How much of what?" Alban inquired.

Her eyes widened. "You *drugged* him?"

"I have a very knowledgeable physician who has travelled the world. Don't worry about Smith. He'll wake up in an hour or so."

"Then what on earth was the point?" Tillie demanded.

"The point is, we'll anchor a few miles up the coast and when he wakes, we'll tell him he's been asleep all night and day and he's in Ireland. Then we'll offer to help him on his way. He'll need it, for he'll feel like death for several hours after he wakes."

Understanding began to dawn. "Then you *are* on our side!" she exclaimed.

"I apologize," Alban said. "It was my men who took you. They were under orders not to harm you, so if you suffered at all—"

Dove rubbed his ribs. "I wish you'd given them the same orders for me."

"Well, we didn't expect *you*. Miss Dawlish was to be enticed from the party. I gather she came before she was enticed, with you hard on her heels. Since they couldn't shake you off, they brought you."

But Tillie had moved on. "The letter I found definitely said Sweden, not Ireland," she insisted.

"Yes, but you found it nearly two weeks ago," Dove pointed out. "Time was, no doubt, moving too fast while Winslow and I kept Smith in Blackhaven. Aren't you tempted to go to Ireland?"

Alban wasn't a man who seemed to smile much. But he brought two fresh glasses and poured a measure into each. "There is more than one way to skin a cat. Your health and happiness, Miss Dawlish."

Doubtfully, Tillie raised her glass and looked at it.

Alban's eyes gleamed. "The drug is not in the bottle. If you noticed, I had already poured Smith's before you came in. And I am still standing."

Dove gave a crack of laughter and drank.

Watching him, Tillie touched her lips to the glass and then lowered it. "Dove, will you take off your coat and let me see your arm?"

Rather to her surprise, Dove set his glass on the table. "Maybe I will." He unfastened the coat, and to Tillie's surprise, Alban helped him off with it. He obviously knew the story of the wound.

Tillie's stomach twisted when she saw the bright red stain on Dove's otherwise pristine white sleeve, but she swallowed back her instinctive cries of distress.

But Dove met her gaze. "Captain. Did you say you had a physician aboard?"

WHEN JAMES, THE Grants' large footman, currently masquerading as the driver of a hired cab, saw the figure of Miss Tillie in her bright red cloak hurrying up the side of the house, he acted quickly. The carriage which had turned and halted in front of him did not block his way. In fact, in obedience to the owner's instructions, he had walked the horses up and down the path twice already while waiting. Now, he climbed back up on the box, and gathered the reins. But before he could move, he glimpsed Tillie vanishing into the other carriage. He opened his mouth to call a warning to her, then, with some relief, saw the unmistakable figure of Major Doverton running after her at full tilt.

James's heart misgave him as the carriage in front began to move. The major leapt in just in time. The door slammed and the carriage lurched forward at an almost instant gallop.

"What the…" Instinctively, James urged his horses to follow, but they seemed to be set in their ways and determined to cooperate as little as possible with their unfamiliar novice of a driver. They strolled to the end of the house, by which time, James could see the lights of the other carriage disappearing off the drive and onto the road beyond. He'd never catch them, and if he did…

"Oh, God," he muttered, helplessly. "I knew I shouldn't have done this!" Clambering down, he abandoned the horses, merely shouted a plea to the stable lads to look after them. He then bolted into the kitchen, demanding someone take a message to Mr. Grant.

"Take your orders out of here, James Taggart," the cook told him roundly. "We have enough to do."

"It's urgent," James pleaded.

"*What's* so urgent?" the cook demanded.

James closed his mouth. The impossibility of explaining without landing Miss Tillie in a mess finally struck him. The story would be all over Blackhaven by morning.

"Never mind," he muttered. "I'll go myself."

"James Taggart, you'll go nowhere in that dreadful overcoat!" the cook exclaimed, scandalized. "In fact, I won't have it in my kitchen!"

James, already striding for the stairs, tore off his coat as he went and rolled it into a ball under his arm. He had no more time to waste. In the footman's livery he wore beneath, he hurried through the house and toward the noise of voices and music. Elegant guests had spilled out of the drawing room, but none of them were either of the Grants. He stopped a scurrying maid. "Have you seen the vicar or his wife? Are they in there?" He nodded at the drawing room.

"Likely," the maid said, shaking him off. She paused. "No, wait, they're with the master in *there*." She pushed him toward a closed door and ran off.

James took a deep breath, knocked, and strode in.

Mr. and Mrs. Grant were with the squire, a tall old gentleman he couldn't recall ever seeing before and a small, near gent who looked like a solicitor or a man of business.

"What?" the squire demanded, then peered at him, frowning. "You're not one of mine."

"No, sir," James said apologetically. "I'm theirs." He nodded awkwardly at the Grants, who had swung on him in surprise at the sound of his voice.

"James?" Mrs. Grant said in clear astonishment. "What are you doing here? It's your night off."

"I need to speak to the vicar, madam. It's important."

In fact, they both advanced on him. He'd always known he would be in trouble for this. He'd probably lose his position, but it had to be done.

"It's Miss Tillie," he blurted, remembering at least to lower his voice. "She got me to help her play a trick on the major, but they got into the wrong carriage somehow and now they're gone, and I don't know where. Too fast to follow."

Somehow, they didn't seem quite so surprised or quite as angry as he'd expected. To his amazement, Mrs. Grant immediately began regaling the information to the others while the vicar demanded, "Which direction? Which road?"

James scratched his head. "South."

"Then they're not eloping," the elderly gentleman said with apparent relief.

"They were never eloping," James insisted. "It was a jest."

"It always is," said the solicitor chap with a sigh.

"Where's this carriage of yours?" the vicar demanded.

"It's a hired cab, sir," James said miserably. "Just at the front drive."

"Come on then," the vicar commanded, striding for the door. "It will be quicker—and more discreet—than getting our own organized so early."

"No, it won't, sir," James protested, following him. Mrs. Grant trotted at his side. "I can't drive 'em fast, and they don't pay much attention to me."

"They'll pay attention to me," the vicar said.

"They will," Mrs. Grant agreed. "James, we may need your size and muscle. And Tillie will most certainly need a chaperone. Mr. Winslow, I am so sorry about this…"

Chapter Eighteen

ALBAN OPENED A cabin door and held it for Dove to precede him. "Dr. Gowan," he said without emphasis, "this is Major Doverton, who has a partially-healed injury he needs you to look at."

Alban closed the door, leaving him alone with the doctor.

At first glance, Gowan looked like an academic. In his shirt sleeves with a pair of spectacles on his nose, he lacked both Dr. Morton's bluff heartiness and Lampton's dour kindness. On the other hand, there was nothing wrong with the muscles in his arms. In the past, however lawfully they behaved now, Captain Alban's crew had almost certainly taken part in acts of piracy and smuggling. Dove expected the doctor had done his part.

He certainly had penetrating eyes as he scanned Dove from head to toe. Then he stood abruptly and offered his hand. "Sit, Major, and let's have that shirt off... Hmm. Neat job. You've just loosened one of the stitches. I'll put in another to replace it and you should do very well. No more fighting, though, Major, for another couple of weeks."

"The fighting was Alban's fault," Dove said provokingly, curious to see what effect such criticism would have.

"I don't doubt it," Gowan replied.

Like Lampton, he was surprisingly gentle. The matter of cleaning, stitching, anointing—interestingly, with a muddy substance that looked and smelled very like Dr. Lampton's—was quickly accomplished.

"I imagine Lampton scolded you for dueling," Gowan remarked, bandaging the wound with swift efficiency. "He is averse to pointless risk."

"I gather you are not."

"That rather depends on what one considers pointless."

Dove hesitated. "You appear to be acquainted with Lampton."

"I have met him once or twice. Interesting man. As are you, Major."

Dove searched his face. "You're the one he wanted me to see."

"That surprises you," Gowan observed.

"A little," Dove admitted. "I expected someone older, more…"

"Respectable?" Gowan guessed.

"There appears to be nothing unrespectable in your current position."

"I gather knowledge, and I use it to heal if I can. There can be nothing more worthy of respect, in my view. Are you going to ask for my formal credentials?"

"No, I see them on the wall."

Gowan smiled. In silence, he finished binding the wound and helped Dove back into his shirt. Then he sat down on the other side of the desk again.

Dove thought of the last three years, the seemingly endless suffering, the bitterness he had thrown off, and the peace he'd found with his fate. He thought of the beautiful, vital girl in the cabin along the passage, who had, for reasons he could not fathom, insisted on tying her fortunes to his. He thought of revived hopes coming to naught, of leaving her alone to grieve. He thought of living with her, of seeing her laugh every day, of learning every inch of her mind and body, of waking up next to her each morning and making love to her. Children. A future.

He didn't know if it was possible, and neither did she. No one knew what their future held. He could have drowned at sea instead of rescuing her. He could have been killed by Luke Dawlish or knocked over by a carriage. Every day should be seized. What did yet another medical opinion matter?

It mattered if this opinion came with a solution to heal him. If it didn't, he had lost nothing. And neither had Tillie.

"Dr. Gowan," he said. "Would you mind taking a look at an older wound of mine?"

ALBAN LEFT TILLIE in a spacious cabin by herself, assuring her she would not be disturbed, before conducting Dove to his surgeon. Tillie hoped this individual would not undo all the good Dr. Lampton had done.

Considering the weather outside, and the wet snowflakes occasionally splattering on the sloping cabin window, it was surprisingly warm below deck. Tillie removed her cloak, then washed her hands and face in the bowl provided, and patted them dry on a soft towel. Apparently, Alban's wife, Lady Arabella Lamont, often accompanied him on his voyages, which probably explained the odd, unexpected luxuries. There was another strange marriage.

Tillie brushed out her hair with the brush on the table and repined it, staring in the glass without really seeing herself. Her mind was on Dove, and her own foolishness in causing this fresh catastrophe.

But she was being silly again. Neither Dove nor Alban seemed to consider the blood stain in any way serious. And if she was going to marry Dove, she was going to have to learn not to overreact to every "scratch". She would have to be strong for him. She *would* be.

She sat down on the seat under the window—or whatever one called it on a ship—gazing out at the gray, choppy sea. She rather liked the roll of the ship and the impression of being in another world, far from everything she was used to. Quite different from the last time she'd been at sea.

She shivered, veering away from the past to the future. There was a lot to think about.

When the knock sounded at the door, she called, "Enter" without thinking. Then, of course, she remembered where she was and jumped to her feet in alarm, just as Dove walked in and closed the door.

"Oh, it's you," she said in relief, falling back onto the window seat. "Come and tell me about your arm."

He was wearing his coat again and showed no obvious signs of pain. "It's fine. He's replaced one of the stitches and put a fresh dressing on it." He eased himself down beside Tillie without touching her. She searched his face, unable to read his expression, which seemed to be both shocked and baffled and yet not quite either.

"Then what is it?" she asked as mildly as she could.

He blinked, as though reminding himself of her presence, which was hardly flattering. But he took her hand is his warm clasp, and that was better.

"It's a funny thing," he said. "It turns out Alban's physician— Gowan—is the doctor Lampton wanted me to see."

"Truly?" she said, startled. "Are you going to let him examine you?"

"That's a funny thing, too. It seems I have already done so."

Her hand gripped harder before she could stop it. "What did he do?"

"Oh, some of the usual. He had a damned good prod around. Then he just asked me a huge number of questions, about the history of the wound and treatment and my convalescence, my eating and drinking habits, my strength, pain, what exercise I do. About my relations with women. And what I plan to do next. For the next fifty or so years."

Her eyes widened. "For the next... Oh, Dove, what did he say?"

Slowly, his intense blue gaze lifted from their joined hands to her face. "He said that to all intents and purposes, I have healed. That even mortal wounds that appear untreatable and unrecoverable occasionally defy every learned opinion and simply get better. He says I am strong as an ox and if I would just refrain from dueling as Dr. Lampton bids me, he sees no reason why I should not enjoy a long and busy life."

She gasped, sliding her arm up over his chest to his neck, and pressed her cheek to his. "Oh, my dear, my love…"

"What is this?" He touched her damp cheek, even as his arm came around her. "I thought you would be pleased."

She choked out a laugh. "Of course I am pleased, you idiot. I've never been so happy in my life! Oh, Dove!" She kissed his lips and frowned with renewed anxiety. "But why aren't you more pleased? Don't you believe him?"

He considered that. "Yes, I think I do. I suppose I am…shocked. A bit like battle, when something explodes right beside you. You can't quite believe you've escaped, but know somewhere that you're pleased to be alive." He took a deep, shuddering breath. "Alive. Alive with you."

Pain twisted through her. But she hugged him tighter. "You don't need me anymore," she whispered.

Abruptly, he pushed her back, holding her by both shoulders as he stared into her face. "What? Tillie, where do you come up with those daft notions?"

"You will have children now, Dove. Aristocratic children if you wish!"

"I don't wish," he said, revolted. "I'll have your children or none. Besides, you abducted me. You have to marry me."

The sudden laughter was muffled in his mouth as he kissed her with fierce passion. She responded with every instinct and emotion she had. His hand at her nape, gently kneading, spread thrills all through her body. Her breasts heaved against his strong chest. He lifted her in his arms, spinning with her, almost dancing to the bed where he laid her down and loomed over her. Slowly, deliberately, his hand closed over her breast and she gasped with bliss as he kissed her, and kissed her again. She felt his weight upon her, his hardness pressing between her thighs, arousing urgent desires she hadn't known she possessed.

She wriggled, aching to be closer, to feel his hands on her naked skin, to touch him.

With a groan, he tore himself from her, and for an instant, stared down at her, his breath coming in pants, his eyes excitingly hot and clouded with lust. "God help me, now is not the time. Alban will be looking for us, assuming we care about Smith and his information."

She swallowed, trying to gather her thoughts. "Do we?" she asked doubtfully.

He let out a breath of laughter. "We had better try since it's our only excuse for being here. And we need something to be rid of your family for good. Besides." He stroked her hair, her cheek, his fingers lingering as they caressed her lips. She kissed them.

"Besides?" she prompted.

"I shan't take you until you're mine."

"I am yours," she whispered.

He gathered her into his arms. "And I will always look after you."

"THAT," CAPTAIN SMITH said with one glance toward the shore, "is not Larne."

It was dark, and Captain Alban had anchored off the Cumberland coast somewhere Tillie suspected he knew from his smuggling days. But it was not far from Whalen.

It was snowing, and the clouds obliterated the stars and just about anything else that Smith could have used to identify his true location. When he'd wakened, Alban had told him it was six o'clock the following evening. Smith had seemed shocked to have been asleep so long, but he still looked like death warmed up, like a man, in fact, who had severely overindulged and was paying the price.

"I'm not mad enough to land at a port," Alban said.

"We have to," Smith insisted. "I have brandy and cotton garments to deliver."

"Then we can do that in daylight after your more nefarious dealings."

"I don't know what you mean," Smith said with dignity.

Alban shrugged. "Please yourself. But you'll forgive me saying you don't look in much condition to get yourself to any…meeting." He called over his shoulder. "Lower the long boat!"

"Aye, sir," came the instant response.

"While you're gone, I can deliver these two." Alban offered, nodding his head at Dove and Tillie, who were doing their best to look chastened as they huddled together for warmth against the ship's rail.

"They only want the girl," Smith snapped.

"Well, Doverton can be their headache, not ours," Alban said carelessly. "Where are the Dawlishes?"

"The Harbor Inn in Larne," Smith said reluctantly.

But Tillie thought he was glad to have that task taken off his hands. He didn't truly want to hand her over to the family who had harmed her already, though he was content enough for someone else to do the dirty work.

Alban nodded. "Off you go then!" he encouraged.

Smith lurched along the deck and paused, pressing trembling hands to his temples as if in some futile effort to stop the pain.

"Damn it, man," Alban said. "You're in no condition to go anywhere. I'll come with you. Where are we going?"

Smith stared at him, made one more effort to climb over the rail to the boat, and then fell back against Alban. With a curse, he lowered his voice and began to speak rapidly.

"People ashore, sir!" came the shout from one of the men.

Tillie glanced toward land, knowing the appearance of people with local accents might give Alban's game away. Lights bobbed along the rocks, illuminating a few indistinct figures.

Alban appeared at Dove's other side, raising a glass to his eye. He made no comment about what he saw, merely passed the glass to Dove.

She heard his intake of breath.

"That's Dawlish," he said, causing her stomach to twist unpleasantly.

Alban gazed at him as he took back the glass. "Are you sure?"

"Of course I am,"

The eyes of the two men met. Dove's fingers curled around hers with a squeeze at once warning and comforting, and she understood suddenly that whoever it was he'd seen on the coast, it was *not* her uncle.

"Let us go, Captain," she pleaded.

"Land us back at Larne and we can easily take another ship back to England," Dove suggested.

"It isn't up to me, sadly," Alban said without obvious feeling. "Captain Smith has chartered the ship and crew. We'll take you with us, kill two birds with one stone."

And so, Tillie found herself climbing down into the longboat, curious and eager. Although it was far too cold to be comfortable, at least the snow had stopped falling and the sky seemed to have lightened a little, which probably helped maintain the fiction that it was some twenty hours later than it actually was.

"You look ill, sir," Tillie told Captain Smith with perfect truth.

"I am ill," he snapped, and clutched his clearly aching head. "I never faint, and I never sleep around the clock like that."

"Captain Alban has a doctor on board," Tillie said helpfully.

"I've seen him," Smith said, grimacing. "He told me it was something I ate and it would pass in a day or so."

"At least you will be well in a day," Tillie pointed out with a sniff. "I shall probably be married to my vile cousin, thanks largely to you. And God knows what will happen to Dove. They will probably kill him."

Smith smiled sourly. "My money's on Doverton."

Tillie smiled brightly. "Truly? Then perhaps there is hope for us."

"What of your hope, Smith?" Dove murmured.

Alban glanced at him, and Tillie had the idea that he wasn't best pleased.

Smith merely grimaced and held his head. "I shall undoubtedly go to hell. But my family will be provided for."

"Do you think so?" Dove asked in tones of deep interest. "In my experience, children prefer to have a father, a woman her husband. Besides that, what is mere *provision?*"

Smith wrenched his gaze free, "I do not intend to die just yet."

Dove shrugged. "Not sure it's your intentions that matter here. What if the people you are here to meet kill you once you have passed on your messages? What if the British have found out and are waiting for you? You'll die a traitor. Forgive me, but how will that help your wife and family?"

"I'm not a traitor!" Smith burst out. "This nonsense will achieve nothing. Don't you see that? The Royal Navy has Elba surrounded. Bonaparte's going nowhere, whatever plots or conspiracies are set in motion."

Dove gazed at him. "And if someone else's father, someone else's husband, dies because of the plot you have facilitated, is that nothing, too?"

"There is a time to look after one's own," Smith said hoarsely, wrapping his arms around his stomach.

"But you're not," Dove said.

Smith turned once more and stared at him.

Alban stirred. "As it stands, you have committed no crime." It seems he had switched from his own plan to extract the information from Smith to Dove's, which might yet redeem him.

It was one of Dove's strengths, Tillie realized, winning men around who had gone down a wrong path, because he still saw the good in them. It was what he had done with Captain Blackshaw, and what he was trying to do now with Smith.

Alban said, "You have received information which it is your duty to pass on to the relevant authorities."

Smith swallowed and closed his eyes. "I gave my word. And Dawlish knows."

"Have you considered *how* Dawlish knows?" Dove said dryly. "Whatever, you may safely leave the Dawlishes to us. For the rest...give the messages to me and tell Alban exactly where you are meant to meet your...conspirators."

"You have until we reach shore," Alban added. "Which is a minute or so."

Poor Smith was in no state to think clearly. Which, of course, had been Alban's aim in drugging him and tricking him into revealing the meeting place when he was unable to find it on his own. It might still come to that. For the moment, he seemed unaware that Alban and Dove were allies.

Two of Alban's men jumped out and waded through the sea to the beach, hauling the boat aground. Unsteadily, Smith rose and climbed over the side with the help of one of the seamen. It seemed Dove had lost.

But they still had Alban's plan. And whoever was waiting ashore surely had to be friends when Alban had been inveigled into bringing herself and Dove.

Dove climbed over the side and reached for her. She went willingly, secretly excited to be in his arms as he splashed ashore and set her on the sand. From there, a path wound up the side of the cliff to a road of some kind, for Tillie was sure she could make out the shape of two carriages at the top. Several people, with lanterns, seemed to be making their way down the path to the beach.

Abruptly, Smith halted in his tracks and recited a string of numbers.

"Thank you," Alban said mildly.

"For what?" Tillie asked, bewildered.

"I think he's just given him the coordinates of the meeting place," Dove said.

Tillie smiled proudly. So, Dove had won after all.

"And some names?" Alban prompted.

"I have no names. Only codes. They're all in here." And Smith took a document from inside his coat and slapped it against Dove's chest. "I've had enough. I can't do it."

"Good man," Dove said, clapping him on the back. "And look, here's just the man we need. Colonel Fredericks."

"Unexpected pleasure," said an elderly gentleman with a military moustache, marching across the sand with a trail of people behind him.

Tillie's mouth fell open.

"That's not Dawlish," Smith said, frowning. "None of them are Dawlish! It's the vicar!" He glared at Colonel Fredericks as if the whole business had been his fault. "If you have no objection, I will find my own passage home. Perhaps you'd be so good as to point me in the direction of Larne."

Fredericks flapped his hand toward the sea. "Somewhere over there."

Smith's eyes widened impossibly.

"We're about five miles south of Whalen," Fredericks said.

Smith tightened his lips into a harsh line as he realized, no doubt, how thoroughly he had been tricked. Tillie understood how he felt, for behind Colonel Fredericks and Mr. Grant trailed the vicar's wife and James the footman, followed by another two men she couldn't yet see clearly.

"Oh, James, I am so sorry," Tillie said contritely. "I mistook the carriage and must have got you into all sorts of trouble! Kate, Mr. Grant, it was all my fault, please forgive him—and me, if you possibly could!"

"Just glad to see you safe, miss," James muttered. Then he grinned. "Besides, it was worth it to see the vicar driving a cab hell for leather up the Whalen road."

Tillie let out a choke of laughter. Dove was grinning openly while Mr. Grant merely smiled beatifically.

Kate took her husband's arm. "He is a man of many talents. We followed your tracks through the mud and snow to Whalen, and there we met Colonel Fredericks, who was about to chase along the coast after *The Albatross*."

"Then Captain Alban and Colonel Fredericks had planned this between them?" Tillie exclaimed. She rounded on Dove. "Did *you* know this?"

Dove threw up his hands in mock surrender. "Acquit me! I knew only what Alban told both of us. But when I looked through the glass and saw the Grants clambering down the cliff, I wanted an excuse to get you to them without alerting Captain Smith to Alban's plans."

"Well, I'm not sure your plans amount to much," Smith said bitterly. "You have the information, but you'll never alert the authorities in Ireland in time. If I don't appear tonight, they'll vanish by tomorrow."

Then it's a good thing it's still the night before," Dove said cheerfully.

Smith scowled. "You make no sense."

"You slept two hours, not twenty," Alban said. "I'm afraid I drugged you. Well, ladies and gentleman, I believe I have information to carry to Ireland, so I will bid you goodnight."

"Wait a minute," someone said as Alban turned away. "Is this the Alban fellow or the damned army officer?"

Alban swung back. "Alban Lamont, sir," he said coldly. "I don't believe I have the honor of your acquaintance." His tone left little doubt as to what he thought of such honor.

"Courtney," said the old gentleman. "Alfred Courtney."

Tillie's jaw dropped again. "Oh dear," she said faintly.

Dove glanced at her with a quick frown of surprise.

And then, adding to her growing sense of unreality, Mr. Hatton stepped into the light. "I'm sorry. I didn't get the chance to warn you that Sir Alfred was coming..."

"There was no need, Mr. Hatton," Tillie said in a cold, disdainful voice she was quite proud of. "Of course, I am always pleased to see you, but I will not be meeting Sir Alfred. Did you really come in the cab, Mrs. Grant? Is there room for Dove and me?"

"I'm sure we can squash in somehow," Kate said with a flickering glance at the elderly gentleman. "But you will find there is more room in the other carriage with Sir Alfred. Would formal introductions help?"

"No," Tillie said baldly.

"Yes," Dove said. "I am entirely baffled by Sir Alfred's presence."

"And I by yours, sir," Sir Alfred said haughtily. "Be so good as to unhand my granddaughter."

Chapter Nineteen

ALTHOUGH DOVE MADE no effort to release her, Tillie held onto his arm with both hands.

"There is no need," she said with equal hauteur. "I do not acknowledge the connection. And I would rather travel with you, Kate, if you won't be too uncomfortable."

"Let's at least walk up to the carriages," Dove said, urging her forward. "It's too cold to linger down here." He turned and called a farewell after Alban's retreating back and received a backhanded wave in return.

Tillie all but dragged him onward, leading the way off the beach and up the path.

"Slow down," Dove said mildly. "There is no race here. So, Courtney is the grandfather who disowned your mother?"

"He is. I am happy to reciprocate on her behalf."

"I don't blame you," Dove soothed. "Only…why is he here?"

"I have no idea."

"Aren't you curious?"

"Not yet," she said with difficulty. "I'm too angry."

"May I ask him?"

"Hatton," growled Sir Alfred behind them. "You may tell that encroaching officer it's none of his business."

Tillie bristled with outrage, but Dove only grinned.

"He won't tell you anything in my presence," Dove said. He took her hand. "It's only a short journey to Blackhaven, an hour, no more. Why don't you go with him? Let Kate be your chaperone."

"Actually, that's a good idea," Kate said. "Because that way, we'll get a better view of Tris driving the cab."

Tillie gave a reluctant laugh. But she was even more reluctant to spend an hour in her grandfather's company. She wanted to be with Dove and allow her happiness to blossom after their adventure. She didn't want to be angry and resentful.

But then, Sir Alfred's very presence had already cut up her peace. She could not *enjoy* her happiness until this, too, was dealt with.

"Would you mind accompanying me, Kate?" she said with difficulty.

FIVE MINUTES LATER, she was in a comfortable travelling coach with Kate and Sir Alfred Courtney. James sat up on the box beside the driver. She didn't see who piled into the hired carriage, but as Kate promised, she did see Mr. Grant driving it, contriving to look at once quite at home and utterly incongruous in his evening dress.

Smothering a giggle, she faced forward once more and regarded the stranger who was her maternal grandfather. Sir Alfred Courtney was certainly a distinguished looking man. She allowed him that much. But she did not care for the haughtiness in his eyes or the superior way he held his head, as though there were a bad smell directly under his aristocratic nose.

"What did you wish to discuss with me, sir?" she asked coolly.

"Your future," he replied.

"I don't believe it is your concern, any more than my past was."

"You bear a grudge," he observed. "Well, I don't blame you for that." He shifted with the first hint of discomfort Tillie had seen in him. "Let me say, I could have dealt better with your mother's marriage. To help you understand, she was the apple of my eye, sweet and courteous, and never disobeyed me but once, and I was angry."

"Did her death anger you, too?" Tillie flung at him, for he had not even acknowledged her father's note informing him of the tragedy.

"No, it crushed me," her grandfather said simply.

"It crushed us, too. You did not even have to visit. A few lines would have comforted my father." *And me.*

The old man's nostrils flared with distaste. "Your father's comfort was never my concern."

"Clearly."

Her grandfather drew a deep breath. "However, I have been brought to believe that I was wrong to visit the sins of the mother upon the daughter."

"The sins were not hers but yours," Tillie interrupted.

Her grandfather smiled faintly. "You are loyal. That is a good Courtney trait."

Tillie stared at him in disbelief. "I am astonished to hear you say so."

He waved that aside. "I was spurred into action when I heard what your vile family was doing to you."

"How did you hear that?" Tillie demanded, frowning.

"My grandson wrote to me, saying he was sure he had met you in Blackhaven and that your cousin was claiming to be your husband but that there was some doubt. And then some matter of a duel, which is unforgivable."

But Tillie had latched on to the beginning of his statement. "Your grandson? Who is your grandson?"

"Anthony Blackshaw."

Her lips parted in wonder. "Anthony Blackshaw is my *cousin*? So *that* is why he acted for Luke against Dove! He thought there was some family connection..." She cast her grandfather a wintry smile. "Making up for your neglect, no doubt."

"No doubt," her grandfather agreed just as coldly. "So that all explains why I am here, why I came via the vicarage and Mr. Winslow's house to find you. We'll say no more about this escapade."

"Agreed!"

"For I have another proposal for you."

She cast him a wary glance. "You have?"

"I will give you a dowry, acknowledge you as my granddaughter. You will be received everywhere."

"I sense a large *if*."

"There is no *if*. I will even find you a husband who is heir to a barony."

"I think *that* is the if," Tillie said shrewdly. "Just for interest's sake, do please tell me who you have in mind."

Her grandfather smiled faintly. "Why, your cousin, Anthony Blackshaw."

Tillie's lips parted. Beside her, Kate inhaled sharply.

Weirdly fascinated, Tillie asked, "Does Captain Blackshaw know?"

"By the way he speaks of you, I know he will be happy to marry you," her grandfather replied.

"I wouldn't be so sure," Tilly said. "However, I am obliged to you for your thoughtfulness, and to Captain Blackshaw for his amiability. Unfortunately, I cannot please you in this matter. I am engaged to marry Major Doverton."

Her grandfather's nostrils flared once more. "Doverton? The Dovertons are nobodies, and what they have has all gone to the elder brother. From what I hear, your major has nothing but his prize money and ill health, both derived in the Peninsula."

"You are wrong on both counts," Tillie countered. "But to quote your own words, sir, that is none of your business."

"You won't say so when you are looking for a place to live!"

Tillie laughed. "Sir, are you really not aware that I am quite vulgarly wealthy? I don't need your money, and I wouldn't take it even if I were starving."

And that, Tillie thought with fierce satisfaction, was that.

But it wasn't. When the carriage finally pulled up at the vicarage, her grandfather helped her down. They barely glanced at each other. Instead, the old man was looking toward the other carriage. Grant had just jumped down from the box, and Dove was striding to meet her.

"Major Doverton," her grandfather said. "Might I have a word? If we may impose on Mrs. Grant a few minutes longer."

"Of course," Kate said cordially.

She took Tillie's arm, urging her through the gate. Now Tillie was uneasy, for she had no idea what her grandfather meant to say to Dove, and how it would affect his innate chivalry. But clearly, Sir Alfred, having committed to this fight, was not giving up easily.

DOVE FOLLOWED SIR Alfred into Grant's study and closed the door.

"I will come to the point," Courtney said abruptly. "You are not the husband I choose for my granddaughter. I believe you to be grasping and opportunistic, in short, sir, a fortune hunter."

Dove ushered him politely to a seat but remained standing, gazing down at him. "You do not know me, sir, and your age compels me to accept from you insults that would be unforgivable in a younger man."

"Yes, yes, very admirable. You are indigent, sir. But since Matilda appears to have a fondness for you, I will grant you a sizeable pension. Provided you leave her alone. She will marry my grandson, Captain Anthony Blackshaw."

Dove blinked. In a bizarre, unexpected kind of way, the relationship made sense. "I beg leave to doubt it, sir."

Courtney shrugged. "Then you are a fool. She has already agreed."

"You lie," Dove said, looking him straight in the eyes.

Courtney smiled. "Do I?"

"Yes, you do. Good evening, sir."

As he turned on his heel, Courtney's jaw had already begun to drop.

"You'll lose the pension," he said with a shade of desperation. "And I'll make sure you never touch a penny of Matilda's money!"

Dove laughed. "Bless you, Sir Alfred. Not everything is about money. Or even birth."

He was still smiling as he crossed the hall to the drawing room. But when he opened the door and went in, he didn't like the anxiety he saw in Tillie's brilliant eyes.

"What?" he said, going to her at once.

"What did he ask you?" she demanded.

"To give you up for a pot of money, I think. He has a very inflated sense of his own importance."

"What did you say?" Tillie demanded.

Dove paused and scowled. "What the devil do you think I said?"

At that, her shoulders relaxed and a smiled wreathed her face, depriving him of breath.

"I'd best go and see him," Grant said, taking his wife's hand and making for the door.

"Wait a second, Grant," Dove called. "If Tillie's agreeable, can we get a license and be married the same day as Lampton?"

"Of course you can," Grant said and went out.

"That is only a week away," Tillie said, awed.

"Is it too soon?" he asked, drawing her down onto the sofa beside him.

She shook her head, her smile now adorably shy, and yet her eyes shone with happiness. It stunned him all over again that he had inspired such feeling in her. "I was just wondering why you wished to be married at the same time as Dr. Lampton."

"The idea just came to me... I'll have to speak to him and to Princess Elizabeth, and of course if they don't care for the idea, we'll change it. It's just..." He smiled a little deprecatingly. "The truth is, I always held myself a little aloof from Blackhaven, and even from my fellow officers—at least those I did not know before my injury. Afterward, because I knew I had not long on this earth, it seemed...unnatural and unkind to make friends."

She took both his hands in hers. "Because you thought you would die?"

He nodded. "I wasn't lonely," he said quickly. "Or I don't *think* I was. I was just...distant. Oh, I did my duty at headquarters and in the town. I went to some of the assembly balls and occasional parties people invited me to. But I was never like Grantham or old Fredericks, never really part of the community." His fingers curled around hers. "I think I would like to be. Since you came, I've realized how much I like and appreciate these people—the Grants and the Lamptons, the Muirs and the Winslows, even Sylvester Gaunt! It just came to me that I would like to be married along with such friends."

He kissed her forehead. "But I don't truly mind. If you dislike the idea in the slightest—or they do!—it doesn't matter. The important thing is to marry you."

Smiling, she held up her face to be kissed.

A LITTLE OVER a week later, Tillie married Dominic Doverton in Blackhaven Church, in the same ceremony that married Dr. Lampton to Elizabeth von Rheinwald. Attending her was Catherine Gaunt, while Dove's brother John served as best man.

Of course, Dove's family was not best pleased by the match, although they were no doubt mollified by the fact that she was Courtney's granddaughter and brought a considerable fortune with her besides. On top of which, Dove had told John and Ellen in no uncertain terms that his wife was to be treated with every respect. And if she was not made welcome to the family, it would cause a serious rift.

"But, Dominic, *Felicity*!" Ellen had pleaded in a somewhat feeble last-ditch attempt to influence matters.

"Felicity does not like to be without a husband to order her life," Dove had retorted. "I could not live with a woman who lies and considers no one but herself. More importantly, I do not love her, and she should never have been led to believe that I still did. I blame you for that, Ellen, however good your intentions. Now you must respect my wishes in this. I hope you can. I hope you both can, for you're my family and I have no wish to begin a quarrel."

Neither clearly did John or Ellen, for they said no more, and even postponed their departure to attend the wedding, as did Mr. Ashley, although Tillie caught the odd rueful look in his eyes.

Several of the regiment came to the church, including Captain Blackshaw. More of a surprise was the presence of Sir Anthony Courtney, glowering from the back of the church.

Annie, now Mrs. Trent, was there, too, with both big and little Georges. The latter was good as gold and didn't cry at all until after the ceremony. With Mr. Hatton's help, the old King's Head Inn had been purchased, and Annie and George were supervising repairs before George's mother arrived from Manchester. They both had great plans for the place, and Tillie was delighted to see them so happy.

If only the inn had been ready on time, Tillie would have chosen to have her wedding breakfast there. Since it was not, everyone repaired to the hotel dining room.

During the breakfast, the brides compared wedding trips.

"I shall love to see Italy with Nicholas," Elizabeth confided. "Beneath the man of logic and science, he hides a deep appreciation of the arts... But oh, I shall miss Andreas. I have never been apart from him before, and I cannot bear the thought that he might cry for me."

"I believe your governess has plans to keep him so occupied, he will have no time to cry," Tillie said. "Besides, only think how delighted he will be when you come back!"

Elizabeth laughed. "There is that! But where is it you are going? Did I ever hear?"

"Probably not. We were waiting for Captain Alban to return from Ireland—oh, did you hear they caught the conspirators?" Who had included her own uncle and cousin, desperate to make money from anything. "Anyhow, Alban is lending us his yacht, weather permitting, to sail to France and from there we intend to travel to Spain to visit Dove's old haunts, and then, perhaps Vienna."

"Then we might see you there!" Elizabeth said, pleased.

"Vienna?" said Sylvester Gaunt, who was passing behind them. "You might come across my sister Anna there, too. Give her my best, if you do. Tell her to write to Tamar, for I probably wouldn't reply."

"The Gaunts are a strange family," Dr. Lampton observed.

"Brought up almost feral and yet somehow grew into decent and charming people."

Before setting out on their trip, Tillie repaired to the cloakroom. While she paused to straighten a hair pin and wonder at the flushed happiness in her own face, Ellen Doverton came in.

Although Tillie smiled in a friendly manner, she did not expect the encounter to be warm. But to her surprise, Ellen paused beside her, as though she had something to say.

"You would have married him when you believed he was dying, wouldn't you?" she said abruptly. "You would have nursed him and suffered with him."

Tillie nodded, a little warily.

"That is no small thing," Ellen said with difficulty.

Tillie tilted her chin. "I love him."

"Dominic also told us it was you who persuaded him to let doctors examine him again. It is because of you we know he will live."

Tillie had always known Ellen's concern for Dove's marriage stemmed from more than pride and snobbery. Ellen cared for him. Now, Tillie recognized the depth of that love and forgave everything.

She smiled. "I think it was just Dove himself. It was the right time."

"Because of you. We won't forget that," Ellen said. She dashed one hand across her face and hastened to a washing bowl.

Tillie blinked after her in some wonder. In this shared affection was the basis of a friendship with her new sister-in-law. "You know we're going to buy a house in Blackhaven?" she told her. "You'll always be welcome there."

Ellen turned. "Then you won't return to Manchester?"

"Not to live. My later memories there are not good. Others will run the mills and the rest, though I will keep an eye on them. I want my workers happy as well as prosperous."

Ellen narrowed her eyes. "Are you a radical, Miss Daw—Mrs. Doverton?"

"Oh goodness, how strange that sounds! *You* are Mrs. Doverton!

Please, call me Tillie. And no, I'm not a radical. But I like everyone around me to be contented."

Ellen's lips curved into a smile. "Funnily enough, I suspect they are."

"I THINK ELLEN likes me," Tillie crowed to Dove some time later. "Secretly, of course. We might even be friends one day."

They stood together on the deck of Alban's yacht as the sun began to set. The sea was quite calm, but the air felt icy on her face. She was glad of her fur cloak and the gorgeous little fur hat that matched. And of Dove's shoulder pressed to hers.

"Of course she does, and I believe you will be." He nudged her gently. "If it makes you feel better, they didn't approve of Felicity when I was engaged to her either. They are older than me, and were always inclined to be overprotective, even before my injury. But this is a new life for you and me, and I believe they want to be part of it. They already like that you make me happy, and that you bully me about doctors."

"I did not bully you!" Tillie protested. "You merely saw sense."

The smile died on his lips. "Because of you, I wanted to live. I wanted you to know. Because of you, I was *afraid* to know, which didn't sit well with me once I'd acknowledged it."

She hugged his arm and rested her head against his shoulder. "Look how beautiful the sky is. I wish I could paint colors like that."

"We'll buy paints and you can try."

In silence, they watched the sun sink below the horizon. A deep contentment filled Tillie's heart, and yet it beat too quickly, too excitedly, for Dove stood close to her. And in the eyes of God and man, she was his.

He said, "Come, it's growing cold. Let's go below."

She turned to meet his warm gaze and her heart turned over.

He cupped her cheek, then bent and kissed her lips. "I want to make love to you. At last."

"At last?" she teased, although her voice was not quite steady. "You have only known me a month!"

"I feel as if I have always known you, always wanted you."

She shivered with delighted anticipation. The crew, well-trained by Alban and Lady Arabella, accorded them no more than a cheerful nod when they passed. Climbing down the ladder to their cozy and yet luxurious cabin, Tillie's heartbeat left her breathless. By the time they stood in the middle of the cabin, almost touching the post of the large bed, she was trembling. Two lamps were lit in the cabin, casting a soft glow over Dove's strong face. He was at once a stranger and her friend. Her husband.

"You are lovely in that hat," Dove said, taking it off with reluctance. He smiled. "But then, you are lovely without it too."

His greatcoat was hung behind the door with her cloak. His hands on her shoulders, he bent and kissed her lips with soft, devastating sensuality. She melted against him, clutching his coat buttons until she found she was unfastening them and could slide her arms around him inside it, even burrow with her hands under his shirt to the hot, smooth skin of his back. His muscles rippled under her caresses while he seduced her with his lips and tongue and nibbling teeth.

Her whole body seemed to be on fire as her gown and underdress dropped around her feet with her stays. He drew back to shrug off his coat and waistcoat, and for an instant, stood gazing at her, breathing heavily. He reached out slowly and gathered up her chemise and drew it over her head.

"Dear God," he whispered, gazing at her as she gasped and trembled with embarrassment. Without meaning to, she took a step toward him, and with a muttered oath, he seized her in his arms, swung her off her feet, and onto the bed. In a trice, his shirt was over his head and his breeches kicked to the floor. She caught a glimpse of the jagged scar across his abdomen and the dark shaft rising over it. And then he lowered his body over hers and she could run her greedy, wondering hands over his hard chest and shoulders and back, over the rise of his buttocks.

He kissed her mouth with breath-taking passion, before moving down her throat and shoulders to her breasts, which he kissed so delightfully that she moaned and wriggled beneath him, clutching him to her. He returned suddenly to her mouth, claiming it with strength as he slid inside her. She cried out with shock, but he whispered her name, kissing and caressing her until she relaxed once more into his embrace. And then he pushed deeper and rocked within her, and she gazed up at him with awe, while her body blindly followed him, deriving ever intensifying pleasure from her every move and his.

The strange, wonderful dance grew wild and overwhelming until it consumed her, shattering her into ecstasy such as she had never imagined. And he felt it, too, collapsing on her with fierce groans of bliss that astonished her more than all the rest.

Slowly, he detached his mouth from hers and turned, drawing her with him so that they lay on their sides, still joined. "I feel I have waited a lifetime for this one moment."

"Just this one?" she said breathlessly. "Won't there be others?"

"Oh, many, many others," he assured her. "If you like."

"I *will* like," she whispered.

And she did.

Mary Lancaster's Newsletter

If you enjoyed *The Wicked Waif*, and would like to keep up with Mary's new releases and other book news, please sign up to Mary's mailing list to receive her occasional Newsletter.

http://eepurl.com/b4Xoif

Other Books by Mary Lancaster

VIENNA WALTZ (The Imperial Season, Book 1)

VIENNA WOODS (The Imperial Season, Book 2)

VIENNA DAWN (The Imperial Season, Book 3)

THE WICKED BARON (Blackhaven Brides, Book 1)

THE WICKED LADY (Blackhaven Brides, Book 2)

THE WICKED REBEL (Blackhaven Brides, Book 3)

THE WICKED HUSBAND (Blackhaven Brides, Book 4)

THE WICKED MARQUIS (Blackhaven Brides, Book 5)

THE WICKED GOVERNESS (Blackhaven Brides, Book 6)

THE WICKED SPY (Blackhaven Brides, Book 7)

THE WICKED GYPSY (Blackhaven Brides, Book 8)

THE WICKED WIFE (Blackhaven Brides, Book 9)

WICKED CHRISTMAS (Blackhaven Brides, A Novella)

REBEL OF ROSS

A PRINCE TO BE FEARED: the love story of Vlad Dracula

AN ENDLESS EXILE

A WORLD TO WIN

About Mary Lancaster

Mary Lancaster lives in Scotland with her husband, three mostly grown-up kids and a small, crazy dog.

Her first literary love was historical fiction, a genre which she relishes mixing up with romance and adventure in her own writing. Her most recent books are light, fun Regency romances written for Dragonblade Publishing: *The Imperial Season* series set at the Congress of Vienna; and the popular*Blackhaven Brides* series, which is set in a fashionable English spa town frequented by the great and the bad of Regency society.

Connect with Mary on-line – she loves to hear from readers:

Email Mary:
Mary@MaryLancaster.com

Website:
www.MaryLancaster.com

Newsletter sign-up:
http://eepurl.com/b4Xoif

Facebook:
facebook.com/mary.lancaster.1656

Facebook Author Page:
facebook.com/MaryLancasterNovelist

Twitter:
@MaryLancNovels
twitter.com/MaryLancNovels

Bookbub:
bookbub.com/profile/mary-lancaster

Made in the USA
Las Vegas, NV
17 April 2021